New Orleans Rush

KELLY SISKIND

everafter
ROMANCE

EverAfter Romance
A division of Diversion Publishing Corp.
443 Park Avenue South, Suite 1004
New York, New York 10016
www.EverAfterRomance.com

For more information, email info@everafterromance.com

First EverAfter Romance edition April 2019.
Paperback ISBN: 978-1-63576-626-4
eBook ISBN: 978-1-63576-627-1

PRAISE FOR KELLY SISKIND'S PREVIOUS TITLES

Chasing Crazy: "With a swoon-worthy male love interest, and Siskind's superb storytelling, this is one of the best New Adult contemporary romances I've read to date."

—*USA Today* best-selling author K. A. Tucker

FALL IN LOVE WITH KELLY'S OVER THE TOP SERIES

My Perfect Mistake, Over the Top #1: "This has easily soared to one of my favorite books of the year and has earned itself a place on my all-time favorites shelf."

—The Sisterhood of the Traveling Book Boyfriends

A Fine Mess, Over the Top #2: "Delicious, sizzling chemistry that leapt off the page! Lily and Sawyer will absolutely win your heart."

—*USA Today* best-selling author Jennifer Blackwood

Hooked on Trouble, Over the Top #3: "...an awe inspiring story packed with humor, heat, passion and love."

—Chatterbooks Book Blog

GET SWEPT AWAY IN KELLY'S ONE WILD WISH SERIES

Legs: "An intoxicating romance that lingers like a great Merlot and leaves you with one hell of a book hangover!"

—Scarlett Cole, author of the Second Circle Tattoo series

Stud: "A sexy and steamy read with loads of flirty and witty banter. Siskind knows how to write characters that have off-the-charts chemistry."

—RT Book Reviews

Licks: "Kelly has blended a mystery into this compelling love story in a way that keeps the reader flipping pages. I couldn't put it down!"

—*USA Today* best-selling author Ellis Leigh

New Orleans Rush

1

Seeing the world through rose-colored glasses was a culti-vated skill. A sunny outlook could brighten partly cloudy skies and refract that brilliance into the world. Most days smiling through adversity was effortless. Tonight, Bea's posi-tivity had fled the building.

"Hit me with another, sir." Her request came out faster than intended, each word knocking into each other.

The bartender in question cocked an eyebrow. "You sure that's a good idea? Looks like you enjoyed a few before coming here."

She squinted at the man's gelled hair and fancy bow tie. He seemed the unflappable sort, the type who could have survived her gray day with a sip of tea and self-deprecating chuckle.

Bea planted her elbows on the bar, briefly grimacing at the sticky surface. "I appreciate your concern, but that was my first drink. And if we switched bodies in one of those body-swapping movies, and you had to relive my last thir-teen hours, you'd realize I could win the Guinness World Record for Worst Luck. Denying me another drink would be barbaric."

Except the alcohol *was* fogging up her usual rosy glasses. Or maybe it was the cold medicine she'd taken when she failed to find Advil in her purse.

The bartender cracked a smile. "Barbaric?"

"A crime against humanity."

He shook his head and reached for the vodka on the shelf. "Maybe don't inhale this one."

Another lemon drop in hand, she swiveled on her stool and scanned the room. The low lighting made her eyelids heavy, the red carpets and mahogany walls adding to the bar's sleepy warmth. It had a Rat Pack vibe, accentuated by the bow-tie-wearing servers and lampshade table lights. Jazzy music joined the hum of the crowd. A crowd as unfamiliar to her as the rest of New Orleans.

Move with me to the Mardi Gras City, Nick had begged. *We'll work the bar scene at night. You can paint all day. We'll live each minute like it's our last!*

Her boyfriend—now of the ex persuasion—had neglected to mention that four days into their adventure he'd change the rules, leaving Bea homeless and jobless in the birthplace of jazz. She also hadn't painted anything but artless amoebas the past month.

Sinking lower on her stool, she cupped her drink with both hands. She didn't sip it right away, letting her tipsiness linger instead. Then a guy in a top hat and cape appeared.

Yep. That just happened.

She looked into her full glass, then back at the mirage, wondering if she was drunker than she'd realized. She *had* consumed her first drink faster than usual, and mixing cold medicine and alcohol wasn't the best idea. She squinted harder at the man. The top hat was still there, making its already tall owner stupendously taller. The cape was still there, too. Not just any cape. A midnight velvet cape with stars stitched through the material.

It was a galaxy far, far away. Right here. In a New Orleans bar.

The cape looked soft and plush. If Bea could rub her face in the fleecy fabric and roll into a cocooned bundle, she was sure she could sleep for a week and wake up in a different life. One that didn't resemble a fifty-car pileup.

The top hat man focused on her, as though sensing the longing in her stare. Or maybe he'd heard her say, "I'd love to nuzzle your cape."

A thought she'd accidentally unmuted.

He walked toward her like she was the only person in the jazzy room and stopped in front of her barstool. "You can touch it, if you'd like."

The fabric looked even softer up close, but the sensual timbre of his low voice had her sitting straighter. "If you're not referring to your cape, things might get ugly."

She wasn't above tossing her drink in his face.

His lips twitched. "I do mean the cape. Unless you'd like to try on my hat." He tipped up the felt brim.

She loosened her grip on her glass, pleased she wouldn't have to waste a perfectly good martini. But the way her day was going, the hat would probably give her lice. "I don't accept hats from strangers. Or capes."

"I believe that applies to candy, not capes."

"What if it carries an ancient spell and whisks me away to some dark castle where I'll be imprisoned and tortured until they learn I can't command the cape's magic?"

The edges of his eyes crinkled. "A valid point."

His languid gaze slid down her body and up again. He studied her so long she finally sipped her drink, then he extended his hand. "I'm Huxley."

The second her fingers—cold and damp from the chilled glass—slid into Huxley's large grasp, heat shot up her arm. The cape most definitely had hidden powers. "Bea," she said. "Fascinating to meet you."

The most fascinating moment of her gray day.

Aside from the subtle blond scruff highlighting dramatic cheekbones and his aquiline nose, Huxley wasn't traditionally handsome. Puckered skin overtook half an eyebrow, part of his right ear was missing, and a thick scar ran down his left cheek. His dirty-blond hair had a slight unruly curl, the ends licking at his neck.

Individually, his features weren't particularly attractive, but as a whole this man was ruggedly elegant. Like when you stepped back from a Monet and all the paint strokes blended into a masterpiece.

Until he said, "Bee, as in the insect?"

Now he was more of a disturbing Picasso painting than a Monet masterpiece. "As in *Beatrice Baker*, but make a bee joke and I might borrow your cape after all. See if I can use its dormant magic to turn you into a colon rectum."

He barked out a laugh. "Excuse me?"

She fixed him with her best menacing stare. "A colon rectum. It's an ugly beetle."

Frequently taunted with "bee" jokes as a kid, Bea had studied insects and animals. The odder the name the better. Using the insults against bullies would often confuse them into silence. It had a different effect on Huxley, whose striking cheekbones rounded, his lips curving upward like he'd stumbled upon a four-leaf clover in a barren land.

She found herself leaning toward him. "Are you from New Orleans?"

"I am. But you're not."

She froze, worry weaving up her spine. He wouldn't know she'd just arrived from Chicago, unless he'd followed her here. Not impossible, but the one person who would have tailed her was even taller, with a slight paunch. Big Eddie could have sent someone else after her—an accomplice to intimidate and threaten. Except a gun for hire wouldn't waltz around, brazenly, wearing a cape and top hat, and Big Eddie had no clue where she was.

She relaxed on her seat. "How'd you know I'm not local?"

"Deductive reasoning."

"Because you're a clairvoyant with a photographic memory and can tell me every meal I've eaten the past week?"

Amusement lit his eyes. "My ways are much simpler than that."

"Do share."

He pointed at her lap. "The keychain on your purse is a dead giveaway."

Right. The Chicago Bulls tag. A gift from her ex-boyfriend on their third date. She didn't love basketball, but the keepsake had been sweet. It was now a sour memory. She removed it from her purse zipper and tossed it onto the bar. "Now I'll blend in."

Huxley's posture shifted, shrinking the distance between them. "A woman as beautiful as you doesn't blend."

Whoa.

Her pulse tapped up her neck, her rapid breaths chasing the erratic beat. She tried to decipher the odd color of his eyes, but the dim lighting made it tough, and a man bellowed Huxley's name from the back of the room, breaking the moment.

Huxley turned, and she gawked at the hollering man... because mustaches like his were extinct. That was a mustache wearing a face, the type of hairy handlebar that could serve as a playground for miniature children. A monkeybar-stache! She snickered at her internal joke and checked her drink again. It was still half-full, but her day no longer felt half-empty, thanks to the cape-wearing man before her.

"I'll be back," he said, all wonder eclipsing from his Monet face.

Once he joined the owner of the monkeybar-stache, Huxley glanced at her, but the mustache man's aggressive hand gestures drew his attention away. She sipped her drink and watched the odd interaction, wishing she could read lips.

When she finished her lemon drop, she turned and flagged the bartender. "One more, please."

He accepted her extended glass. "How 'bout we call this your last? You should head home after, sleep this Guinness Record Day off."

A brilliant idea, if she had a home, or a bed.

It hadn't taken much effort to stuff her clothing and paint-brushes back into her duffle bag this morning. She'd then loaded her yellow Beetle—the trusty automobile being the only mainstay in her life—and had sat in her parked car for an unhealthy length of time, replaying today's disaster.

"Here's the thing," Nick had said when she'd woken up this morning. "I've changed. I don't want to be in a committed relationship. It's best we know this now, before we get in too deep. It's been fun, and you're great, but it's time we moved on."

She had tugged at her ear, sure her hearing had failed her. "I'm sorry, but it sounds like you're breaking up with me?"

His answering nod had been all sympathetic puppy-dog. "It's for the best. I mean, I was getting coffee this morning, and a girl in line asked me out. I wanted to say yes, which means there's something missing between you and me. If we stay together, I might regret it and hurt you in the process. And you know I'm a stickler for honesty."

Getting dumped four days after following Nick to New Orleans had been humiliating. Listening to him admit he'd accepted the coffee girl's date *for tonight* had driven her mortification home. All because Nick believed in honesty. So much so, he reminded her the apartment he'd rented was in his name. He then graciously suggested she crash there until she found something new, no hint of irony in his voice.

Bea had stared at him. And stared. She hadn't screamed and cursed, because she wasn't a screamer or curser. She'd simply looked at the man who'd convinced her to quit her waitressing job, leave Chicago, drive across four states, upend her life for a dream, and she'd said *nada*.

The fact that he'd never blessed her when she'd sneezed should have been a red flag, along with his Kardashian-sized shoe collection. But Bea had wanted to escape and delve into her art and forget about her father, and the mess her sperm donor had made of her life. The matter of a certain loan shark threatening her bodily harm may have also expedited her departure.

Now here she was, the victim of another sabotaging man.

She dragged her newly filled martini glass closer, ignoring the pull of the caped man behind her. She was in no state to find any man intriguing. Not on a Guinness Record Dumping day. Sipping her lemon drop was no longer an option, either. She tried to suck that puppy back, but the straw jammed into her cheek. Huffing, she pushed it aside and downed the martini, finishing by wiping her wrist across her mouth. The room took a lazy spin.

She sat awhile, twirling the empty glass, waiting for her equilibrium to settle. The weight of her troubles hunched her shoulders. She still had no job. No place to live. The alcohol provided no insight, nor did the monotony of the spinning glass. She couldn't reverse time, so telling Nick where to shove his *"it's for the best"* face was off the table. Time to call it a night.

Tip left for the bartender, she hopped off the barstool. The walls did a tilt-a-whirl—a questionable sensation. She'd only had three drinks. Enough to make her mind feel loose, but not enough to turn the room into a merry-go-round. The cold medicine she'd used to Band-Aid her headache must have been the culprit. The aching no longer plagued her, but the room's drowsy spin could pose a problem.

Bathroom. She just needed to make it to the bathroom, splash a little water on her face, and she'd be rain as right. Or right as rain. She'd shake this wooziness and figure out a plan. Translation: she'd sleep in her car tonight and hope to wake up in one of those body-swapping movies.

Maybe she could become Emma Stone. That girl had a sassy spine, no qualms about mouthing off to deserving men. They both had the red hair, freckle thing going on. Emma's boobs were smaller, so wearing fitted tops wouldn't make Bea feel like a Hooters waitress trolling for tips. But Bea had an hourglass figure with a daylight saving's hour padding out her rear, which she loved. Come to think of it, Bea liked her body just fine. It was her life and backbone that were in need of swapping.

So lost in her hypothetical switcheroo, she didn't recall walking to the bathroom or flushing the toilet or even leaving the stall. She hoped she hadn't sat directly on the seat.

Beside her, a black woman with peroxide blond curls re-applied red lipstick. She cut a look Bea's way and whistled. "Someone's had a rough night."

Bea sighed at her bleary reflection. "I made a bad decision."

One that shouldn't derail her life. Nick's name *did* rhyme with prick, but she was in New Orleans. A colorful city with men in capes and monkeybar-staches. The perfect place to replenish her drained creative juices. She didn't need Nick the Prick to start fresh. To prove her capability, she fumbled for the watermelon lip gloss in her purse and managed to paint on a layer. Everything in the world could be made better by watermelon gloss.

The woman curled her top lip and wiped some excess red from her tooth. "You're preaching to the choir. My bad decision is named Miles, and he has a special ringtone."

She pocketed her makeup and pulled out her phone. A few swipes of her thumb later, Carrie Underwood's "Before He Cheats" blared from her rhinestone-covered cell. Bea bobbed her head as Carrie sang about keying her cheating boyfriend's car and smashing his headlights.

When the chorus ended, the woman shoved her cell into her purse. "That, girlfriend, is how you remind yourself to avoid bad decisions. Miles calls every few days. He leaves a voicemail apologizing, and I don't call back. I could block his number, but I like remembering I'm no man's doormat." Her pointed look was as fierce as her leopard-print dress.

Bea was still wearing the pink pedal pushers and turquoise polka dot blouse she'd pulled on this morning. The outfit exuded more bubble gum cheer than Hot Tamale attitude, but she'd always been a Double Bubble gal. She also wasn't sure Nick had earned a Carrie Underwood ringtone. Definitely a Taylor Swift lyric jab or two, but Carrie could be pushing it. They had, after all, broken up prior to his date tonight, but accepting the date *before* his "it's for the best" speech made the situation suspect.

Still, she didn't want to key his 1978 Mustang Cobra, which he loved more than his shoe collection. Life was too short for revenge.

With a wink, the woman left the bathroom. Bea followed. A little too fast. One hand on the wall, she closed her eyes as the tilt-a-whirl whirled again. Eyes open were preferable. Air was also in order. She tried to strut outside with Hot Tamale attitude, but it likely resembled a dizzy stumble. She made it outside and sucked back air like a drowning swimmer breaching the water's surface.

Her first breath cleared a layer of fuzz from her head. The second restored clarity to her blurry vision. She wished it hadn't. There, across the street, was none other than Nick, walking hand-in-hand with his date.

The bar wasn't far from his apartment, something she should have considered before setting up camp inside, and her uncharacteristic anger returned. She didn't love Nick. Moving to New Orleans and leaving her past had been as much for her as for him. But she'd trusted the man wouldn't leave her high and dry...for another woman. After four days.

Because he was honest.

She contemplated stomping across the street and telling him to screw off. She detested confrontation more than she hated green lollipops, but calling him a spiny lumpsucker or tufted titmouse would leave her with a modicum of satisfaction.

Then she noticed his black Mustang. Half a block down, his treasured automobile sat parked at the curb. A gift from the Carrie Underwood gods. Nick was walking the opposite way, and Bea's attention lasered in on his vehicle. She wasn't a malicious girl. Her back was basically made of Teflon, all resentment and stress sliding to its demise. Yet she was ogling Nick the Prick's muscle car with devious intent, and she barely recognized herself.

She'd worked since she was old enough to deliver papers. She'd then cut lawns and babysat and eventually waitressed. She'd dabbled in house painting—anything to add color to the world and money to her pocket, all while pursuing her art in private. Growing up, she'd been the levelheaded one who had kept the electricity on and heat flowing. She prided herself on being the only member of the Baker clan to never procure a mug shot.

See? Totally levelheaded.

Which meant her next action could only be blamed on Nick's "honesty" and the brilliant Carrie Underwood. She'd also revised her cheating theory: dating a woman the same calendar day of a breakup was definitely considered running around.

She walked to the side of his Mustang.

If he wants honesty, he'll get honesty.

She lifted her car keys from her purse.

I honestly think you're a fungus beetle.

Fisting the keys, her mind drifted to her father. To the feeble shrug of Franklyn Baker's shoulders when he'd admitted to gambling away her life savings, and how she'd caught nothing but a mouthful of flies in reaction. Her wicked grin faded. Her keys bit into her palm.

I am no man's doormat.

2

Huxley Marlow was used to being the center of attention. He'd spent the majority of his teen and adult years on stage. He had no qualms walking around in a top hat and costume, but it wasn't often a sexy redhead asked to nuzzle his velvet cape. Most women giggled and gawked, understandably. Some even winced when they noticed his scars. This woman wore the brightest pink pants he'd ever seen, her turquoise polka dot top had his lips curving into a smile, and her imaginative cape story had him struggling not to laugh.

Him. Laugh. A guy who spent most of his days scowling.

Then there was her colon rectum comment.

Before he could ask her to explain her odd animal insult, or why she was alone with a hint of sadness behind her playful quips, his beady-eyed archnemesis dragged him away.

The Great Otis Oliphant narrowed his gaze at Huxley. The curled ends of his mustache twitched. "You cheated."

"Of course I cheated."

"Your skills are uncultured. Nothing but a bag of cheap tricks."

Huxley offered a condescending smirk. "Who's walking out of here with a stack of twenties and a new gold Rolex?"

Oliphant ran his thumbs under his suspenders, his evil glower locked on Huxley's wrist. The heavy Rolex hung loosely. Oliphant glared harder. "Your execution is sloppy."

Huxley tipped up his hat. "Call my handwork sloppy again, and I won't give you the chance to win back your cash and save your pride."

"That's against the rules."

It was. Huxley knew it. He also knew his comment would get under Oliphant's twitchy mustache.

Three rules governed Club Crimson's weekly underground poker games.

Rule One: Only skilled magicians were permitted.

Rule Two: The winner always gave his or her competitors a rematch.

Rule Three: Sleight of hand was not only allowed, it was encouraged.

If you could count cards, false shuffle a deck, or exploit other handwork skills to win, you deserved to rule the poker table. You also gained bragging rights as king or queen of the New Orleans magic scene. Huxley's winning streak was the stuff of legends.

And so went their usual post-poker chit-chat, with Oliphant lamenting his losses, shit talking like the little brat he was. He may have been ten years older than Huxley's thirty-five, but the man was a snotty former street urchin, whose mustache was larger than his IQ. Huxley had even caught the man picking pockets at the bar, preying on drunk patrons. If the owner, Vito, knew Oliphant was jeopardizing his livelihood, Oliphant's suspenders would be the only part of him left.

Huxley glanced over his shoulder. Beatrice Baker was gone, and disappointment sunk into his chest. Instead of chatting with an alluring woman, he'd gotten stuck with

Otis Oliphant. Annoyed, he made a show of checking his new Rolex. "As exciting as these conversations are, I need my beauty rest. See you next week?"

Oliphant grumbled under his cigar-tinged breath and shoved past Huxley. He'd take that as the yes he needed. The burst pipe that had flooded his theater boiler room this morning was just another addition to his ever-growing Fix-It List, right below tending to the warped ceiling, patching the crumbling plaster, and avoiding electrocution from the sparking spotlights. At this rate, it would take five years of poker games to repair the dilapidated building.

Rubbing his eyes, Huxley pictured his father scowling down on him with regret, wondering why he'd entrusted The Marvelous Max Marlow legacy to his eldest son.

His father couldn't have been clearer about the items bequeathed to Huxley in his will. The theater, where he and his four brothers had grown up learning magic and watching their father mesmerize crowds, would thrive under Huxley's caretaking. The 1977 midnight blue Mustang Cobra, with the white pinstripes down the hood, would be his to keep pristine. Max Marlow had passed his prized velvet cape to his eldest son, with the message: *Be magical.* He'd also left him a small puzzle box.

The attached note had read: *If you can open it, the world will be your oyster.*

Max Marlow died nine years ago. For those nine years, Huxley had tried every trick imaginable to open that damn box. Needless to say, the world had not yet become his oyster.

The box tormented him with endless frustration, but it was the aging theater that ate at him most. The Marvelous Marlow Boys were supposed to honor their father with a successful dynasty and extravagant shows. Instead his two youngest brothers had disappeared without a trace, leaving the remaining three to perform in front of half-filled rooms, while the building sagged under the weight of Huxley's self-reproach.

He needed to do better. He *would* do better.

His cell vibrated and he frowned, unsure who'd be calling. Pushing back his cape, he pulled his phone from his pocket and tensed at Ashlynn's name. There was only one reason his assistant would be calling, and it wasn't good. He could ignore her call, claim a drained battery, but delaying this conversation wouldn't change the outcome.

Moving to a barstool, he forced bravado into his voice. "Just the lady I wanted to hear from. I've had an idea for a new number, something that'll highlight your skills." Which included folding her thin frame into a myriad of boxes.

Her answering sigh told him all he needed to know. "Hey, Hux. I got the job. The one that actually pays me money." A pause. Another sigh. Then, "I was hoping to give you notice, but they need me to start tomorrow."

Huxley swore under his breath. "You can't quit on me, Ash. You know we're great together. And I just won a big poker round. I have a Rolex with your name on it."

"You know I love you boys, but I can't keep living poker game to poker game. You'll have to rework your acts without me. I'm sorry, but tonight was my last show."

The world was *most definitely* not his oyster.

Huxley's father had drilled teachings into his kids, one of his mainstays being: distract your audience with beauty. Man or woman, it didn't matter, as long as their allure drew focus and mesmerized the crowd, pulling attention away from your trickery. Huxley was now a magician without an assistant, a performer without a beautiful distraction. A man losing hold of his dream one calamity at a time. "I understand, Ash. Thanks for everything."

They hung up and he pocketed his cell. He ran his thumb over the puckered scar on his pinky finger. He needed to think, regroup. Find a new assistant and more consistent cash flow.

There was only one place where Huxley did his optimal problem solving, and that was behind the wheel of his Mustang. The purr of the engine lulled his mind, soothed his nerves. He'd worked on every inch of that car with his father: nights drinking Scotch, tinkering, talking.

Max Marlow would wax on about the time he'd made an elephant disappear while traveling with the Newbright Circus, how he'd ruled Club Crimson's poker room for a decade. Their sweat had rebuilt that engine. Their bonding had turned it into a prized possession. Aside from nights alone in the theater, it was where he felt most connected to his father.

Cape flowing behind him, Huxley stalked out of the club, ready to put his mind to work and his pedal to the metal.

He stepped outside. He turned toward his car. He saw red.

A redhead, to be precise, the one with the cape-nuzzling fetish. Beatrice Baker was hunched beside his car, intent on something. The disappointment he'd felt at her disappearance lifted. As did his curiosity. He cocked his head, unsure why she'd crouched by his Mustang. Normally Huxley enjoyed unpuzzling unpuzzleable puzzles. His appetite for understanding the bizarre made him an exceptional magician. In this case, the ear-splitting squeal of metal-on-metal clued him in to this woman's nefarious activities.

He saw red for a different reason.

Five furious strides later, Huxley latched his arm around Beatrice's waist and hauled her away from his car. Breathing hard, he gaped in horror at the words scratched into the side of his beloved Mustang: *Assface. Isopod. Kerivoula kach…*

Deciphering the final word proved challenging.

He read it several times, ignoring the writhing woman locked against his chest. He should yell at her, demand to know what the *fuck* she was doing. Instead he asked, "What's a kerivoula kachi…*nini?*"

"Not kachi*nini*. Kachi-*nen-sis.*"

The pronunciation seemed to drain her energy, plus it clarified nothing. It also wasn't exactly what she'd written. "What's a kerivoula kachinensis?"

She sagged into his chest. "An ugly bat. The kind that breaks promises and goes on dates in the same calendar day. The worst kind of bat."

Huxley replayed their bar interaction, wondering if he'd said something rude, offending her in some way. But she'd been the one who'd called him a colon rectum then, and a kerivoula kachinensis now. "And why did you key its name into my car?"

She deflated farther. "He wants honesty."

Her voice trembled and hitched, but the longer he looked at his vandalized car, the hotter his anger burned. He'd been drawn to her in the bar, would have been happy spending the evening talking with her about magic capes while enjoying her colorful outfit and beautiful profile. All he saw now was his damaged paint job.

Hand still secured around her waist, he tried to dig his cell from his pocket. "I'm not sure who wants your honesty, but I'm calling the cops."

Her spine snapped straight. "No. God, please. *No.*"

Huxley tipped to the side, ready to give this woman an earful, but the sight of her face had him swallowing his tirade. Tears streamed down her cheeks and her pale skin had turned red and blotchy. The sadness he'd noticed behind her playfulness earlier was on full display, as was the extent of her drunkenness. He should dial nine-one-one, place her under a citizen's arrest, but instead he found himself gentling his tone. "Who wants your honesty?"

"Nick the Prick."

He knew no magicians by that name. All signs pointed to boyfriend trouble. "And you thought he wanted it scratched into *my* car?"

"Not your car. *His* car. He lied to me. They all lie to me. They think they're being honest, but they're not." She shook her head, and her cheek rubbed against his cape. She nuzzled closer, mumbling, "Soooo soft."

His stomach tightened. He didn't remember the last time he'd held a woman this close. She was three sheets to the wind, had vandalized his beloved Mustang, but her distress loosened something in his chest. He glanced again at the jagged letters keyed into his perfect paint job and gritted his teeth. He arranged her boneless body against the side of his car and waited for her to gain her equilibrium.

"Sorry about the prick," he said, stepping back. "But this isn't his car. This is my car."

Her half-mast eyelids shot up. "No, no, no. It's *his* black Mustang. 1976. A Cobra! I know this car. There was sex in this car."

That visual heated his blood, but he reined in his focus. "Sex may have happened in a *black* Mustang, but this lovingly restored *1977* Mustang Cobra is midnight blue, not black. And it belongs to me."

"No."

"Yes."

"No, no, no," she said again. She stared at the paint job, her eyes growing impossibly wide as she traced the white pinstripe on the hood. "No." This time it was a whisper.

"Afraid so. Which means you'll have to pay for damages."

Her tormented gaze didn't stray from the scratched car. "I can't believe...I mean, I'm so, so sorry—this isn't me. I don't do this." More tears followed her fumbling apology. "I'll pay for it. I don't have a job, or money, but I'll find a way." She sucked in a sharp breath and clutched his shirt in desperate fists. "I'm the only one without a mug shot. I can't be arrested."

When he caught up with her verbal whiplash, his agitated mind settled, and his call with Ashlynn suddenly became less troublesome. *Jobless. Broke.* Maybe he didn't need a long drive to puzzle out his current dilemma. Not when one Miss Beatrice Baker had offered him an answer in a petite, drunk package.

Gingerly, he loosened her fists from his shirt and eased her back against his car. "If you can't pay me now, and you don't want the cops involved, I have a solution."

She bit her lip. "I thought it was his car. I swear. I didn't mean it." A dreamy look overtook her sad features. Her attention moved to his face. Like in the bar, she didn't cringe at his scars. "I really like your hat. And the galaxy."

Her fascination with his costume was unexpected. As was the animal vocabulary, the mug shot quandary, and her criminal activities. This woman was both mystifying and infuriating. He should still be livid with her, but Huxley found himself entranced by her as she spoke. Beatrice had spectacular lips and stunning gray eyes. Even unfocused, her eyes resembled the stirrings of a rainstorm.

Huxley loved tipping his face up to the rain.

Beautiful women didn't usually care for his cape or hat or line of work. They often frowned at the burned half of his eyebrow and scarred cheek with disgust. She likely would, too, when sober. "Well, Miss Beatrice Baker, if you didn't mean to key my particular car, then I might be willing to offer you a deal."

Her reply: "You're tall."

"You're short."

"That's rude."

"So is calling someone tall."

She pursed her kissable lips.

"As I was saying, I can offer you a compromise." When she didn't interrupt with random nonsense this time, he went on, "I'd like you to work for me." The proposition wasn't ideal. It meant living with his father's defaced car, the insults visible for everyone to see, but he'd dealt with worse.

She scrunched her face. "Are you a pimp?"

"I am not a pimp."

"Do I have to wear skimpy clothes?"

He considered her request. "Yes."

"But you're not a pimp?"

"I am not. I'm an illusionist. You can work for me, as my assistant, until this damage is paid off. But if that doesn't suit you, I can call the cops." The threat had a hint of blackmail to it, a new low for him. But the theater came before everything, and letting her off with unpaid work was kinder than charging her.

Her gaze lingered on his cape, in particular on the stars embroidered on the blue velvet. She ran her fingers over the fabric. "People say I'm too trusting. It usually gets me hurt." Her rainstorm eyes caught him in a downpour. "Can I trust you?"

He was unprepared for the lucidity in her voice, the honesty in her pained gaze. He also didn't like hearing people had hurt her. "You can trust me."

"Okay." She petted his forearm. "Sign me up. As long as you're not a kerivoula kachinensis."

Unsure how to reply to that odd statement, he reached for his phone to enter her details, but she swayed. Huxley caught her before she slipped to the ground.

3

Bea's mouth felt like it was filled with sawdust. Her head throbbed and there was drool caked on her cheek, but something soft swaddled her tender body. She tugged the blanket higher. It smelled faintly of cigars and brandy, like a gentlemen's club. Not that she'd ever been to a fancy club, gentlemanly or otherwise. Still, its cozy weight dulled the stabbing in her temples, its warmth gradually lulling her. She began to drift back to sleep.

Then someone clapped by her ear. "Time to wake up."

Bea went to pull the blanket over her head and cuddle deeper into the sheets, when she remembered she didn't have a bed to sleep in. She cracked an eye open. "Where am I?"

A tall man stood over her, arms crossed. His unusual features reorganized themselves as she focused, becoming handsome. And familiar. "You're the Monet."

The corner of his mouth kicked up. "Not sure about that, but I am Huxley Marlow, and you're in my theater. You passed out last night, so I brought you here."

Passed out? Bea shot to a sitting position and regretted it instantly. Her head felt slushy and her cozy blanket slipped to her lap. She took stock of her clothes, pleased her polka dot top and pedal pushers were still on. At least sex didn't happen. Then she noticed the blanket on her lap wasn't a blanket at all. It was a cape, midnight blue, embroidered with gold stars. She remembered this cape. Specifically, wanting to nuzzle it.

Snippets of her night floated back: mixing cold medicine with alcohol. Cape. Nuzzle. Carrie Underwood. Keys. Car. *Holy hell.* "I keyed your car," she croaked.

"That you did. Which means you now work for me."

He wasn't wearing the top hat she remembered, or any fanciful clothing. He was in dark jeans and a fitted thermal shirt. Ordinary by all accounts. That didn't mean he wasn't dangerous, and she didn't remember accepting a job from him. She smoothed her hands over the cape. Only vampires wore capes, or superheroes, or seedy characters. "Are you a pimp?"

"We established my non-pimping last night."

"Do you sleep in a coffin?"

"I prefer beds."

She massaged her temples. "Last night is hazy."

"I imagine it is. I brought you coffee and beignets."

There were a barrage of questions she should have launched, but her brain snagged on the word *beignet*. She rolled her tongue around her stale mouth, salivating at the thought. "I've never had a beignet." The longing in her voice was almost embarrassing.

"That, Honeybee, is a travesty in need of reform." Huxley jerked his chin toward a table by the far wall.

Ignoring the Honeybee chide, she approached his offered gifts. The coffee and beignets sat on what looked like a makeup table—a mirror filled the wall behind it, bright lights framing the rectangle. Tucked in the corner was a pretty cage that housed three doves. Its inhabitants regarded her sternly. On the opposite wall, a closet overflowed with glitzy, shiny, velvety clothes.

Her hazy mind, still seeing the world in slow-mo snippets, connected the surrounding dots: Top hat. The cape. The theater. The birds. Extravagant clothes. Dressing room. "Am I being sold to the circus?" As she spoke, she snagged a still-warm beignet and shoved it into her mouth. She moaned and sank onto a chair.

She'd been dying to try a beignet. It had been one of Nick the Prick's selling features when pitching their runaway adventure. They were going to try every beignet New Orleans had to offer. Her anger from yesterday returned, but there was no sadness. No desire for the man who'd dumped her on a whim. Only frustration with her own naiveté, always assuming the best in people.

Pollyanna, her history teacher had labeled her as a teen. Idealistic. Too trusting. Too *nice*. The woman had claimed Bea was a dormant volcano packed with unaired grievances that would one day erupt and bury her friends under suppressed anger.

The volcano imagery may have been overkill, but Bea probably shouldn't have thanked her teenage nemesis, Tanya Fry, for trying to dye her hair orange for a football game. The offer had seemed genuine, even if Tanya had recently scratched "loser" into Bea's locker. Bea had wound up with green strands that had fallen out in clumps.

Most people would turn cynical after enough setbacks, but Bea wanted to live life in full color, face adversity with a smile. Give people the chance to change. Unless she was drunk.

Drunk Bea was the definition of bitter and sullen.

Now she was sober(ish) and she had a beignet in her mouth. It was everything she'd hoped it would be, crispy and chewy, rich and light. She couldn't control her throaty sounds as she nibbled on the dough and sucked powdered sugar from her fingers. This was heaven wrapped in a deep-fried package.

"I think I'm in love," she murmured.

One of the doves cooed.

Huxley cleared his throat, drawing her attention from the pastry in her hand to his unhandsome-handsome face. He was watching her eat, staring with abandon, as though she was his to stare at. Warmth unfurled in her belly, mingling with the decadent beignet.

"Wait until you try the cream-filled ones," he said in a rumbling baritone, his gaze locked on her lips.

Was that a hint of innuendo in his voice? He *had* called her beautiful last night. Something else she remembered. His eyes darkened slightly as she studied him, and their colors, *plural*, took her aback. The left was a sky blue with brighter flecks. The right was brown, darker and more serious. "Heterochromia," she said.

She'd learned the term from researching the world's ugliest dogs. That Google search had produced an onslaught of Mexican hairless dogs, oddly followed by Siberian husky puppies with two-toned eyes, fluffy fur, and a whole lot of adorableness. She'd also gotten a face full of horse-on-horse porn.

Huxley blinked. "Most people don't know the name of the condition. They also don't know what a kerivoula kachinensis is."

She licked more sugar from her fingers, ignoring the paint caked under her nails. His two-toned eyes followed the movement. "With a name like Bea, I had to defend myself against insect insults. Calling someone a kerivoula kachinensis or banana slug or mole rat, or anything to throw them off, proved helpful."

"Why not go by your full name?"

"Beatrice?" She wrinkled her nose. "Beatrice is a ninety-year-old woman who removes her teeth at night, wears massive sunglasses, and drinks Metamucil instead of martinis. No thank you."

Huxley's half-eyebrow twitched and his light blue eye sparked with...mirth? "Or maybe Beatrice is a feisty red-head who moans when she eats fried dough, can't handle her liquor, and likes to scratch misspelled insults into strangers' cars."

That hit below her high-waisted belt. Shame turned her voice into a whisper. "I'm sorry about your car. I can't believe I did that."

He stepped closer. "I'll make sure to work you extra hard, *Beatrice*."

Again with the possible innuendos, but he didn't smile. He studied her as if waiting for some kind of reaction. She couldn't tell if he was teasing or angry. It was hard to focus with the fuzziness in her head. The sugar melting on her tongue distracted her further, as did the way he'd said her name: *Beatrice*. Slowly, with a sensual roll to the syllables. No one in the history of ever had made "Beatrice" sound sexy. Until one Huxley Marlow tried her name on for size.

Unsure how to process her strange circumstances, she popped the last bite of beignet into her mouth. She moaned again while cataloguing the framed pictures adorning the walls, all featuring the title: The Marvelous Max Marlow. They seemed dated, a series of older posters. Huxley's father, maybe? She wiped her sticky fingers on her pants, only to realize Huxley's cape was still scrunched on her lap. A cape now covered with her sugary fingerprints.

She cringed and held out the defiled garment. "I'm sorry about this, too."

Brow furrowed, he took his cape. He didn't accept her apology or offer an understanding nod. He simply folded the garment delicately over his forearm, like it was a precious thing. "Do you need to get home? Let anyone know where you are?"

"No." The harshness of her reality swiftly sank in. There was no home to go to, no one who would miss her. Just as quickly, she realized sharing this fact with a virtual stranger wasn't in keeping with any stranger-danger rules. "Actually, I'll send a text to my friend. She'll be wondering where I am. I'll tell her I'm at the..." She waited for Huxley to fill in the blank as she moved to the bed and found her purse. Her wallet and EpiPen were still safely inside.

"The Marlow Theater. On Decatur Street."

She tried to power up her phone, but the screen remained dark. The more she charged the battery these days, the fewer hours it functioned. Another fact Huxley didn't need to know. Keeping the device angled away from him, she typed nonsense and pretended to hit Send. Spying a charger on the makeup table, she made a mental note to use it once he left.

She returned her defunct cell to her purse and fixed him with a pointed stare. "My friend knows where I am now."

Translation: if she went missing, her invisible friend would raise hell.

Unconcerned by her proclamation, he said, "Good. We'll start right away." He walked to the glitzy, shiny, velvety closet and pulled out a garment. "This should fit. You'll wear it tonight."

The miniscule outfit looked like an ice-skating costume. "So you're not a pimp, but you *did* sell me to an ice show to cover the cost of your car and the cape dry-cleaning? Now I'll be forced to skate as an extra in the ice performance of *Pretty Woman*. Am I close?" Bea may owe this man money and would avoid his calling-the-cops threat like the plague, but a woman of the street she was not.

He lay the sequined bodysuit and micro-skirt on the bed beside her. "I didn't sell you to a circus or an ice show. No prostitution is required. You're now a member of the Marvelous Marlow Boys magic ensemble, along with me and two of my brothers. Five nights a week, you'll perform on stage as our assistant."

"Whoa there, magic man." She would have laughed, but the beignet in her belly was searching for an eject button. "You must be mistaken."

She hadn't performed in public since the sixth grade Chrismukkah assembly where she'd frozen so badly someone had physically carried her off stage.

Panicked, she sneezed. Twice. Her nervous tic.

Huxley paid her freak-out no mind, but he did bless her, so quickly she didn't have time to thank him. "There's Advil in the drawer," he went on, a bit more irritation in his tone. "I suggest you take a couple. There's a shower and bathroom across the hall. I left a toothbrush in there for you, and my former assistant stocked it with womanly essentials. In your few coherent moments last night, you mentioned something about a car parked near Club Crimson. If you give me your keys and tell me what make it is, I'll drive it over."

"I can't perform," she squeaked again, twitching her nose to keep from sneezing. "I have stage fright."

Exasperation pulled his features tight, especially his scars. She wanted to ask about them, touch them, paint them. Imperfections made people unique, each story and flaw mixing the colors that mapped their lives. She wondered what colors had shaped Huxley's past. Until he said, "If you want me to call the cops, just say the word."

Now she wanted to flick his funny bone. Blackmail, that's what this was. He was blackmailing her to stand on stage in front of a crowd, where she would no doubt turn into a petrified statue. He had her number, and he knew it. That was okay. She'd agree for now, then she'd find a way to out-blackmail his blackmailing.

He took her silence as an agreement. "I need your keys."

She stuck her hand back in her purse, delaying as she reassessed her situation.

She was doing it again, assuming the best in someone. Trusting her father had been unequivocal proof her intuition often failed her. Even worse was dealing directly with his loan shark, suggesting he allow her to cover Franklyn Baker's debt. On layaway. Over ten years. All to save her father from his own bad decisions. The goateed criminal had given her a much shorter deadline, one that came with bodily harm if missed. She had smiled and thanked him. And fled to New Orleans.

Which brought her to the here and now, and another man testing her instincts. She would never again let her father, or any hint of gambling, back into her life. But Huxley could have made a much bigger deal about the damage to his car. He seemed genuinely nice, had put her to bed, fully clothed, under his precious cape. He'd bought her food and coffee. She also had nowhere to live and couldn't afford rent.

If she asked to sleep in this scarlet dressing room, Huxley would likely request money upfront. Working in the theater, however, might allow her to sneak in and crash in a corner. Not ideal, but better than sleeping in her car.

Decision made, she tossed her keys toward him. "I drive a yellow Beetle."

He caught them one-handed and smirked. "A bee driving a Beetle. You could make that into a picture book."

Maybe he wasn't so harmless. "Or I could use your magic wand and turn you into a blobfish."

Her threat didn't keep him from ordering her around. "Rehearsal starts in twenty minutes. Meet me on stage. Don't be late."

Her fuzzy head may have been crippling her ability to focus, but she still couldn't fathom why he'd concocted this arrangement. Who would want a girl with stage fright and no experience working with them? Thoughts of capes and vampires plagued her once more.

As Huxley turned to leave, she asked, "What happened to your last assistant?"

A pirate smile shifted his features into another startling masterpiece. "I sawed her in half."

4

Huxley's trip to move his new assistant's car took longer than intended. Beatrice Baker was a conundrum, one he intended to solve. It didn't take a genius to know she'd typed gibberish into her phone, when supposedly texting a friend, and her agreement to work for him instead of facing the cops was suspect. Still, he didn't snoop through her belongings. It wasn't the civilized thing to do. He did, however, lose track of time once inside her yellow Beetle.

The first thing to hit him was the smell of watermelon. He'd noticed the sweet, fruity aroma last night, whiffs of it curling past his nose when she'd cuddled his arm.

As enticing as the watermelon in the car was, it was the interior of the old Beetle that distracted him most. Small paintings adorned the dashboard and doors, detailed sections of faces, whimsical in nature: a nose and lips here, eyes and eyebrows there, almost like slivers of people lived in the vehicle. Paint splattered the floor. A rainbow dangled from her rear-view mirror. But her steering wheel gave him the most pause.

One word was written on the rim in block letters: *SMILE.*

He did just that—he smiled. Huxley couldn't help himself. Like he couldn't help hitting on her the night they'd met. If the paint caked under his new assistant's fingernails was any indication, this artwork was hers. An eccentric honeybee.

He wondered what she saw when looking at his face, how she would paint the burn on his eyebrow, the fibrous tissue of his scars. The ugly marks on his chest and abdomen. It made sense now, the way she'd studied him earlier, calling him a Monet as though fascinated. Not the flicker of interest he'd hoped he'd seen. It was how Huxley watched a fellow illusionist, picking apart each movement instead of enjoying the show. He was a curiosity to her. A subject.

The notion disappointed him.

He got lost studying her miniature paintings, picturing Beatrice, brush in hand, bringing these peculiar portraits to life. The corners of his lips lifted again, muscles that had atrophied over the years, until this firecracker had asked to nuzzle his cape. There was just something about her quirky paintings and watermelon smell that affected him while he sat in this unusual car that swelled with her uniqueness.

By the time he parked and walked toward the theater, he was late. Huxley hated being late. Lateness was a sign of irresponsible laziness and disorganization. His brother, Axel, was the poster child for that affliction. Strides quickening, he went to cross the street but stopped halfway. A man in a green Polo-style shirt and khakis was taking photos of his theater. The man dropped the camera around his neck and scribbled on a clipboard. Not a good sign.

A car honked. Huxley finished crossing the street, halting a foot behind the stranger. "Can I help you?"

The man kept scribbling. When he turned, Huxley bit his tongue to keep from cursing. On the right side of the man's shirt, the name *Evans* was stitched. On his left side were words that had Huxley running a mental tally of his bank account and every City of New Orleans housing code his theater might have breached: *Code Enforcement Inspector.*

"The name's Larry Evans." The enforcer thrust his hand forward. Huxley returned the handshake robotically as his mind ran a mile a minute. Evans went on, "We had a blight complaint lodged a month ago against this building. I'm documenting the infractions. A hearing will be set afterward, usually thirty days from when we complete a title search on the property. Gotta say"—he shook his head at the deteriorating façade—"you have your work cut out for you."

"The place is a dump." Edna Lisowsky shuffled past them with her usual sunny demeanor. His two-hundred-year-old employee had worked the Marlow ticket booth since opening day. Her glasses were twice the size of her face. None of her teeth were her own. But her snake-headed cane doubled as a bludgeoning tool when pesky teens came sniffing around. The brats didn't give them trouble.

Huxley was scared of the woman, too. "You can work from home anytime you like," he told her, as he often did. "I'll reroute calls there. We'll open the booth in the afternoon instead."

She shriveled her already shrunken mouth and tapped her cane on the cement. "My husband is at home. All day. Every day. Working in that stuffy booth, in this rundown theater, is a vacation. Come to think of it, you should open seven days a week. Lord knows you need the cash."

She meandered off, and Huxley dragged a hand down his face. He didn't need to be told how strapped he was for cash or that the theater was rundown. The shortcomings haunted him daily. The red-and-gold paint job was peeling in sections. The cornices and lintels were chipped, as were the bases of a few decorative columns. Two second-story windows were cracked, the exterior lights had rusted, and the fissures running through the foundation were probably why rats inhabited the building. There was also the broken fire escape and warped gutters.

After trying and failing to upgrade the property over the years, Huxley had studied the ins and outs of code enforcement, researching his worst-case scenarios. If this was a blight complaint, only the exterior would be analyzed, but it would hit hard. Without the cash to fix every violation, he'd be slapped with a Notice of Judgement. The City would put a lien on his theater, and they'd auction off his father's pride and joy in a sheriff's sale. If they somehow discovered his electrical wiring and plumbing weren't up to code, they could shut him down *now* until it was fixed. Thank God it was only a blight issue.

He faced the enforcer. "Who lodged the complaint?"

Evans checked his clipboard. "A Ms. Loretta Welsh."

Huxley fisted the car keys in his hand, mulling over the name. He didn't know a Loretta Welsh, but he did know a Great Otis Oliphant, who would give his left nut to acquire the Marlow Theater. A horrifying prospect. He could picture Oliphant at their poker games, bragging about buying his birthright for a song and dance, relishing twisting that knife in his gut. He sensed Oliphant's twitchy mustache all over this development. That didn't change his predicament.

Without the money to get the building up to code, he'd lose everything.

"Got it," he told the enforcer, unable to curb his curtness. "I came into some cash. The theater will be good as new before the hearing." The lie tasted bitter.

Evans cowered slightly, shoulders hiked, like he was waiting for a sucker punch. When none came, he relaxed. "Well, that's swell to hear. I usually get yelled at or assaulted. Maybe it'll take me a bit longer to request the title search."

It was a decent gesture, but he'd need more than an extra few days to fix this mess.

Leaving Evans to finish estimating the theater's time of death, he entered the building, his temper growing with each stride. Oliphant was a weasel in need of neutering, but the fact that Huxley had let the Marlow Theater fall into this level of disrepair was the bigger blow.

Before his death, Max Marlow had planned to restore the declining building, returning it to its pristine glory. The dream had died with the great man, when he'd shackled his wrists and sealed himself in a water-filled barrel. He'd normally had sufficient room to execute his dramatic escape, but a dent in the side had sealed his father's fate and lungs.

It had also thrust Huxley into the role of Surly Brother, as Axel often quipped. The responsible one. The demanding one. The one who couldn't even convince their sorry excuse for a mother to lend them money.

Now the Marlow Theater was reduced to one ugly word. *Blight.*

He needed to increase daily attendance. He needed to up the stakes at his weekly poker games. He needed a goddamn miracle.

What he had instead was a new assistant with stage fright and no experience, whose perfectly odd uniqueness had already caused him more distractions than he could afford.

Bea sat on the stage, legs dangling over the edge, her head still soupy from last night's events. When Huxley finally walked in, she pretended to study the watch she didn't own. "You're late."

"You're wearing the same thing you slept in," Huxley said, terse. "Where's your costume?"

Since he didn't glance at her, she wasn't sure how he knew she was still in last night's outfit. Maybe it was one of his magic skills. "I didn't think I needed to be half-naked for the rehearsal. Plus, it's cold in here."

"You need to get comfortable in the costume. If you put it on your first night, you'll be self-conscious." He said this while stomping up the stage stairs, eyes on the ground. He disappeared behind the side curtains.

Bea picked at the paint forever stuck under her nails. She *had* been late meeting him and worried he'd be annoyed. Turned out she'd been more on time than he was, which was a first for her.

Bea was the type to forget a minute only held sixty seconds. There were just so many *things* to explore in every given moment, and this theater was teeming with fascinations. Aside from old posters on the walls, and the other dressing rooms filled with fanciful costumes, she'd stumbled into a prop room laden with dummies and cages and feathered hats. She'd even found a dinosaur skull. A mecca of magical curiosities. So magical, her fingers had twitched, as though her creative dry spell might come to an end.

Excited to sneak in at night and paint, she'd found a cracked second-story window and had opened it a smidge— her perfect secret entrance.

Squatting in this theater at night could be just what Bea needed. She didn't, however, relish the idea of rehearsing in the chilly space wearing little more than a bathing suit. Not that it mattered. She may have been pretending to go along with their arrangement, but she wouldn't be performing in front of a crowd *ever*, so Huxley needn't worry about her self-consciousness.

He remained behind the curtains, but another man strode in from the entrance, clad in worn jeans. He wore a pair of

Secret Service sunglasses, and his white T-shirt was printed with the word *Jenius*. He stopped inches from her kicking legs. "You're not Ashlynn," he said.

She looked down at her torso, confirming she had not indeed swapped bodies with anyone. "Nope. I'm Bea."

He pulled his glasses down his nose and peered at her over the frames. "What happened to Ashlynn?"

Deducing that the mysterious Ashlynn was the assistant Bea had replaced, she said, "I believe she was sawed in half."

The man nodded as though death by saw was the most normal thing in the world. "I'm assuming the surly brother hired you. I'm Axel, the charming one."

He offered Bea his hand, and she extended hers in response. Gaze a smolder, he brought her knuckles to his lips for a gallant kiss.

Axel was indeed a charmer, and a looker. His reddish eyebrows were both intact, and there were no scars on his clean-shaven cheeks or flesh missing from his ear. His strong chin and defined biceps were attractive, but she found herself wanting to search for Huxley. To catch another glimpse of the surly brother who'd bought her a toothbrush and had tucked her under his cape. She also had no urge to paint Axel's pretty profile.

He removed his sunglasses and hooked them on the front of his shirt. "Who have you worked for?"

She studied the cracked plaster ceiling, silently running through her résumé. Fresh murkiness clouded her thoughts, like she was there but not there, but she powered on. "Depending how far back you'd like me to go, there were the Debrovsky and Wheeler families. The Debrovskys had a hot tub, so babysitting there was fun, but the Wheelers stocked Skittles. I worked for Ace Painters on and off for a few years. I painted interiors and exteriors for them, but only if the owners wanted rainbow colors. Taupes make me itch. My waitressing list is long, mainly because I—"

"Let me stop you there, Rainbow Brite." Axel's lips flattened as though holding in a laugh. "Magic experience only. I don't need your biography. Just tell me which shows you've worked."

The edges of her vision turned hazy, and she pressed her hand to her temple. It didn't help much. "None."

"None?"

"Zero."

Axel no longer looked ready to laugh. "And *Huxley* hired you?"

"Yep. The surly brother." Her joints joined her head's mutiny, all extremities turning heavy at once. "Is it okay if I lie down?" Not waiting for his answer, she lay on her side and tucked her knees into the fetal position. Today was not an upright day.

Footsteps sounded from the entrance of the theater again. The owner of the slow stride appeared next to Axel. He didn't question Bea's horizontal status or ask who she was. He simply stared at her so long her eyelids drooped. Then he said, "Why did Huxley replace Ashlynn with a drunk painter?"

She forced her eyes open. "I'm not drunk." She didn't like being anything like her father, and the word *drunk* character- ized the man whose gambling and drinking had been respon- sible for Bea going to work instead of finishing high school.

The new arrival lifted a skeptical eyebrow.

She called his eyebrow and raised him a stink-eye. "I'm in a *sleep fog*, for your information, from last night's cold medicine and martini combo. And how'd you know I was a painter?"

"Ignore Fox," Axel said. "He reads minds and performs as a mentalist. He's the clever one."

More like the sneaky one. Where Axel was affable with a thick head of messily styled auburn hair and casual threadbare clothes, Fox's tailored black ensemble emphasized the serious set of his sly features. His ponytail was precisely tied.

She blinked at their sideways selves. "So Max is your father, and there's Huxley and Axel and Fox…I'm sensing a pattern here." Stuck with the name Beatrice, she'd spent countless hours obsessing over other people's names.

Axel scratched his chest lazily. "Our other brothers are Paxton and Xander. Dear old Dad thought the letter X was an underused consonant."

She smiled. Overusing an underused consonant was quirky perfection. "You should have—"

"The name was taken," Fox cut in before she suggested they name their magic ensemble the X-Men. Mind reader, indeed.

Fox continued his silent staring.

Axel beamed at her. "You'll fit in fine here. Where did Hux run off to?"

She gathered her knees tighter and yawned. "I couldn't say. He was late to meet me, then he disappeared. He was angry I wasn't in costume."

Axel crouched until they were nearly nose-to-nose. "Did you say Huxley was late?"

Another yawn. "Late as a bad date."

He stood and faced Fox. Fox did his crafty mind reading and said, "Yes."

Bea tried to follow the remainder of their one-way conversation, which involved Axel's tone rising in worry over Huxley's lateness while Fox did an excellent impression of a brick wall. Apparently, Huxley was a time stickler. A rule stickler in general, if she had to guess.

The longer Axel spoke, the heavier her eyelids became. "Is it okay if I go lie down for a bit?"

"You're already lying down," Axel said.

She patted the hard floor. "The dressing room cot is a tad more comfy. I'll just take a quick nap."

Fox didn't add his two cents.

Axel shrugged. "As long as you don't mind dealing with a pissed-off Huxley, go for it."

She hadn't quite figured out Huxley yet. He'd been flirty last night, kind but gruff this morning, and bluntly curt not long ago. Pissed off didn't seem a stretch for him, but her body felt heavy, the ache in her temples crowding her vision. A bit more sleep was worth poking a growly bear.

5

Bea woke to the sound of an all-night rave. It took a moment to remember why she was in a dressing room, and that she was supposed to be rehearsing, not sleeping. At least she felt halfway human. Instead of a cape, a ratty quilt was draped over her body—one she didn't recall finding—and techno tunes pumped through the walls. She tapped her toes and wiggled her hips, doing a jig in her cozy position. If music played, she danced. It was a sickness.

As she shimmied, she lifted to sitting.

One glance in the makeup mirror suggested her intended cat nap had been more of a dead-to-the-world sleep. The pillow creases on her cheek were far from attractive. She rummaged through her purse, popped a mint into her mouth, then swiped her lips with a splash of watermelon. Beignets plus Advil plus sleep, plus her trusty lip-gloss, and she no longer felt like she was drifting underwater. A change of clothing would have completed her recovery, but she felt fairly ready to take on the world.

Or at least discover the source of the trance tunes.

Before leaving, she checked her newly charged phone and froze. There were no messages, but today's date seemed to glow, a reminder of the past she'd hoped to leave behind in Chicago. With her recent traveling and lack of work schedule, the date had eluded her. There was no avoiding it now.

Today was the day she'd told Big Eddie she'd pay the remainder of her father's debt. She still wasn't sure how she'd gathered the courage to meet her father's latest loan shark, let alone bargain with him. The bar she'd entered had been the sort of dive flashed on the nightly news with words like *gunshots* and *arrests*. Big Eddie had jolted at the sight of her and stared, oddly slack-jawed, until she'd introduced herself.

Immediately, he'd curled his lip and said, "Of course he sent you."

Bea had almost run out in her kitten heels, but she'd pictured her father bruised and battered and forced herself to stay put. She had blabbered about Franklyn Baker's gambling issues and drinking issues, while begging for leniency. She'd promised to pay the ten grand he owed slowly over ten years. A fib to buy her father time to gather cash. Big Eddie had stared at her so long, sweat had descended her spine. At a loss, she'd forced a plaintive smile.

He'd muttered, "Shit," an inscrutable look on his face, then his dark eyes had hardened. "You can tell your father his plan backfired. This debt's now on you, and the deadline stays. Ten grand *plus* an additional five in interest. And don't think I ain't serious. You'll lose one finger for every day your payment's late."

Without the money, she'd latched onto Nick's New Orleans offer and left town, desperate for a fresh start that didn't involve her father or threatening loan sharks. Today's date was either the start of that new beginning, or a ticking clock toward its end.

Refusing to dwell on her past, she stood. She'd been discreet about leaving and had changed her number. She no longer owned a credit or debit card, thanks to her father. She'd even disabled her phone's GPS. It was time to focus on her future and the trance tunes teasing her ears, not her father's unfixable mistakes.

Bea followed the sound through the narrow hallway. Once at the theater's stage, she tucked herself next to the tall crimson curtain and peered out.

If this was the crowd the Marvelous Marlow Boys drew nightly, maybe performing on stage wouldn't be so terrifying. Six senior citizens sat in the center of the darkened room. Two were nodding off, the other four in a catatonic state. A few families were spread out, comprised of teens on their phones, while most adults paid cursory attention to the stage.

Watching her first Marlow Boys show from the wings didn't seem appropriate, so she snuck back the way she'd come and poked around until she found the auditorium entrance. She slipped quietly into a seat, but it collapsed on one side, nearly spilling her onto the floor. Squishing to the left, she studied the dark interior again, looking for Big Eddie or any other unsavory sorts, then she chided herself for her paranoia. She was untraceable, and her father had probably paid off Big Eddie by now. That man had a knack for landing on his feet.

She forced her focus to the stage spectacle.

A Milky Way of stars smattered the black curtain behind the three brothers. Only Huxley wore a cape and hat, strutting around the stage with command. He moved; the cape swished. Silently, he communicated with his brothers to flank a central coffin-like box.

She side-eyed the contraption.

Huxley had said he didn't sleep in coffins, except his wording had leaned toward the vague. *I prefer sleeping in beds*, he'd claimed. Maybe he was a vampire after all. A blood-drinking, forever-living, garlic-hating undead person. She'd have to test his skin for sparkles.

The techno beat turned trippy. Huxley worked the stage, motioning to the coffin-box, while Axel and Fox spun it round and round, proving there were no escape hatches.

Although all men wore black slacks and oozed charisma, each had a persona. Huxley, in his gold button-down, walked with authority, his broad shoulders squared, head held high. Axel was all swagger in a blood-red shirt, easy grin in place. Fox moved with feline grace, striding smoothly while mind reading. His button-down was a sneaky jet black, of course. They made quite the team.

Until they stopped spinning the coffin.

One of the spotlights sparked. A kid ran up the aisle, complaining about the music. Someone's phone rang. Huxley froze, frustration in his jerky movement. He either hadn't noticed Bea, or he was ignoring her.

Standing taller, he made a final circle around the black box, but Fox moved toward the back as well. The two bumped shoulders and Huxley's jaw tightened. Fox closed his eyes briefly. To the beat of a heavy bass, Huxley pushed on. He opened the top third of the box. Fox climbed in and attempted to lie down. More like he shoved his tall body inside. His ponytail caught on the edge, and it looked like he jammed his knee.

Finally, his black wingtips poked out the bottom end and wiggled. He grimaced, hinting that this wasn't his usual role. This was likely Ashlynn's role. Which meant it was now Bea's role. She bit her lip.

If she were up there, Huxley wouldn't be scowling at Fox and Fox wouldn't be contorting himself to fit into a too-small coffin. Not that Bea's stage skills would have done the Marlow Boys proud. They'd have been forced to manually shove her stage-fright body inside the contraption. Still, their bumbling made her rethink evading her assistant duties. Helping friends in need was as important to her as avoiding all things taupe. She also strived to better herself, a side effect of watching her father walk the path of least resistance.

She wasn't sure Huxley was a friend, but performing in this near-empty theater could help her conquer her stage fright.

A snore sounded. A quick glance showed four of the five seniors now dozing. Granted, the act had hit a small snag, and the music was painfully dated, but the boys were alluring and mysterious. How could anyone not watch their show with bated breath?

She shifted on her wonky seat as Huxley and Axel spun the coffin again. Fox wiggled his shoes some more, proving they were his. The spinning ceased. Axel passed Huxley a massive metal sheet. The two handed it back and forth, banging the thin sides and flipping it around. The music built into a *bow-chicka-boom* beat. Half porn, half techno. Huxley's cape billowed as he twirled and positioned himself behind the coffin, metal sheet raised over the middle. Bea squeezed her bouncing knees together and leaned forward.

Widening his stance, Huxley slashed the metal down, like an axe to a block of wood. She gasped loudly. He halted just before hitting the coffin...and looked right at her. The corner of his lips lifted. Returning his attention to his boxed brother, he repeated the false swing, then he did it again. She gasped each time. She wasn't sure when she'd clutched her hand over her heart. One buzz-cut boy clapped from his seat, equally as rapt. Huxley gave the kid a wink.

With the sheet raised a fourth time, his gaze swept the auditorium. "This might hurt a little."

Her shoulders shivered at his devious tone, her racing heart more aflutter than afraid. She wasn't sure afluttering should happen one calendar day post-breakup, but here she was, aflutter, imagining that devastating voice whispering in her ear.

Down came the metal, cleaving the coffin in half. She squeaked.

Axel and Huxley pulled the coffin apart. Fox, now sliced in two, twisted his head and smirked at the crowd. He pointed and flexed his toes. Huxley walked between the severed body, and Bea couldn't help herself. She clapped wildly, excitedly, horrified by Fox's current state of halfness, but mesmerized. Her face hurt from grinning.

————

Huxley didn't remember the last time he'd loved performing so much. The audience was pitiful. Fox was furious about standing in for Ashlynn. They had to pay a kid to fold himself into the sawing box to become Fox's feet. Yet Huxley felt fifty feet tall. He executed his Reappearing Dollar Bill number with flair. He shot fire from his hands and released doves as though entertaining thousands at the Superdome.

All because of Beatrice.

She squealed and winced and clapped like a kid at Christmas. The fire in his hands may as well have engulfed his chest.

After the show, Axel cornered him in the stage wing. "Fox is fuming."

"I know."

"And that audience was craptastic."

"They were." Except for one redhead who'd enjoyed the shit out of it. And that cute kid whose jaw had hung open for the last half. Even with those unexpected diversions, he could feel his good mood draining, his troubles marching a line across his tensing shoulders.

"Not sure how much more of this I can take," Axel said as he undid the buttons of his red shirt. "We need to shake things up. Make a change. And if you go on about the type of show Dad wanted in his theater, and that we have to honor him—yadda yadda yadda *puke*—I'll deck you."

Huxley removed his hat and scratched his head. "We have bigger problems than shaking up our shows."

He hadn't spoken of his morning encounter yet. His brothers knew the theater needed major work, but Huxley never let on how rough things were. They didn't know how high the bills had piled, or that he'd been struggling to pay Ashlynn. If they questioned the state of affairs—Fox, in particular, was attuned to details—he'd brush off their concern with vague answers about plans and money coming in. He was the oldest brother. The theater had been left to him. It was his responsibility.

Instead of telling them it was spiraling out of control, he'd spent the day brooding. He'd marched into the dressing room, ready to find Beatrice and lay down another ultimatum: the cops or her assistant duties. If she wasn't all in, there was no point training her. Finding her curled up and fast asleep had derailed his plan. She'd looked so peaceful, the antithesis to his unraveling life. He'd covered her with a blanket instead and had watched her sleep longer than was decent, unsure why he didn't want to leave.

He'd finally forced himself out and had driven his vandalized Mustang awhile, followed by a session with his father's puzzle box. He'd hunched over the small contraption, hoping to find his oyster. He still didn't have a plan, or an oyster, and there was no hiding the blight complaint from his brothers.

Axel whipped off his shirt, a nightly habit. The snake tattooed around his ribs writhed as he stretched. "I'm scared to ask, but what could be worse than performing while people play Candy Crush on their phones?"

"We could lose the theater."

His Jane Fonda moves ceased. "Lose it how?"

Before Huxley could reply, Fox joined the duo, his face still sour from his assistant duties. Fox folded his arms and regarded them. His lip curled in irritation. "Was it Oliphant?"

"He's my best guess." Not having to explain much to Fox was always appreciated.

Axel waved his fisted shirt to remind them he hadn't vanished. "You two mind filling me in?"

Huxley fingered the edge of his top hat. It was slightly big on him, like the cape. Like the responsibility of running the theater and ensuring his brothers got paid. He went on to describe the blight complaint and the cost of upgrading the exterior of their real estate under a tight time frame. He tugged at his shirt collar as he spoke.

Axel looked as venomous as his tattooed snake. "First, you're a dick for not telling us right away. Second, if Oliphant is behind the complaint, I'll fill his theater with termites."

"Fact is," Huxley said, "it doesn't matter. The building is rundown. It's become an eyesore, and that's unacceptable. I consider this the push I need to turn it around. I've got it under control."

Fox focused on an indeterminate spot above their heads. "I agree on the dick part, and nothing about this is under control. If Oliphant is the culprit, he won't add more poker games. So unless you've learned how to make cash appear out of thin air, we're in serious trouble."

Fox didn't know the half of it, and Huxley planned to keep it that way. The last time things had fallen this far off track they suggested selling the theater. "Oliphant's always happy to up the stakes, and I have something else on the go." A total lie, but he'd become adept at looking Fox in the eye and feigning confidence.

"We need to modernize the show," Axel said, voicing the same lament Huxley had endured the past few years.

The Marvelous Max Marlow hadn't subscribed to modern. He'd done classic. Elegant. He'd expected Huxley to uphold their family tradition. "More shows," Huxley told them instead, heeding Edna's blunt advice. Their ticket salesperson may have been a crotchety old woman, who often poked her nose where it didn't belong, but she could be shrewd. "We'll go from five days to seven, starting next week. With my other plans, it'll be a cake walk."

"I can do six, not seven," Axel said. "I can't give up my Monday street magic gig. But I'll ramp up those shows, too. Contribute what I earn." His quick agreement eased some of their tension.

"Six works for me, but"—Fox fixed Huxley with a hard stare—"you need to keep us in the loop. And I'll bring in what I can."

Ignoring the "keep us in the loop" jab, Huxley rounded on him. "No pickpocketing."

Fox didn't reply.

"Huxley?"

They all turned at Bea's intrusion. She had a musical voice—innocent in its higher pitch, breathy when questioning. Like now. The boys took their cue, heading to their dressing rooms with a promise to think on their woes. Huxley needed more hours in his day.

He had to speak with a contractor, scrape together cash for a deposit, then scrounge for the rest over the next month, while practicing counting cards and shuffling before his next poker game, all while training his new assistant. Exhaustion overtook him.

He joined Beatrice on the edge of the stage, close in their quiet corner. "You bailed on your training." He'd rather tell her how her enthusiasm had added life to his shoddy theater, but the words stayed packed under his troubles.

She fiddled with the hem of her polka dot top. "Last night was obviously rough for me, and I think I was emotionally drained. It won't happen again. But thanks for covering me with the blanket, assuming it was you who did that."

"It was." He was also the one who'd invaded her privacy, unable to tear his eyes from the slight part of her lips as she'd dozed. He wanted to ask if she was feeling better, but he didn't want to speak. He wanted to listen and let her sweet voice blanket his worries.

She did just that. "I loved your show. I mean, the cape was spectacular, as I knew it would be. The top hat as well. But sawing Fox, the fire and the doves, and the way you all worked the stage—it was mesmerizing. I haven't had this much fun in, well…ever. I hope you know how stupendously magical you are."

"Stupendously magical?"

"The most stupendous."

He stepped closer, feeling like he was walking on air. A magic trick he'd never performed. "Are you still afraid to be on stage?"

She nibbled on her glossy lip. "Yes? But the crowd wasn't quite what I was expecting. I'm willing to give it a shot."

The reminder of the meager crowd renewed his worries, and his briskness. "We have the next two days to rehearse, then we're upping the shows from five days a week to six. I'll ease you into things as much as possible, but you'll need to work hard. The more personal flair you add, the better."

She twirled on the spot. "I can do flair." But she glanced toward the auditorium and paled. Abruptly, she sneezed. A sharp, high-pitched chirp.

Even her sneezes were sweet. "Bless you."

"Thank you," she said, but her eyes were unnaturally wide.

Her stage fright, he surmised. He couldn't afford to pay an assistant, and Fox filling in reduced his brother to testy tantrums. Beatrice and her fears would have to do. "Your car's across the street," he said. "Near Odel's Grocery. But you can use my parking spot in the back tomorrow. Rehearsal starts at ten a.m. It'll just be us. Fox and Axel will join us Tuesday, same time. Don't be late."

She studied her shiny pink shoes, toes knocked together, like she was delaying her departure. "Tomorrow it is," she said eventually, walking backward. "I'm rooming with a friend who lives close, so I can practically roll out of bed and land on stage. The timing shouldn't be a problem." She punctuated the comment with a cheeky smirk.

He nodded, still preferring listening over talking.

"*You*, however, shouldn't be late," she said.

"I'm never late."

"You were this morning."

"First time in my life." Because he'd sat in her car, studying her peculiar paintings, surrounding himself with her watermelon sweetness.

She flicked a hand, dismissing the comment. "Liar."

A liar, Huxley Marlow most certainly was not. "Shall we bet?"

She stopped abruptly, all teasing leaching from her face. "I don't bet."

"Even if I make it worth your while?" He shouldn't be goading her. Or was he flirting? Something else he shouldn't do when he'd been abrupt more often than kind with her. But, hell, she was beautiful. Unique with her fifties flair and glowing innocence. He'd told her as much when they'd met, but nothing had gone according to plan since.

She didn't smile or return his feeble flirting. "I don't bet," she said crisply. *"Ever."*

6

"I'm sorry, did you say *fifteen* thousand dollars?" Huxley paced the sidewalk, unable to still his pulse or dizzying momentum.

Trevor snapped his measuring tape closed. "I'd never gouge you, Hux. But I gotta pay my guys, and there's a shit-ton of work here. If my last job didn't get canceled, I wouldn't even be saying yes."

Witnessing a pickpocket nab Trevor's watch five years ago had served Huxley well, especially since the timepiece held sentimental value. Huxley had then picked the pickpocket's pocket to return the keepsake—a skill he never should have taught Fox, who often trolled the streets like Robin Hood of New Orleans. Huxley rarely performed the service, preferring to avoid tangling with street urchins who preyed on the innocent, but instinct had taken over that day.

Now Trevor owed him. Huxley had sat on the favor, waiting until it would pay off, but material goods and wages weren't costs the big man could swallow.

Huxley rubbed his jaw. "Can you get it done in twenty-nine days?"

"Twenty-nine?"

He nodded. Always best to leave a buffer. "And I can only pay you a couple grand now, but I'll have the rest when the job's done."

Trevor squinted one eye and fiddled with his measuring tape. "Fine. But then we're square."

They shook on the deal, but Huxley's stress levels spiked. He never welched on a promise. If Trevor did the work, Huxley had to pay him, and that two grand would nearly wipe his savings clean. And this was just the exterior. Not the major interior issues he'd have to tackle later, before someone tipped off the City to that disaster.

Agitated, he stalked into the auditorium at 9:28 a.m.

Beatrice wasn't there. So much for her rolling out of bed and falling onto the stage. Heavy with his burdens, he slumped into a theater seat. He came here late some evenings, using the cavernous room as his confessional, sharing his fears and thoughts aloud, as though his father could actually hear him.

Today he waited in silence. The longer he waited, the more he stewed. The more he stewed, the faster his frustrations knotted into anger. Outside of gambling, the only person he could go to for cash was his mother. Last time he'd asked Nadya Marlow for help, she'd looked him in the eye and said, "I hope that theater crumbles to dust."

Beatrice trotted onto stage at 10:04 a.m.

"You're late." Huxley couldn't control his growl.

She raised the cups in her hands, a sheepish smile on her face. "I thought I'd bring us coffee, but the line was longer than expected."

He sighed and rubbed his forehead. "Thank you, but I already had coffee, and we need every available minute for rehearsal. You'll have to drink yours after."

Horror eclipsed her face. "If you knew me, you wouldn't suggest that. I'm liable to fall asleep on my feet."

No, he didn't know her, or her coffee habits. But he'd spent half his evening reliving how she'd beamed and applauded while watching him perform. He couldn't shake thoughts of her. He wasn't sure why. Maybe because he'd wanted to ask her out before his stressful life had kicked him, once again, in the nuts. He *still* wanted to ask her out.

After nine years of putting his theater and brothers first, he couldn't think of anything he'd rather do than court this singular woman. Act on a spontaneous desire for once in his adult life, but she was his assistant. Not exactly a faux pas, but dating led to feelings which led to complications. The last thing he needed was more headaches.

She placed his coffee—that she'd been sweet enough to purchase—on the floor and sipped hers.

Goddamn, his life wasn't fair. "I told you to wear the costume."

"I know, but it's cold in here. And I'm making alterations."

"Did it not fit?"

"It wasn't colorful enough."

He couldn't handle any more color in his world. "The costume is fine as is."

She didn't reply.

Freshly frustrated, he tried not to look at her fitted flower-print pants or ruby off-the-shoulder top. He tried not to imagine her in the silver bodysuit Ashlynn had worn. He stood and began Beatrice Baker's magical education.

———

Huxley's rule-stickler status had been confirmed. Bea had sensed his sternness yesterday, but there had also been a hint of teasing tenderness, along with a shot of caring in the way he'd bought her food and had covered her with a blanket. At the end of the night, he'd seemed to soften briefly as they'd chatted in the darkened theater. He'd even flirted some.

Today he looked like his head might explode.

"Left," he ground out. "When I circle right, you need to turn left. We meet at the back of the stage, then you take my hat when I hold it out." His tone had twisted from irksome to irate during the past three hours.

"Maybe if you explained instructions instead of barking them, they'd be easier to follow."

"If you stopped playing with the props, you'd hear me properly the first time."

She slowly removed his top hat from engulfing her head. "It doesn't fit anyway." But goofing around had kept her from glancing at the large auditorium and imagining it filled with people.

He stalked toward her and snatched the top hat away, cape swishing around his jeans. "It's time to move on. I'm getting the zigzag box."

Bea didn't know what a zigzag box was, but if she could hide inside it, performing might be easier. When she realized he was heading for the prop room behind the stage, her nerves switched tracks.

She'd barely slept last night, thanks to that amazing room and an artistic epiphany that had finally coaxed beauty from her fingers. If she'd left evidence of her paints while tidying, Huxley would likely kick her out. She might struggle to paint again, which was unacceptable.

Bea had been a starving artist since birth. Chocolate syrup finger paintings and mashed potato carvings had occupied her early years. Icing smeared walls and peanut butter sculptures followed. She'd built chewing gum castles and Skittles worlds, all to her mother's delight, using every available food source, choosing art over eating. Starving for her craft.

Then she'd found paint. Glorious, bold, titanic paint. She'd painted windowsills, doorknobs, cutlery, toothbrushes, using surfaces to study portions of people and animals. She'd stolen sections of the world to make them shine. The past seven years, she'd worked odd jobs, while exorcising the muses from her mind and finishing high school through evening classes. She'd saved her pennies and planned to attend the California Institute of Art.

Until Franklyn Baker had ruined that dream.

But dreams were intangible things. They could bend and stretch, appear in black-and-white or color. At twenty-eight, the notion of saving for school again had lost its luster, but the larger problem, the devastation plaguing Bea the past month, had been her creative rut. Since her father had undermined her kindness again, everything she'd painted had been bland, like all her colors turned taupe the second they hit a surface. Lifeless studies. Flat portraits.

An artistic dry spell that had ended last night.

All it had taken was found two-by-fours of wood, her minimal paints and brushes, and a cacophony of magical inspiration. Her mind had bloomed with imagery, the brush an extension of her hand. Squatting at the Marlow Theater was no longer a last resort. She needed this assistant position. She needed this splendiferous building to feed her soul, even if it came with a surly Huxley Marlow and a raging case of stage fright.

A standing coffin-box rolled from the wings, Huxley walking behind it. The frame was electric violet and black, with a white female figure painted on the surface. A cut-out at the top awaited a human face. Two smaller holes—one at the waist, one by the head—seemed to be for hands.

Huxley positioned the box beside her. "This classic illusion has been performed since the sixties. It's called Zigzag

Girl, and we usually do it every show. Since Fox doesn't fit in this box, we did the sawing-in-half piece last night, but you should fit fine."

He barely glanced at her while speaking, an oddity he'd exhibited all day. He'd talk to her knees, her elbows, her shoulders, getting grouchier with each interaction. He held this particular conversation with her hair.

She tried to meet his eyes. "Why is it called Zigzag Girl?"

He palmed the middle section and shoved. The painted body divided into three, its tummy zigging to the right. "That's why."

She beamed. "Give me a sec while I take a picture." Without an audience and her curmudgeonly tutor, this magic gig wasn't half bad.

But Huxley said, "No."

She froze partway to her phone. "I just want to send a quick text to my mom. She'll think this is really fun."

His rigid stance drooped slightly. "I don't have time for texts or fun."

The wistfulness on his face squeezed her heart. "That's the saddest thing I've ever heard."

He finally met her eyes, a piercing gaze that made her feel like she'd eaten a handful of Pop Rocks. "Sadder than passing a homeless child on the street?"

She refrained from rolling her eyes. "Don't be obtuse. And I said *heard* not seen."

"Shall I be isosceles?"

"I'd say you're equilateral. The even-steven sort. And a serious stickler."

His lips pulled up at one side. "A stickler, you say?"

"Of the anal sort."

This time he chuckled. "That could be, but it doesn't change the fact that I don't have time for fun."

"Do you *want* to have fun?"

His attention fixed on her lips. His cheeks hollowed and his breath stilled, like he was slowing his pulse to pass a lie-detector test. "I very much want to have fun."

Yep. Bea had a serious case of Pop Rocks, and she didn't want to frustrate him further. She would photograph the painted box tonight. Text her mother with the tagline, *Guess who's getting zigzagged?* Her mother would probably reply with a picture of a pig's face or fried crickets, or whatever daring meal she'd recently enjoyed, with an equally cheery description.

Bea had once asked her mother, a woman who spent her life chasing fun and adventure, why she'd married Franklyn Baker, a man who often sucked *said* fun out of life. Her mother had stared at her wedding ring, a sad smile on her face. "We loved each other very much back then. He was wild, so full of life. I was dating someone else when we met, a man I cared deeply about, but your father was irresistible. And we had you. I have no regrets."

Molly Baker had left six months later, before Bea's thirteenth birthday. Now her mother snapped photos of her adventures, from skydiving to visiting animal sanctuaries, choosing her whims over family obligation. She and Bea shared snippets of their lives through texts and pictures, like a couple of hashtag friends. Mothering or daughtering never entered into the equation.

The zigzag photo could wait until later.

To Huxley, she said, "Let's get back to work."

He opened the door to help her into the box. "The illusion is the size of the space. The way it's painted on the outside makes it look narrow, but there's extra room inside."

He gripped her hips and moved her to the left. "When I close the box, you place your hands through the two openings.

I'll pass you yellow handkerchiefs, and you'll wave them around. This confirms the hands throughout the number belong to you. After I make a show of proving the metal blades are solid, I'll insert two blades into the box, here and here." He gestured to her neck and waist. "But it's also an illusion. The black handles cover the full width, but the blades themselves are shorter. They only cleave the right side. By squishing yourself to the left, they'll miss you. Then I shove the middle of the box."

Huxley's voice was brisk, but she kept replaying his moment of vulnerability, and his pained words, *I very much want to have fun.*

"I'm sorry," she said hesitantly. "About my goofing off before. I mean, it's not odd for me to act silly, but it's also my nerves. Even being on stage without an audience is making me sweaty."

He looked her in the eye again, staring so long she glanced at her red heels.

"It's not uncommon," he replied, drawing her attention back up. "I used to get nervous before going on stage."

"Yeah?"

"Full sweats. Could barely swallow. But Fox helped me out."

"By reading your mind and telling you to picture the audience naked?"

"Yes and no. He was the only one who figured out that I panicked, but the naked thing never worked for me." Huxley's attention dipped down her torso, and his jaw slackened. Was he picturing her naked now? Her body responded to the possibility, but he strode past her and said, "I'll be back."

He returned swiftly and pressed something silky into her hand. "Fox gave me this. Told me it belonged to the Great Blackstone—a famous magician in the twenties and thirties.

He said it would calm me. He didn't make a big deal about it, but I kept it in my pants pocket and would hold it before I walked on stage. I'd picture Blackstone levitating a woman off a couch or vanishing a bird cage. It turned my focus from the audience to the acts. Maybe it'll help you."

Bea stroked the red handkerchief in her palm. "I can't accept this."

"Nonsense."

"What if your stage fright returns?"

He raised an eyebrow. "I think you need it more than me."

The gesture touched her, but she couldn't accept it without offering something in return. As it stood, he was driving around in a car she'd vandalized. "Okay, but..." She grabbed her purse from the stage edge, which was filled with essentials, including glitter pens and stickers, and pulled out the perfect gift for Huxley. "I insist you take this."

She held out her miniature Cotton Candy My Little Pony doll.

His serious façade threatened to crack. "You want me to have a pink pony?"

"Not just any pony. It's the thirty-fifth anniversary re-issue of the 1983 classic."

Forget cracking. A smile stretched across his handsome face. "Thanks, but it's not necessary."

"That's where you're wrong." She forced it into his hand and touched the corner of his mouth that no longer tilted down. "See this? You don't smile enough, but I bet when you look at Cotton Candy you won't be able to fight the feeling. She'll make your life more fun."

Her hand drifted back to her side, and the amusement on Huxley's face shifted into something more intense. July-fourth-fireworks intense. A marching-band-playing-in-her-chest intense.

"Having you here makes things more fun," he murmured while thumbing his pink toy. "Even when you're testing my patience."

His chest swelled more deeply, rising almost as quickly as hers. Her heart raced so fast it made her dizzy. Huxley was kind one minute, barking orders the next, with glimpses of vulnerability in between, but this admission made her weak in the knees. It also gave her a mission.

She tucked the silky handkerchief into her pocket, sucked in her middle, and flattened her twisted waist against the side of the box. "Then let's master this trick, shall we?"

Huxley's moment of vulnerability vanished, and his lie-detector face resumed, but that didn't change her plan. Since she couldn't pay to fix his Mustang and was crashing in his theater, she owed him more than free assistant services. Her mission unfolded before her, daunting yet critical. Not only would she try to overcome her stage fright and wow their paltry audience, she would do her best to inject more fun into Huxley Marlow's life.

7

Injecting fun into Huxley Marlow's life proved harder than Bea had anticipated. Today's rehearsal had her securing Axel in a straitjacket and locking him in a Plexiglas box. Fox instructed her in the art of choosing the best audience members for his hypnotic hypnosis acts. They then blocked the Flying Playing Card number, where she would have an audience member choose and write on a card. The boys proceeded to pass the marked card from one to the other, without touching it, each of them retrieving it from the oddest places.

She clapped like mad during the demonstration.

On short breaks, she stole Huxley's top hat and wore it until he snatched it back. She danced with his cape like the fabric was a person. Huxley's scowl only grew more severe.

Bea quit trying to make him smile and sighed. "Playing the part of Surly Smurf won't win the crowd."

Axel flashed her a sparkling grin. "I guess that makes me Sexy Smurf."

She would not be duped by his excessive charm. "Nope. That makes you Cocky Smurf. And that one"—she winked at Fox—"is Sneaky Smurf."

Fox's expression remained as stark as his black wardrobe.

"Come on, Smurfette," Axel said. "You haven't even seen me with my wand yet. I'm Sexy Smurf all the way." He swiveled his hips.

"I saw your wand, *Cocky Smurf*. It was smaller than expected."

"You haven't seen it in my hands, though. It's an impressive sight."

"His wand has a tendency to backfire." This from Fox.

Huxley's reddening face looked minutes from erupting, but playing along was too much fun. "Does it shoot sparks?" she asked.

Axel dialed up his smolder. "We should test it and see."

"Enough!" Huxley's face had morphed from tomato to eggplant, the puckered skin of his scars whitening. "Messing around won't prepare us for tomorrow's show. Or bring in more business."

Bea pulled up her polka dot thigh-highs, stalling. She'd mused on their show since the other night. On the snippet she'd caught, at least. She wasn't sure Huxley wanted outside advice from a novice such as herself, but sometimes fresh eyes cast illumination. "I had a thought about the show in general."

"I'm all ears." Axel snatched his straitjacket from the floor and began fastening the buckles. Fox tried to read her mind, but she made sure to only picture unicorns.

Huxley regarded her warily.

She clicked her pink patent heels together, a trick she used growing up when sharing her art with her father. No matter his faults, he'd never fail to praise her work and proclaim her a genius, but sharing her creations had always felt like baring her soul. Clicking her heels together made her think of the *Wizard of Oz* and finding her lioness confidence. "It's about the music," she told Huxley.

"There's nothing wrong with the music," said the surly brother.

That didn't stop Bea. "Not if you're a nineties club kid high on ecstasy, but that's not who attends your shows."

Axel tossed up his hands, praising the heavens. "Finally, someone who agrees with me. Modernization, that's what the Marlow Theater needs."

His agreement fueled her argument. "Popular music might get the teens off their phones. It would jazz up the numbers. I bet it would even motivate you to mix up your routines."

Fresh music had certainly worked for her. Since recharging her phone, she'd chosen a new playlist and had spent a portion of her two illegal-squatting nights reworking her assistant costume. Having a theater with fabric and sewing accoutrements came in handy. She'd then painted into the wee hours of the morning. She doubted Huxley would be impressed she'd appropriated wood boards lying around his theater for her project. Or that his fascinating face had become her muse: his two-toned eyes filled her imagination, punctuating how people had so many colors trapped under their skin, layers of traits and quirks and desires.

He didn't seem taken with her suggestion, either. "There's nothing wrong with our routines, or the music. We simply have to market ourselves better."

Straitjacket tucked against his side, Axel slung his free arm around Bea's shoulder. "Maybe Bea and I will set out on our own. We'll wow New Orleans with my wand and her cool music."

She bumped her hip into his. "They already have those shows here. They're called male revues."

Huxley zeroed in on Axel's hand on her shoulder. His light blue eye darkened to match his brown one—quite a possessive look for someone who growled at her more often than he spoke. "We're taking a lunch break," he said.

"It won't work," Fox told Huxley, apropos of nothing.

The odd comment earned him a Huxley Glare.

Ignoring that cryptic statement, Axel released Bea's shoulder and blew her a kiss, which she caught and planted on her cheek. Huxley stood, his spine snapped straight as his brothers left the stage.

She pulled a snack from her purse and peeled the wrapper. "Did you lose Cotton Candy already?"

"Lose *what*?"

"The My Little Pony doll. You're grumpier than usual."

"She's at home," he mumbled while watching Bea nibble her fruit-and-nut bar. "What are you doing?"

"Eating lunch."

"That's not lunch, Beatrice."

"On my budget, it is. I don't earn a paycheck." A sad state of affairs. She'd checked wanted advertisements this morning and had booked interviews for waitressing jobs. Until something panned out—a daytime job that didn't interfere with her assistant duties—she'd have to ration meals.

She was so busy savoring her meager snack, she didn't notice Huxley's approach until he'd clasped her elbow. "You're coming to lunch with me."

Fox was right, as Fox usually was: fighting his interest in Beatrice Baker was a losing battle. All rehearsal, Huxley had been ready to deck Axel. His brother had been as obnoxious when rehearsing with Ashlynn, his charisma gene always switched to high. But watching him flirt with Ashlynn had never made Huxley want to punch his brother in the face. Beatrice had laughed when Axel had joked. She'd beamed when he'd done the running man while wearing his straitjacket.

Huxley had nearly ground his molars to dust.

In his life, he'd never experienced this kind of irrational jealousy. And here she was, existing on granola bars because he'd blackmailed her into working for free.

Ashamed, he took her to a small café. The hostess smiled when she looked at Beatrice. The other patrons grinned, too, as had every person they'd passed on the street. It could be the polka dot thigh-highs she wore, or her flared pink skirt, or the black-and-white halter top that turned her into a fifties pinup girl. But Huxley knew better: it was the Beatrice Baker Effect. Her natural brightness was contagious.

"You don't have to do this," she said, tucking her napkin on her lap.

"I believe I do. I'm the reason you're eating bird food for lunch."

"Technically, *I'm* the reason. I'm the one who keyed your car and couldn't pay for it."

Technically, she was correct, but he didn't like being inadvertently responsible for her grim situation, and his curtness this morning had been unacceptable. He also wanted to know about her art and the name of her favorite book and if she brushed her top or bottom teeth first. He settled on asking her the question he'd mulled over since their fateful meeting. "Speaking of the car keying, you said something odd that night."

"Besides calling you a kerivoula kachinensis?"

"Besides that." Scents of coffee and bacon drifted from the back of the all-day-breakfast café. She studied him, expectant. "When I suggested calling the cops, you said you were the only one without a mugshot."

"This is true." She didn't elaborate.

The glass doors were open to the street, fresh air drifting in. Across the road, a mule clipped and clopped, towing a vintage carriage. Tourists ambled down the sidewalk, sugar-dusted beignets in hand. The sun disappeared behind a cloud, shading this peaceful section of the French Quarter. Although mornings along these streets usually smelled like a frat party gone wrong, the sourness was absent. Music swirled from different directions: a violin, a horn of some sort, the pounding of a drum. It felt like years since Huxley had simply sat and soaked in a New Orleans afternoon, especially with a beautiful woman. One he wanted to understand.

"Care to clarify?" He prodded her, unable to let it slide. "After all, you're part of the Marvelous Marlow Boys now. I'd like to know if nefarious sorts will be chasing after you."

She pulled her gaze from the passing mule-drawn carriage. "Don't you love the word *nefarious*? It's very nefarious-sounding."

"I do." He also couldn't get enough of how she enjoyed the minutia of life. "But you're ignoring my question."

Their small table held a single carnation in a vase and salt and pepper shakers. She tipped a pile of pepper in front of her and began moving it around. "There is one man who'd like to dismember my fingers, but he shouldn't be a problem."

"You have a vivid imagination." She shrugged like she wasn't joking. He wasn't fooled. "You're evading."

She didn't glance up from her pepper art. He didn't know her that well, but she'd always tried to meet his eyes when talking, even when Huxley had avoided it. Looking into her rainstorm eyes reduced him to nothing but a pounding heart.

"Unlike your big brood," she said, "I'm an only child, but my father was one of four kids. The mug shots vary, but most were a result of petty theft and drunken behavior. Their kids followed suit. No mass murderers or anything, just a DNA pool with addictive personalities, famous for making bad decisions."

"Which bad decision did your father make?"

She finished drawing a pepper flower and met his gaze. "He's a drunk. Not the abusive, angry sort. More the pathetic, sad sort. He's sweet when he's sober. He's also a compulsive gambler. He did some low-level theft to support his habits while I kept the electricity on."

"And your mother?"

"Mom is more of a Facebook friend than an actual parent. She's a free spirit and a band groupie. She travels and dances where the music takes her. Her arrest record involves public nudity."

Having a dancing, hippie mother suited Beatrice Baker. That didn't mean her childhood had been easy. "Being the only responsible one of the house is rough."

She cocked her head. "Sounds like familiar territory for you."

More familiar than he'd like. "I'm the oldest of five by four years. My father was great growing up, but he spent his nights performing. I was often stuck cooking dinner and making sure my brothers did their homework. My mother worked as a fortune-teller, preying on the desperate. Something she still does. They come to her for answers, and she swindles them out of cash."

Beatrice wrinkled her nose. "My father did that to me."

"He's a fortune-teller?"

"No. But I was the desperate one he took advantage of. I always believed he'd change."

Huxley couldn't count how often he'd hoped his mother would magically transform. With his father's death, he'd thought her maternal instincts would kick in. His youngest brothers had spiraled out of control and needed support. Fox and Axel had hit rough lows. As had he, but he'd been older. He hadn't had the luxury of focusing on his own pain. Nadya Marlow had all but disappeared, leaving Huxley, unqualified and out of his depth, thrust into the role of guardian. It was no wonder Xander and Paxton had moved away without a trace.

His failure to keep the family together was Huxley's cross to bear, and he was older now. He no longer wished for the impossible with his mother, but he despised the thought of Beatrice being let down by her parents, too.

He shifted forward, his knees touching hers under the small table. "How'd your father take advantage of you?"

She nestled closer as well. "It's my own fault, really. I hate assuming the worst in people. I mean, if we all walked around thinking *nefarious* thoughts"—her eyes sparkled at the use of her preferred word, as though they weren't discussing degenerate parents—"the world would be a pretty awful place."

"It would, but what did he do?" He couldn't let the subject go.

She didn't sigh or frown. She wiped the pepper flower aside, ruining her impromptu art project. "I had to work too much during high school to get my diploma, but I finished it gradually afterward, taking night classes. I planned to attend the California Institute of Art and spent years saving for it. A month ago, my father came to me and claimed he was turning his life around. He said he was sober and had a chance at a steady job, but his employer required a credit check. He asked if he could co-sign on my bank account, just for the check. He promised we'd remove his name afterward."

She didn't say more, but she didn't have to. That bastard had drained her account to gamble. It also clarified her harsh line when she'd said she never took bets.

"So you have nothing?" Anger edged his tone.

"Don't be ridiculous." She gestured outside the open café doors. "It's sunny. I'm in New Orleans, although I've barely seen any of it, and I'm about to order bacon and eggs for lunch. I'm also a zigzag girl."

Her genuine happiness, in the face of such betrayal, shocked him. Granted, he'd seen her last weekend, face blotchy, tears flowing, anger guiding her shaky hand as she'd defaced his Mustang. But that wasn't the woman facing him now, full of light, able to let go and move on.

He envied the ability, but it was her weather comment that pitted his gut. He glanced outside and only saw a partly cloudy sky. "How do you do it?"

"Do what?"

"Find joy in everything."

She studied him a moment, then said, "I smile."

She punctuated the comment with a dazzling grin, but he worried for her. Smiling was a quick fix, a mask to cover what lay beneath. Discovering hard truths you'd buried could be more damaging than facing them head-on.

Their waitress interrupted them. Beatrice fussed over the woman's bottle-cap earrings, the two gossiping about the nearby French Market. But Huxley fisted his hands. Sweat dripped down the back of his T-shirt. As strapped as he was for cash, he couldn't, in good conscience, allow Beatrice to work off her debt, ruined Mustang or not. Giving her money for food outweighed repairing his car.

She ordered bacon and eggs, sunny-side up. "And please don't bring ketchup, unless..." She studied Huxley like he might have a contagious rash. "Do you use ketchup?"

"I enjoy it."

"Can you live without it for this lunch?" He nodded, and her features relaxed. "Then we can share the table. It's the worst condiment. The smell makes me gag."

He filed that fact away and ordered his eggs. He asked for them partly cloudy, with a side of watermelon. The waitress side-eyed him.

The second she left, he faced Beatrice. "I'll pay you. The theater's in trouble, so I can't afford much, but I'll get you some cash. And if you haven't seen much of New Orleans, we need to remedy that."

She ignored his dismal attempt to ask her out and said, "The theater's in trouble?"

He waved off her concern. "I'm figuring it out, but I'll pay you."

"No."

"If you can't afford a proper lunch, how are you even paying rent?"

Her attention meandered, drawing invisible lines over his head and down the café's peach wall. A bee flew around close by, then hovered over their table. Instead of answering him, she said, "Bee."

"It seems to like you."

She became immobile. "Please make it go away."

Her stiff posture... The trepidation in her widening eyes... "Are you afraid of bees, *Bea*?"

"I'm allergic."

"A girl named Bea is allergic to bees?"

"If I get stung because you're making jokes instead of shooing said bee, my tongue will swell and choke me before I can tell you you're being a white-bellied go-away-bird."

"Is that a real bird?"

"Yep. And it's staring right at me."

Amused, he swatted the insect away and it went to annoy another table. "Are you really allergic?"

She petted the purse she'd hung over her chair. "My EpiPen is always close."

He suddenly wanted to exterminate all bees from the stratosphere. He also wasn't letting her off from answering him. "How are you paying rent?"

This pause didn't last as long. "The friend I'm staying with isn't charging me right now. And if the theater's in trouble, I won't accept your money anyway. I've booked interviews for later today. I should have a job soon, something with daytime hours that won't interfere with the show."

He wondered if her roommate was the same friend she'd pretended to text from the theater. More untruths, possibly. "I still want to pay you. And if things fall through with your living arrangements, I have a spare room. You can crash there anytime." Except the offer had his blood rushing. Beatrice in his apartment, living in the adjacent room, was as terrifying as it was exciting. The little sleep he did get would likely vanish.

"Thank you for the roommate offer. If things get dicey, I'll let you know, but I still won't accept a paycheck." Her tone turned serious. "Everything happens for a reason, Huxley, including Nick convincing me to move here, him turning into a prick, and my terrible decision to ruin your car. I'm still sick about the car part, not so much the Nick part, but it brought us together. I think I'm meant to be in your magic act. I also think you should consider the music change."

"Okay." His quick agreement would have both pleased and shocked the hell out of Axel, but it was Beatrice's vehemence that drove his consent. As had her comment about fate bringing them together. He felt it, an invisible thread binding them. He'd gradually leaned forward as they'd spoken. A gravitational pull. His heart beat faster, reaching for her.

"Really?" She shifted closer, too. "But you shot me down at rehearsal."

"I didn't want Axel to gloat. He's been pushing to make changes for years. It's not what my father would have wanted, and I hate the idea of letting him down, so I've held off. But I'm running out of options."

Refusing Beatrice seemed a worse offense.

"*Would have* wanted?" She reached under the table and placed her hand on his knee. "Does that mean he passed?"

"It was a while ago." It seemed odd she didn't know this defining detail of his life. He felt a strange familiarity with her, like they'd grown up comparing parental scars. She also didn't know about the other scars on his body, marks that often turned women off, or the tiny detail that he played a regular poker game. Considering her father's issues, the latter fact could cause her to stop touching his knee. He liked her hand exactly where it was.

"If you won't accept my money," he went on, covering her hand with his, keeping them connected, "at least let me help with your job search. Fox's friend Della works at the market the waitress mentioned. Last I heard, her stall was busy. I could put you in touch."

She pressed her thumb over his, warmth emanating from her brightening face. "I have interviews booked. If they don't work out, I'll holler. But thank you *again* for another generous offer."

He was learning there wasn't much he wouldn't do to earn a Beatrice Baker smile.

8

Walking the French Quarter with Huxley after lunch was more fun than the time Bea had attached scrap metal to her shoes and spent a month tap dancing. Moves she dusted off as they passed a busking saxophonist. She shuffled her toes and stomped her heels. Huxley watched her like he'd made alien contact. She grabbed his hand and led him into a vampire shop.

Face pinched, he eyed the shelved fangs and coffin purses. "Why are we here?"

Bea released his hand and picked up a gothic umbrella. She twirled it over her head. "You said we needed to remedy my limited New Orleans experience. We're touring the city."

"This isn't the city. This is a tourist trap."

"A fun tourist trap." She spun her umbrella. His eyes didn't stray from her face. His stare was so intense, she looked away. "I'm also on a fact-finding mission."

There had to be some explanation why her pulse fluttered around him. Why her hand still tingled from holding his a moment ago. Her skin felt flammable when he was near. All lunch, his knee had grazed hers under their small table, an intimate pose that had satisfied her as much as the tasty food.

Her only hypothesis: Huxley Marlow was indeed a vampire, and he'd cast her under his spell.

Two girls pushed into the shop and giggled at the corsets and fishnet stockings.

Standing too stiff to be comfortable, Huxley shoved his hands into his pockets. "The answer is five minutes."

"Five minutes?"

"If your mission is to discover my attention span for kitschy New Orleans shops, the answer is five minutes."

Then she'd better up her investigative activities. She dropped the umbrella and brushed her hair over one shoulder, exposing her neck to him. "Do I have a bite here? It feels itchy."

He stepped closer and lowered his voice. "Looks fine to me." Not only did his attention remain locked on the delicate skin, but he feathered his fingers over her pulse point. "Looks perfect," he murmured.

He eyed her neck like he wanted a bite, and goose bumps erupted along her shoulders. It was a point in the Vampire column. Not a good sign. Neither was his intimate voice. A Huxley murmur was a surefire way to distract her from her purpose.

Flustered, she picked up lacy thigh-highs, the perfect pair to add to her collection. "Do you like these?"

His nostrils flared. "I do."

His darkening eyes darted from her exposed neck to the lacy vampire stockings. They'd just had lunch, but he looked ravenous, and her belly tumbled at his hungry gaze. Her stomach shouldn't flip-flop when his stocking approval was a second check in the Vampire column. This called for drastic measures. The store was dark and cavernous, all vampire accoutrements equally as villainous-looking. She dragged him into a shaft of sunlight and examined his hand.

His warm breaths brushed the top of her hair. "Is this part of your fact-finding mission?"

"It is." His skin was darker than hers, a hint of olive in the tone. Nothing out of the ordinary, unless she counted the way she wanted to kiss the center of his palm. "I'm checking for sparkles."

"Is that a *Twilight* reference?"

The vampire shop must have given her away. That didn't account for his specific question. She glanced up at him, eyebrows raised. "Have you read *Twilight*?"

"What's your favorite book?"

His subject change made her dizzy. Or maybe it was how he'd curled his fingers around hers. They were now holding hands. In a vampire shop. In New Orleans. She couldn't keep from grinning. "You read *Twilight*." A statement this time.

"You didn't answer my question."

Because she couldn't stop picturing this imposing man on his back, book hovering over his face, flipping pages as Bella Swan swooned over Edward Cullen, and Edward Cullen fought his feelings for the mortal girl. Huxley was a romantic. "Do you read Harlequin novels, too?"

His eyes flicked to the left, then to the floor. "Of course not."

That unsteady gaze was an admission if she'd ever seen one. Instead of making him more uncomfortable, she focused on his favorite-book question. Although she'd overworked her library card in recent years, her answer was a childhood comfort. "The dictionary," she said.

"The dictionary," he repeated. When she didn't contradict him, he said, "A specific volume? Or the dictionary in general?"

"In general. Aside from *Playboy*, it was the only reading material in my house growing up. My father pawned our TV at one point, and I didn't have many friends. I'd spend my free time turning baked beans into food sculptures, and I'd read the dictionary. Although *Playboy* did have interesting articles."

His eyes swept over her face, a mix of wonder in his thorough perusal. This dashing man looked at her like she was the unicorn he'd always hoped existed. Then he smiled. A full-teeth smile, and heat flooded her chest. That smile was too tender and open to belong to a jaded immortal. It was a check in the Mortal Man column.

Another followed when she purchased the lacy thigh-highs, and Huxley blushed. Immortal men didn't blush.

They visited a witchcraft shop next. Huxley pressed his hand to the small of her back and followed her inside the musty store. He indulged her as she picked up poppets and invented voices for the stuffed figures. He smirked when she modeled a selection of cloaks. Before she could coax him to try one on, her cell buzzed with a text.

Pay me or you'll lose more than fingers.

The stale air thickened in her throat. Swallowing became an effort. She glanced around the dank shop sure a masked man might leap from a darkened corner.

So immersed in stage magic and painting and Huxley, she'd put her father's loan shark out of her mind. She'd assumed he'd given up on finding her, or that he'd been paid. Her deadline had come and gone. Big Eddie was in Chicago. She was in New Orleans. The distance had given her a sense of safety, but there was no doubt the threat was from him.

She replayed their encounter in the dive bar, his shock at her arrival and comment that Franklyn's plan wouldn't work. There had been no plan beyond buying her father more time to gather money, and other people had been present in the bar that day. If Big Eddie didn't recoup his money, his reputation would nosedive. He needed to save face.

She cursed herself for agreeing to help her father, but he'd begged and she'd given in as usual, *after* he'd painted a vivid picture of his potential torture. Big Eddie must have gotten her number from him, or he'd found her father's phone. She wasn't sure if that meant her father had been roughed up, a possibility that had her feeling ill. But there wasn't much she could do to help him. At least he didn't know where she was, three states away. Which meant Big Eddie didn't know, either. The text was just an attempt to scare her.

She hit *Delete* and blocked the number. She'd double check that her GPS was still disabled later.

"Everything okay?" Huxley loomed over her, worry in his drawn brows.

She ignored the shakiness in her legs and did what she did best—she smiled. "Everything's fine." She was, after all, in a witchcraft shop, enjoying a New Orleans stroll. She even had job interviews lined up. Still, faint nausea persisted.

Huxley tilted his head, eyes narrowed. Could he sense her lingering discomfort? Chronic anxiety she could do without. Determined to shake her unease, she bumped her hip into his and resumed her silly fashion show. They outstayed his five-minute limit, and she didn't glimpse his lie-detector face for the rest of their city tour. Her concern over Big Eddie took longer to fade.

9

Bea's two interviews were a bust. Both jobs required evening shifts, and the bars smelled like rum-marinated gym socks. Sneaking back into the prop room to paint was a relief. Her phone played a mixture of swing and big band music. The volume was low, in case anyone happened into the building, but that didn't stop her from jigging to the beat.

She was painting a small square of wood, trying to match the brightest flecks of Huxley's lighter blue eye. Every so often, her brush would still, her mind wandering to today's lunch and their kind-of-date. New Orleans was proving more fun than she'd imagined. Proof that when life gave you lemons they could be turned into lemon meringue pie.

Her art project was the whipped cream on that dessert.

It was possible she'd bitten off more Double Bubble than she could chew with this concept, but every stroke of paint before now seemed like practice for this main event: her self-portrait.

Similar to Monet's work and Huxley's unhandsome-handsome profile, she would build her portrait with dozens of tiny monochromatic paintings, small sections that, when put together, formed a different whole. Close up, each would tell her story, old and new: a slice of watermelon lip-gloss, her mother's smiling mouth, Huxley's eyes, a section of his cape, the tail of her childhood My Little Pony doll, a bee's wing, the tip of an EpiPen, three numbers from her empty bank account, the key that had defiled Huxley's car, and on and on until Bea would eventually have poured her life onto wood planks.

Lined up two-by-fours became her canvas, an intriguing surface, easy to separate and hide. Her history drove her paintbrush. The magic of the Marlow Theater inspired her creativity. It unfortunately came with construction work that woke her at ungodly hours, temperamental electricity, and a rat she'd encountered when searching for the fuse box, but she'd been a starving artist since birth. Suffering for her art gave it meaning. Plus thoughts of Huxley made her smile, and she always worked best when she smiled.

She couldn't paint fast enough.

Huxley walked into his dark theater, heart heavy and full at once. It was frustrating meeting Beatrice while struggling to save his birthright. Having the opportunity to date a fascinating woman, only to be too overwhelmed to properly ask her out, was a cruel twist of fate. Today had been a date of sorts, eating lunch together, touring the city. But good dates ended with kisses. When Beatrice had announced she was heading to interviews, their rehearsal done, all he'd done was thank her for her work.

He sat in the middle of the empty theater now, as he often did, eyes closed, resinous scents mixing with the lavender floor cleaner they'd used forever.

He pictured the Marvelous Max Marlow on stage, making the audience laugh by finding a disappeared candy bar in his pant pocket, eliciting gasps when sawing his assistant in half, shocking patrons by locking himself into a water-filled barrel. He'd done the latter number yearly to a standing-room-only crowd. Huxley's brothers had tired of the routine and stopped attending. Not Huxley. He'd watched every spectacle, including the last one.

The fateful one.

He wished he didn't remember it so clearly: the barrel staying closed too long, the agitated crowd. He should have jumped on stage, but Max Marlow would have reprimanded him for ruining the illusion, so he'd delayed helping. Huxley had been too late in the end. He'd taken too long cracking open the barrel. The water had flooded out. His father's lips had been blue. Attempted resuscitations had been futile.

Now Huxley had a face full of scars from unleashing his grief and anger on the wrong people. He also had a head filled with images he'd like to burn.

"I'm sorry," he whispered, the same two words that always began his evening confessionals.

———

Bea's cadmium red was the wrong tone for the corner of her lip-gloss study. She needed to blend alizarin crimson but didn't have the color, which meant she needed a paycheck pronto. The waitressing gigs may not have panned out, but Huxley had mentioned a market job. Asking for his help when she was squatting in his theater wasn't ideal, but needing paints took priority.

Paintbrush between her teeth, she freed her hands to text him: *Can I have Della's number?* If Fox's friend ran a market booth, it would operate during daytime hours, allowing her time to be a zigzag girl and paint. She wasn't sure what type of woman was friends with a sneaky Fox, but she needed cash.

Sure thing, Huxley replied swiftly. He sent Della's info, the speed of his response revving Bea's heart. She wasn't looking at him or talking to him, but she had his handkerchief in her pocket, the slight connection filling her with fresh lightness. She thanked him and shot off a text to Della, buoyed by the prospect of securing work.

She chose a different section to paint and squeezed a small amount of lemon yellow on her plywood palette. Music quietly trumpeted from her phone. She mixed in a dash of white and raw umber. She touched the tip of her brush to her impromptu canvas.

Then her phone died. Its cannibalizing battery consumed her swing tunes, leaving dead air. Until she heard a muffled voice.

"I had fun with you," Huxley murmured to his silent phone after messaging Beatrice. He was glad she'd reached out, but he should have told her how refreshing their afternoon had been. He wished she was wrapped up in his arms now, not somewhere in the city, reading his succinct reply.

He massaged his neck and locked his sights on the ceiling's peeling paint. "Things are bleak," he said to the empty theater. To his father. "It feels like it's all slipping through my fingers. No matter how much I love this place, I can't pull it together." He slouched lower and stretched his legs into the aisle. "We're switching up the music, which you'll hate. No doubt about that, but I probably should've done it ages ago. I'm wondering if we should shake up our acts, too."

Revamp the whole damn place. He hated the notion of modernizing, but something had to give. He also planned to raise the stakes at next week's poker game.

The Rolex would return to the pot, with Oliphant's necklace hopefully joining the loot. If Ms. Terious showed up, he'd coax the gold from her fingers. He'd lure the stacked bills from Dazzling Delmar's padded wallet. The crème de la crème was Horatio Heinzinger. That imposter couldn't perform an illusion to save his life. He'd also inherited his father's millions.

It would be a start, but not enough. Not if his acts didn't bring in more business. "You made it look so easy. People loved you. There were lines out the door. Now I can barely usher people inside. You'd be ashamed of this place."

He wasn't living up to his father's expectations. He wasn't living a functioning life, period. For nine years, he'd dated a total of two women, both relationships ending over two years ago. Fixing up the deteriorating theater had taken priority. He'd become handy at basic plumbing and drywalling. Paying bills filled in his remaining hours. He'd watched as Axel had dated—carefree, living life no matter the cards he'd been dealt. Exactly what he wanted for his brothers, but a hint of bitterness often colored Huxley's jokes when teasing him. Envy for what Huxley didn't have: women, free time, *fun*.

Then Beatrice Baker had given him a pink pony and a smile, offering a glimpse of what he'd been missing. All he wanted to do now was test if she truly tasted like watermelon.

You'd be ashamed of this place. Bea had crept up to the theater wings and tucked herself into the curtain, scanning for the interloper invading her makeshift home. Instead of an interloper, she'd found Huxley, by himself, desolate voice adrift in the auditorium, and her heart splintered.

He must have been sitting there when texting her, so close, yet so far. He seemed to be talking to his late father now, sharing his troubles. She wasn't sure how much the

Marvelous Marlow Boys were struggling financially, but Huxley's lament about not having time for fun, his blatant surliness, and his confessions at lunch and now, all pointed to an uphill battle.

It wasn't her business. She'd only known him three days, yet she couldn't paint her self-portrait without pieces of his profile filling in her gaps. She'd thought about him on and off all evening, returning to the warmth of his hand on her back, how he'd indulged her whims in the shops, his occasional smiles. He didn't offer those smiles freely, each twitch of his lips a gift earned. It made her want to be sillier, goofier. Crazy. Anything to loosen up his stiff cheeks.

She also couldn't imagine losing her father. Leaving Franklyn Baker to face his threats had been a first for her. In the past, she'd allowed him to apologize, accepting him for who he was. She would help scrounge for cash and lie for him. Because Franklyn Baker wasn't all bad. Growing up, he'd thrown her the best birthday parties. Her classmates rarely showed, often leaving just the two of them, too much pizza, buckets of chocolate ice cream, and colored markers. He'd let her draw kingdoms on their walls. He'd get drunk and fall asleep and would wake up with a colorful mustache.

She'd always have those memories of him, but gambling was a sickness, one she didn't want infecting her life. Not when it bred loan sharks who wanted to cleave her fingers. Leaving Franklyn Baker behind had been necessary, but dealing with his death would be harder.

Huxley's obvious despair was partly linked to his father. She couldn't help with that, but the theater problem could be solved. Huxley had listened to her music suggestion. The change hadn't been implemented or proven, but she could divine more ways to fill the seats. For now, he deserved his solitude.

She peeked around the curtain, stealing a glimpse of him before she left, and her belly zigzagged at the sight of his handsome face. She told herself to turn. She tried to walk away.

Then Huxley Marlow of the Marvelous Marlow Boys said, "I met a girl."

———

Understatement of the millennium. He hadn't just met a girl. He'd met a fascinating woman who'd reminded him all clouds had silver linings. She'd been ridiculous today, making voices for dolls, tap dancing on the street. Each goofy display had had him drawing closer to her like a flower seeking the sun. He'd wanted his hand on her back or touching any place he could reach. He'd ached to put those lacy thigh-highs on her just so he could roll them down.

He'd just wanted to fucking *live* for once in his life and take a chance on kissing a beautiful girl, even if it complicated things.

"You'd love her," he went on, but he chuckled, imagining his father's outrage over their vandalized Mustang. "Actually, scratch that. You'd hate her. She destroyed your car. But she's one of a kind."

If he could redo today's goodbye, he'd have circled his arm around Beatrice's waist and drawn her close. He'd have dragged his nose up her neck and ear. He'd have told her he was ready for her brand of fun. That, in a few short days, she'd hijacked his life in the most *stupendous* way. He grinned, picturing her using that word.

Sadly, time travel wasn't a trick he could perform.

"She makes me excited about magic again, about revamping the theater. The pressure sucks, and I'm drowning most days, but this watermelon girl manages to make me laugh. And I think I forgot how to do that—just laugh. Which is pretty damn sad."

Until Beatrice Baker had sat on a barstool in bright pink pants and had called him a colon rectum, a fiery spark in her stormy eyes.

Bea pressed her cheek to the wall and flattened her palm on the surface. Her breaths brushed the velvet curtain, each one warming as Huxley spoke. She'd had boyfriends before, long term and short. She'd told a couple that she'd loved them, but she'd never felt this kind of ethereal lightness, like at any moment her feet would lift from the floor and she'd float away.

"I want to make you laugh," she whispered, too quiet for him to hear. "I want to be your watermelon girl."

She also wanted to show herself, walk on stage, and tell him he'd reinvigorated her art, too. That pieces of him were filling her self-portrait and she didn't know why. But she wasn't supposed to be crashing in his theater. She was also invading his privacy—the larger offense in her mind. And she had keyed his *father's* car? Not Huxley's car. His *late* father's car.

Having defaced his Mustang was bad enough, but ruining something that sentimental was unforgivable. Yet he hadn't held it against her. This solid, good man had let it slide.

If she thought she owed Huxley for damages before, she basically owed him a kidney now. And his privacy. She tried to leave again, tried to turn away and slip into the darkness, but he was talking about her. He'd called her one of a kind. She flattened her back against the wall and slid down its length, tucking her knees to her chest.

Huxley pictured his father sitting beside him, the two men shoulder-to-shoulder, sharing their hearts. He wondered how Max Marlow had wound up marrying Nadya, if his mother had been different back then. If she'd cared about things other than herself. She certainly didn't now.

She'd yet to quit her conwoman activities. She may have inherited a sizeable chunk of change from Max Marlow's life insurance, along with a letter asking her to support the theater, but she'd refused to help repair the building. She hated their block of real estate as much as she'd hated the man she'd married. Maybe his father had worked too much. Maybe they'd married too young. Either way, her numerous affairs had been far from secret, and she'd sooner hug one of her sons than donate a dime to the theater.

Then there was Beatrice, a woman who didn't seem to have a selfish bone in her body. She didn't even hold a grudge against her betraying father, because she smiled. She'd been swindled out of her savings, had been forced to start over from scratch...yet she still smiled.

What would it be like to wake up to her brightness every morning? To have that unbridled joy in his life. To slip his fingers through her red hair whenever he wanted, claim her lips in a bruising kiss. Every muscle in his body flexed at the fantasy.

"How do I do it all?" he asked the father who'd gotten ripped from his life too soon. "How do I focus on fixing the theater and find time to have a life? Because honestly, if you'd met her, you'd understand. She's beautiful and sexy and fun, and she has this way about her that makes everyone around her smile. I'm different around her." When he wasn't fighting his interest in her, at least.

Huxley wasn't looking to meet someone. Not now, with so much stress boxing him in. But he'd put her pink pony on his coffee table and found himself staring at it sporadically, unconsciously smiling despite his troubles. That one simple gift had already made his days better. A ridiculous doll.

He sighed into the empty auditorium. "I know a distraction is a rotten idea right now. I'm just not sure I can stay away."

Don't stay away, she thought. *You can do both. I'll help you.* She pressed her hand over her breastbone, covering her pounding heart, worried he'd hear its booming beat. Like the trumpets from her swing music had taken up song in her chest.

He'd called her *beautiful* and *sexy* and *fun*. God, how she wanted to show him fun. Not just goofiness to loosen him up. She wanted to ride a Ferris wheel together while the world spun around them, their arms and hands linked. She wanted to feed him beignets and lick the sticky sugar from his lips. Get him messy so she could strip him down and clean him up, slowly, with soapy hands. Explore every scar on his body.

Her body tingled at the possibility.

She closed her eyes, reveling in the imagined scenes. She strained to hear his every breath. She wanted to inhabit the silence between his words.

10

The next day Bea stood stock-still, staring at a set of jagged teeth and beady eyes. The alligator's leathery jaw looked ready to chomp her to bits. She'd never seen an alligator up close, dead or alive. This specimen was certainly dead, as were the thirty-odd severed heads on the vendor's table. Kids and spouses posed with the lifeless reptiles, cute photos taken that would be blasted on social media.

Bea sent a picture to her mother, titled, *Caught in the wild!*

Della's stall was at this market, somewhere at the back end. She'd replied to Bea's text, offering to meet about the job. Knowing the sights and sounds of the busy spot would drive Bea to distraction, she had allotted meandering time. It was a good thing. She salivated at the stacked muffuletta sandwiches and overstuffed po'boys. Oysters on the half shell glistened. Fruity cocktails whizzed in blenders. If her wallet weren't nearly bone-dry, she'd try one of everything.

Inhaling the spicy, briny smells, she perused the shelves of hot sauces and art vendors, slipping down the rows with other tourists. She dragged her fingers through piles of necklaces and masks in pinks and purples and neon blues. Even with her meandering allotment, she barely found Della's table on time.

But Della wasn't there. Until she was.

A woman popped up from behind the table, her long braids swaying as she chewed something and licked her lips.

"If that's a po'boy down there," Bea said, "I might have to steal a bite."

Della swallowed. "If you're not Beatrice, this might get awkward."

"Call me Bea, and awkward makes for good fun."

Bea stepped aside, letting a few women browse Della's jewelry. Unlike much of the kitschy pieces inside the main building, her work was striking. Colorful crystals and beads filled small circles, ovals, and squares, the shapes then linked together into bracelets and necklaces. Earrings dangled with intricate patterns. "Your work is as magical as the Marlow show."

Della's deep brown eyes twinkled. "I like you already. When can you start?"

"Shouldn't I be interviewed?"

"Okay." She ducked down, took another bite of her sandwich, chewed, swallowed, then faced Bea. "Will you steal from me?"

"No."

"Can you use a calculator?"

"Yes."

"Are you good with people?"

"I adore people."

Bea's potential boss wore slim jeans and a funky white top with cutouts in the shoulders. Her turquoise and yellow necklace—as intricate as a Greek mosaic—hung over delicate collarbones, a beautiful contrast to her dark skin. Her interviewing skills weren't top notch, but she didn't appear the sort to cozy up with a sneaky Fox. Until she narrowed her eyes at Bea. "Is Huxley one of the people you adore?"

Maybe she'd misjudged Della already. "Is this part of the interview?"

She shrugged. "I'll let it slide. I'm just protective of the boys, and Huxley's been through a lot."

"At least he doesn't try to read my mind." Like his mentalist brother, although he'd done a fine job of it last night. Every confession spoken into the empty theater had echoed her feelings, his deep baritone nearly lulling her to sleep. When his one-way conversation had shifted to talk of his brothers, Bea had returned to her art, giving him back his privacy.

She hadn't seen him since, and hearing he'd been through a lot made her even more curious about the man behind the fascinating face. As it was, her pulse raced each time he crossed her mind, or maybe it was the fact that seeing him tonight meant she'd be performing. On an actual stage. In front of people.

"If a brother is reading your mind," Della said, "you must have met Fox."

"The sneaky one."

"You could say that." Something unreadable flickered across her face. "I've known the boys since we were kids. They tend to—"

"If I buy these three, can I get a deal?" An older woman with liver-spotted hands held up a matching bracelet and necklace, as well as a pair of earrings.

Della chatted with the woman, explaining how she used a magnifying glass and tweezers to assemble the more detailed sections. Her half-eaten sandwich forgotten under the table, she closed the sale.

A steady stream of customers continued. So steady, Bea hopped into the booth and handled the money as it came in, calculating and making change. Della pointed here or there, asking her for a gift box or small bag. They worked around each other in the cramped space, hips bumping, apologies offered. Laughter followed one hand-boob collision.

An afternoon lull later, Della offered Bea half of her half-eaten po'boy. "Some big blogger mentioned my table recently. It's been nuts since."

Bea tried to reply, but her mouth was filled with fried-shrimp goodness. She answered between heavenly bites. "Your work is the nicest in the market. There's a flow about the pieces—rhythmic almost. It reminds me of Van Gogh's *Starry Night*, but with crystal."

Della licked sauce from her palm. "That means a lot from a fellow artist."

She didn't recall writing that information on any interview questionnaire. "Do you read minds, too?"

"Don't I wish." She wiped her mouth and tossed her napkin in the garbage. "Huxley mentioned you were a painter of sorts."

Bea froze mid-swallow. Had he found her hidden art supplies? Her self-portrait? If that were the case, he'd no doubt have tracked her down and demanded answers. Or money. Then she remembered their lunch conversation about the art school she couldn't attend. He'd also driven her decorated Beetle briefly and would have seen her portrait studies. She wondered what he thought of those. "Painting is more of a hobby. For now, at least. But I started a new project I'm excited about."

"If you need to bounce ideas with anyone, I'd love to check it out."

"I'm happy to share my art with anyone who shares a po'boy." Even though the prospect made her queasy.

Her previous experimentations had been private work, studies in her car, her old apartment, sketchbooks she'd left in Chicago. Only her father had seen most of her work, his easy praise one of his few good qualities. Sharing it with others was a daunting prospect, but it was what a friend would do, and she didn't have many of those.

Her Chicago acquaintances were waitress colleagues who griped about crap pay and long hours, not girls who messaged or kept in touch. Painting had always come first for Bea, saving her pennies second. She'd assumed she'd meet her people once in art school, but maybe she'd meet them at magic theaters and flea markets.

Della rearranged a few bracelets. "How's the assistant training going?"

"I'm a regular Vanna White. I do lots of walking in circles and fanning of my arm. I've also learned how to fasten a straitjacket, which will pad out my résumé nicely."

"Important skills," Della agreed dryly.

"I spend the rest of my time dodging Huxley's growls."

She snickered. "That man gives good gruff."

He also had a voice that could melt butter. Bea couldn't keep from nosing around for gossip. "What did you mean before, about him having been through a lot?"

"They lost their father a while back."

"He mentioned it."

"Huxley was there."

Her heart pinched. "When it happened?"

Della's dark eyes turned hazy, like the memories filled too much space to focus. "He blames himself, I think. Went on a bender that night and got in a shit-ton of trouble. Nearly died in the hospital."

Bea pictured his mangled ear and burned eyebrow. "The scars on his face?"

"The ones on his body are pretty gnarly, too. Not my story to tell, but it's all a reminder to him of what he lost. And being older, he's taken on the responsibility of the theater and keeping his brothers in check. Their mother's also a piece of work. Basically, he spends his time treading water."

"He doesn't have time for fun," she murmured, repeating his words.

Last night's quiet confessional took on new meaning, the load Huxley carried bigger than stacked bills and chipped paint. To watch a parent die and feel responsible? She couldn't imagine the weight of that pain.

Della smoothed the lengths of her braids, her probing gaze traveling down Bea's polka dot top and pink pedal pushers. It was now her lucky outfit, since she'd worn it for this job interview and when keying Huxley's late father's car. A lucky-unlucky fate.

"You're into him, aren't you?" Della asked.

Her candid nature took Bea aback. "Is it that obvious?"

Della lowered her voice, the two of them head-to-head like schoolgirls. "I think he digs you, too. The Marlow men aren't exactly open books, but there was something in his voice when he talked about you."

Bea may have eavesdropped on his confessions last night, but the confirmation set off fireworks behind her eyes. "I kind of overheard as much, but it's nice to hear it from you. I'm the worst at reading men."

Case in point: Nick the Prick.

"I'd say he's smitten. But if you're unsure, you could pass him a note during your next rehearsal. Ask him to rate you from one to ten. Or..." Della cocked her head, as though considering a presidential vote. "You could go with a 'Which

Disney Princess Would You Bang' quiz. Those can be illuminating."

If Bea had thought of that in school, she'd have polled every boy. "I'd do Princess Jasmine."

"I'm more of a Moana girl," Della said. "She's got a feisty streak."

They grinned at each other.

Della was proving more fun than her last boss, who'd spent his bartending time talking about fiber intake and bowel movements. "Hard to believe a string of awful events led to this."

"To what?"

Bea gestured vaguely. "Everything. If I didn't get dumped four days ago, I wouldn't have met Huxley or learned about your Moana crush. Life is odd like that."

Absolutely, oddly perfect.

But Della's playful demeanor hardened. "You just got out of a relationship?"

"Yes?" She answered hesitantly, unsure why their princess conversation had derailed.

"And you're into Huxley now? So soon?"

Oh. Right. "It's not like that."

"Like what?"

"Like *that*. A rebound."

"It kinda sounds exactly like that."

She appreciated Della's protectiveness. Reveled in it, actually. It meant Huxley had someone who worried after him, family or not. But it gave her pause. She thought back to his hands on her hips in the zigzag box, to the smiles she'd earned, his fingers covering hers under their lunch table. Each experience had guided her paintbrush last night, adding more color to her world. She felt fate had brought Huxley and the kaleidoscope he'd inspired into her life, or was Della right?

Was she boomeranging from Nick to him? Using Huxley to get over a breakup?

"It's all still new," she said, uneasy now.

She believed in destiny and good things happening to good people. She hoped meeting Huxley was exactly that, and not weakness on her part.

Della didn't look appeased. "I like you, Bea, but the Marlow boys mean a lot to me, and Huxley has dealt with more than his fair share. If you're after a fling, make sure he's on the same page."

Della looked around Bea's age. Maybe a few years younger, but her sharp expression gave her an air of maternal authority. Della turned to help a customer, her scrutiny diminishing as the booth got busier. Their banter gradually returned, chatter about music interests and artists easing the tension. They cracked up over a passerby's manicured mullet.

Still, Bea's mind whirred.

Last night she couldn't wait to tell Huxley she wanted to be his watermelon girl and test if their chemistry truly sparked. She'd itched to curl her fingers into his cape, pull him close, and brush her lips against his. She would see him in a few short hours, but apprehension curbed those fantasies. She couldn't shake the notion of Huxley being a placeholder. Unimportant. A Band-Aid for a healing cut. But that possibility didn't explain why she'd been painting pieces of him into her self-portrait or smiling at the thought of him.

If she had a relationship with her mother, beyond sharing pictures of food or Molly Baker's latest band crush, she'd lament her worries and seek guidance. She'd ask her if choosing Franklyn Baker over the guy she'd been dating had been easy, or if her emotions had felt as strong yet uncertain as this, even though her marriage hadn't ended well. She'd ask if the Baker girls were flighty by nature, destined to hop from man to man, adventure to adventure.

But Molly wasn't a Dear Abby type of mother. She was the first friend you'd invite to a party, and the last one you'd ask for advice.

Without a motherly mother, Bea focused on how right things felt with Huxley, and what she'd accomplished since her move: landing jobs as a magician's assistant and jewelry seller, acquiring somewhere to sleep and produce her art. All things to improve her life. New beginnings that, if nurtured, would keep improving, as long as Della was wrong about Huxley being a boomeranging rebound.

11

Time needed to slow down. It needed to freeze or travel in reverse. Anything to stall the inevitability of stepping on a stage in front of people. Bea couldn't force her hand to open her dressing room door. Her knees shook. The incessant knocking on the door didn't help.

"Show starts in ten, Rainbow Brite. Get your colorful self out here." Axel knocked as he spoke, tapping his knuckles to the tune of "We Will Rock You."

She *was* colorful in her fishnets and silver sequin bodysuit, especially since she'd sewn herself a half-skirt of red and gold feathers. It extended from her lower back to just behind her knees, like a wide peacock tail. Her matching headpiece gave the costume a seventies flair. Her lips were Cherry Bomb red. Her eye makeup made her gray eyes pop.

She still wanted to fold herself inside the closet until Christmas. "There's been an incident. I can't perform."

"Sure you can."

"All my hair fell out."

"Bald is in fashion."

"I stabbed myself in the eye."

"I'll give you an eyepatch and call you Pirate Brite."

"I'm narcoleptic. I'll pass out in the middle of the routines."

"We'll charge extra for people to watch."

Axel's quick-witted retorts weren't helping. A heart attack was imminent. She smooshed her red handkerchief between her fingers and tried to focus on the silky fabric. It made a feeble dent in her fear.

"Beatrice, it's Huxley."

Her irregular pulse went extra haywire at the sound of his voice. She didn't reply. She couldn't. This was the first she'd heard his deep baritone since his confessional. He'd been conspicuously missing when she'd hurried in from her day with Della, and she'd spent the last hour locked in the dressing room, freaking out. She was vibrating with excitement to see him, chastising herself for that pleasure with Della's concerns in mind. She was also a second from face-planting and chipping a tooth.

The sound of a key fitting into the lock clicked. The knob turned. "I'm coming in."

The door opened.

Huxley stepped inside.

She swayed on her feet.

He didn't glance at her until he'd closed the door. When he did, the remaining air in her lungs evacuated. He was in full costume: gold button-down, galaxy cape, top hat, that striking face. His eyes looked different, wider and warmer. He stared at her like they'd never met.

"I'm Bea," she said, in case her outfit had confused him.

"You're breathtaking," came his rough reply.

She swayed again. "Is that why I can't breathe?"

He swallowed and passed a hand over his mouth. "Nervous?"

"I can't move. My feet are stuck."

He glanced at her shiny red heels. "Breathtaking," he murmured again, then shook his head as if to clear it. "Do you have the handkerchief?"

She raised his generous gift with a trembling hand.

"Good. And do you remember how many people attended our last show?"

His tone was all business now, even though his hooded eyes darted to her lips. She couldn't contemplate those sexy looks, or the fact that she'd imagined gripping his cape and hauling him to her for a kiss, or that she shouldn't kiss a possible boomerang. She could barely produce saliva.

Instead she pictured the sleeping seniors and distracted teens who'd attended the last show. "Not many."

"There are less tonight."

"But they'll be watching me."

"They're watching me, not you."

"But...I can't."

He stepped closer and closed his fingers around hers so they were both touching the handkerchief. He lowered his voice. "You can, and you will. Think of it as a rehearsal. Focus on the routines. On the crappy music we haven't switched yet." He stroked his thumb over her knuckles. "Focus on me."

God, how she wanted to focus on him. She tilted up her chin, tried to see only the soft curls that brushed his neck, the shadow from his top hat that darkened his scarred eyebrow. *That.* She wanted to paint that and turn his lips red with her Cherry Bomb lipstick. Leave marks on his Adam's apple and shirt collar. Surely she wouldn't crave branding him Cherry Bomb red if he was a mere Band-Aid.

He tightened his grip on her hand. She whimpered.

"Showtime," he said and tugged her after him.

"No."

"Yes."

"No." But the door was open and she was stumbling in his wake. She didn't want to kiss him any longer. She wanted to buy a voodoo doll, paint his face on it, and stab it full of needles.

They arrived at stage left too soon.

"Is she going to puke?" This from Axel.

"No. But she might faint." Fox, of course, read her mind.

Huxley didn't release her hand. "You two do the intro. We'll be out for the Flying Playing Card number."

Fox slicked his hand down his ponytail and sauntered onto stage.

Axel leaned into her ear. "You look hot." Then he was gone, *after* a low growl rumbled from Huxley.

The surly brother turned to her. "I get that you're scared, but I'm not sorry I put you in this position."

"That you blackmailed me, you mean?"

"Maybe so, but this is your chance to face your fear."

"I want that, I do. But..." Her legs were numb. Sweat clung to her palms. "What if I freeze?"

"I'd rather you try and freeze than give up."

She sucked in a shaky breath. She didn't want to be anything like her father, a man who'd earned gold in giving up. He couldn't escape his addictions, because he was afraid. Scared to feel sadness or pain, choosing the rush of a bet over dealing with getting laid off or divorcing his wife. Bea didn't want her life ruled by fear, no matter how small or inconsequential. That wish didn't make performing for a meager crowd any easier.

She released Huxley's hand and tucked the handkerchief into her cleavage. The only opening on the tight costume. "I'll do it," she said.

She clicked her shiny heels together, finding her lioness confidence.

Pride flashed across Huxley's face. "That's my girl."

His girl. Those words struck a chord in her chest. A chiming bell, clanging so loudly it cleared her fog. She wanted to be his girl, perform with flair and prove how strong she was. Impress this magical man. Share with him the emotion she'd swallowed when listening to his late-night confession. Della had been right to be concerned, but being here, face-to-face with Huxley, she knew he wasn't a placeholder. She wasn't boomeranging.

Meeting him had been fate.

But when the music amped up and he turned to strut on stage, she resumed her statue impression. She no longer wanted to paint Huxley's face on a voodoo doll. She would write *stage fright* over the stuffed body and slash it to bits.

He turned, probably sensing her absence, and his jaw tightened with determination. Before she realized he was closing the distance between them, his fingers bit into her shoulders...and his lips descended on hers.

He kissed her hard, rough. She didn't curl her fingers into his cape like she'd imagined. She didn't even kiss him back, until his tongue brushed her bottom lip. She moaned into his mouth, opening for him. His answering grunt fanned her budding flames.

Then her hands moved.

Then she curled her fingers into his velvet cape.

Then she forgot her name and where she was and that she was supposed to perform.

He broke away. His lips were Cherry Bomb red, his eyes darkened with hunger. She was still on her tiptoes, leaning into him. "Wow."

He caressed her upper arms. "Perform for *me*, Beatrice. Not for them. Just for me."

"Will there be more kissing?"

His fingers stroked seductive figure eights on her bare arms. "After. There will be lots of kissing after."

She wanted lots of kissing. And more figure eights. So she said, "Okay," but her voice wobbled. Her belly was a mix of nerves and inebriated butterflies, throwing her off-kilter. Inhaling deeply, she shimmied her shoulders and forced a smile.

"Okay," she repeated, steadier this time. She followed him on stage.

12

Huxley knew coercing Beatrice on stage was a risky move, but her deer-in-the-headlights performance still shocked him. She froze a handful of times. She turned the wrong direction more than the right. She grappled with Axel's straitjacket buckles so long a teen heckled her. Her stunning eyes snapped wide with worry when Huxley shoved the first metal sheet through the zigzag box, and she fell onto an old man's lap while working the audience.

Pleasure swamped him at each fumble.

Axel punched his shoulder afterward. "That color lipstick suits you."

He touched his lips, remembering the feel of Beatrice against him. He hadn't bothered wiping it off. "I'll add eyeliner next time."

"I'll bring the blush." His brother glanced down the hall, to where Beatrice had disappeared. "She was pitiful."

Pitifully perfect. "She'll get better."

Axel removed his shirt. "At least she didn't puke."

"She did great."

He smirked. "Man, you have it bad."

He wasn't sure how to define his feelings for Beatrice Baker, vandalizer, below-average assistant. All-around astounding girl. He just needed to see her and make sure she wasn't crashing after her performance. Her adrenaline had no doubt ebbed. Anxiety could be setting in.

He strode down the hall and knocked on her dressing room door. When she didn't reply, worry snaked through him. He shoved the door open. To find her dancing.

She twirled on the spot, face lit with joy. "I did it!"

Her brightness filled the room...and his chest. "You did."

"I mean, I sucked, but I didn't pass out."

"We'll call that a win."

"I think I'm ready for the Bellagio."

"Let's get a few more nights under your belt first."

She twirled again, ignoring him, but he couldn't take his eyes off the fishnets that clung to her shapely calves, the feathered accents she'd added, the red handkerchief poking up from her cleavage, which matched the ruby lips he'd kissed.

Her lips had been exquisitely soft, as he'd expected, her little sounds of pleasure ruining him. He hadn't planned to kiss her. Not then, at least. He could declare he'd done it to distract her from her stage fright, but the truth was simpler. He'd *needed* to kiss her. Claim her. Give in to his desire. Desire that surged through his bloodstream now.

She stopped spinning and her red curls fell over her shoulders. She stared at him, breathing hard. "Are you going to kiss me again?"

"I am."

"I'll be better this time. Less like a cardboard cutout."

He closed the distance between them and cupped her cheeks. "Just be you. I only want you. Although I was surprised you didn't taste like watermelon."

"Oh, wait!" She twisted from his grasp, and he missed the contact instantly. She grabbed a tube from the makeup table, applied a layer of something shiny, then danced back into his arms. "Try this."

He wanted to do more than try. He wanted to wake up with her in the morning and make her coffee and cook her breakfast. It would mean exposing his body to her, not always a smooth event with women. Some who'd seen his scars had winced at the sight, excuses eventually made as to why they'd had to leave. One woman thought they were cool and loved touching them. He could only hope Beatrice would look at his scars the same way she beheld his face: with passionate heat.

For now, he'd *try*. He pressed his lips to hers, a soft brush that made his body ache. There was no halfway with Beatrice. No way to tamp his cravings for this woman. She made him ravenous, and she *did* taste like watermelon.

"Delicious," he murmured.

She cooed like his doves. She knocked off his hat, twined her fingers into his hair, pulling him closer, and swiped her tongue along his. His answering groan was dredged from a slumbering well deep in his chest. One kiss, and she pulled his desire to the surface, opened up the fun and excitement he'd denied himself for so long. Her body continued to dance, bumping against his. His hands fell to her full bottom, perfect and lush.

"Beatrice." Her name escaped him between smaller kisses.

She hummed against his busy mouth. "I used to hate my name."

"I love your name."

"I love how you say it." She feathered her fingers through his hair, grazing his mutilated ear. He stiffened, but she didn't. She swayed against him, explored his ugly defect, and kissed him harder.

Lust blasted through him. "Come home with me tonight. I'll whisper your name all over your skin." It was a bold request, but he was past sense and worrying about her reaction to his body, or her becoming a bigger distraction in his too-distracting world. She was the first woman he'd connected with in years.

She pressed her watermelon lips to his neck. "I would—"

"You two need to get a room." Leave it to Axel to interrupt their moment.

Sighing, Huxley rested his forehead against hers. "We're in a room. You invaded it."

Beatrice poked her head around Huxley's arm. "I didn't pass out."

Axel chuckled. "You also took an hour to fasten my straitjacket, but I won't fire you."

"You can't fire me if I don't get paid."

"Why don't you get paid?" At his brother's aggressive tone, Huxley turned to find a still-shirtless Axel glaring at him.

Fox strolled in. "Because she keyed his car."

Axel cringed. "The Mustang?"

Huxley thought he'd parked it far enough to avoid detection. Nothing was ever far enough from Fox.

As a teen, Huxley would "borrow" his father's cape and sneak out to perform on street corners. The all-seeing Fox would file away Huxley's misdemeanors until he'd need an alibi for his villainous endeavors, such as filling Mr. Wessick's car locks with cement. The math teacher had told their youngest brother, Xander, he was dumb as a post, and Huxley had been coerced into corroborating Fox's cover story. The time the jock who bullied Paxton got a sudden case of the shits "supposedly" happened when Fox and Huxley were riding their bikes.

Fox considered himself judge, jury, and executioner when family was involved. If he'd known about the vandalized car and hadn't retaliated against Beatrice, he must approve of Huxley bribing her into performing.

That didn't ease his guilty conscience. "I offered to pay her."

"After he blackmailed me," she piped in. "But I deserved it. I mistook his Mustang for my ex-boyfriend's, after mixing cold medicine with alcohol and hearing a Carrie Underwood tune. It wasn't pretty, and I couldn't cover the damages."

Axel scratched his head, a move that allowed him to flex his arm. "I'd like to meet this bitter, feisty Beatrice. She sounds fun."

Huxley tucked her into his side. "You will do no such thing."

Fox's annoying contribution: "That color lipstick really brings out your eyes."

He needed new brothers. He also liked being branded by Beatrice, red lipstick and all. He imagined burying his face between her thighs, drinking her in, covering his scruffy chin and cheeks in her feminine scent. Not thoughts he should entertain in front of his aggravating siblings. "If you two are done annoying me, it's time to move along."

And for Beatrice to reply to his request. He'd bet the theater she was about to agree to spend the night with him. But she extricated herself from his possessive hold, approached Axel, and studied his snake tattoo. Axel tipped his lips into what he deemed his lady-killer smile.

Beatrice stood back and planted her hands on her hips. "Is that a puff adder?"

He angled his inked ribs toward her. "A woman who knows her snakes. I think I'm in love."

Huxley considered tampering with Axel's straitjacket so the thing would imprison his obnoxious brother. "Why are you still here?"

"Because your girl is staring at me."

"I bet the ladies love that ink," she said.

Axel winked. "You know it."

"Which gives me an idea."

"You want to touch my snake?" Axel waggled his eyebrows at Beatrice, while Huxley glowered.

Fox tapped his middle finger against his thigh—his mind-reading pose. "It's not the worst idea."

Huxley wasn't sure which brother to smack first, but Beatrice faced him. "Have you told the boys about your music decision?"

"We're modernizing the music," he told them. Now they knew. And they could leave.

"Seriously?" Axel's eyes lit up like the Christmas their dad got him his pet gopher snake. He loved that reptile more than flexing for beautiful women.

"I'll work on the music," Fox said. "You have enough going on with the construction, and I don't trust Cocky Smurf."

Beatrice clapped. "You made a joke!"

Fox remained straight-faced. "We'll see who's laughing when you suggest the performance change."

Huxley's spine went rigid. "Performance change?"

She clicked her heels together, an adorable move he'd noticed a few times. She gestured to Axel's bare chest. "He's quite the looker, and those *Magic Mike* shows do bring in crowds."

Axel dialed up his smolder to eleven. "If you want me to strip for you, all you have to do is ask."

Huxley grumbled.

Beatrice shushed him. "I did some research, and there are a couple Australian magicians who perform half-naked. It's a gimmick, but the ladies love them. I thought it would be a great way to shake things up, market yourselves to women for girls' nights or bachelorette parties."

"No way." Huxley wouldn't put his damaged body on display for a bunch of drunk women. As it stood, he was hesitant for Beatrice to see his angry scars and puckered skin. Not enough to keep him from pursuing her, but not all women could handle the sight.

"Count me out, but he'll do it." Fox jutted his chin toward Axel.

"Damn straight. First the music, now this. Rainbow Brite keying your car could be the best thing to happen to the Marvelous Marlow Boys."

Huxley couldn't argue with that. He was also desperate enough to let his brother perform commando if it brought in business. "We'll try it."

Beatrice looked at him like he'd hung the moon. "Really?"

His throat turned scratchy. He undid the top button of his shirt. "Thank you for thinking about us. About the show."

"My pleasure." Her low tone matched his.

They stared at each other, an electric charge vibrating between them.

For a moment, his brothers disappeared. His worries vanished. Her gray gaze slid down his body, and his blood trumpeted. He craved this consuming connection, to feel like they were the only two people in the world. If her rapt attention was any indication, she was as eager as he was to pick up where they'd left off.

"Time for you two to get gone." He spoke to his brothers but kept his focus on Beatrice. "We'll start the new act and music Saturday."

"I'll work on promoting it," she said, sliding closer to his side.

"This is gonna be a blast." Axel smacked the door jam on his way out. "Look out New Orleans!"

Fox dipped his hand into his pocket and pulled out a gold ring and watch. He dropped them on the makeup table. "Use these at Saturday's poker game. And make sure you win big. I've got the music covered."

Half his attention still on Beatrice, Huxley didn't miss how her head jolted, like she'd been slapped, or the slight heave of her belly in her tight bodysuit. Her gaze was fixed on Fox's loot—spoils he'd likely picked from a pickpocket's pocket. The risky stunt would normally send Huxley into a rage, but he couldn't focus on much besides Beatrice's glassy eyes.

The poker game. Gambling. He expected this to be a trigger for her. He'd just hoped to get to know her better, build a foundation, before explaining the games.

His insides twisted.

Fox left, taking the warmth in the room with him.

"It's not what you think." Huxley spoke too fast, the way a guilty person spewed untruths. She was looking everywhere else but at him. His words flowed into the tense silence. "It's a game between fellow magicians. We're allowed to cheat. We do it for bragging rights more than to win, but I need the cash to fix the building. It's not an addiction for me. Not like your father."

The more he went on, the more her shoulders curved forward. He was talking himself into a sinkhole and didn't know how to stop. "Beatrice, please. It's just a stupid game. It's not a big deal."

She flinched, and he regretted his words instantly.

"It shouldn't be a big deal, but it is for me." She met his imploring gaze, her usually rainstorm eyes drizzly and somber. "I won't date a man who gambles, and I know we haven't known each other long, but hooking up with you would be too intense to be casual."

Her admission of their undeniable attraction lodged in his throat. He'd joined the poker match nine years ago, because his father had played. It was another way to keep Max Marlow's legacy alive. To feel close to the man. It was fun and challenging and sharpened his sleight of hand. It paid the bills now, but it didn't make him see sunshine on a partly cloudy day. It was a pastime. Nothing more. One that was coming between him and a woman who'd painted the word *smile* on her steering wheel.

"There's been a blight complaint against the theater. If I don't get it up to code in a month, I could lose it. Your suggestions to increase attendance have been great, and more appreciated than you know, but it won't be enough. I need to play."

"The fact that you *need* these wins is too much for me. I can't have that in my life." She picked a stray feather from her hip and released it. His hope hovered with the plumage, until it hit the floor. "If you don't mind, I'd like to get changed and head home. I told my friend I wouldn't be too late."

Right. Her friend. She was seconds from agreeing to a night of abandon with him, but his obligations had once again derailed his life. Angry with himself and his situation, he turned to leave, but paused. He couldn't let her go, couldn't walk out the door without leaving it open a crack. "I'm sorry for saying it isn't a big deal. It is. It was insensitive of me."

"Thank you," she whispered.

He swallowed roughly. "You were right about something else, too."

"About what?" Her breathy voice was hesitant.

One foot out the door, he said, "Nothing between us would be casual."

13

Huxley used to enjoy his weekly poker games. He'd get off on pulling the wool over his associates' eyes or calling them out when catching a false shuffle or sloppy deck stacking. He'd head home with a piece of jewelry or two, a stack of bills and an easy contentment, then pawn what he could to pay his brothers. It kept Edna on the payroll, so she could doze in the ticket booth and terrify potential vandals. The rest of his winnings would cover his rent and get siphoned back into the building. The gambling had been his mainstay, a moment away from his worries and a way to keep afloat.

Tonight was the second game since meeting Beatrice, and he resented every puff of Oliphant's cigar, every bat of Ms. Terious's gold eyelashes. The only place he wanted to be was with a woman who had quit him cold turkey.

The past ten days he had rehearsed and performed with Beatrice, but her natural brightness had dimmed. She still laughed with Axel and poked fun at Fox until both men were putty in her hands. With him, her interactions had felt muted, like an invisible fog separated them. She hadn't tried to dance with him or tease his surliness. When their routine had her touching his arm or back, she'd break contact at first chance.

She'd steal glances at him, though, lingering past discretion, her brow lifted in longing. Frustration and hunger would pool in his gut.

They both wanted each other. They both kept away. Him, out of respect for the hell her father had put her through. Her, out of fear. He understood the why of it and had given up hope they could surmount their differences. That didn't make inhaling her watermelon scent easy to bear.

"Call or fold."

Oliphant's blunt tone tore Huxley from his melancholy. A reminder why he was here. "I'll raise you fifty." He added his bills into the growing pot. At least the poker game was going according to plan.

Oliphant's mustache twitched, predictably. Huxley had forced a slow play, folding on hands he could have won, drawing out the games to let his money dwindle and feign desperation. Until his final deal. Five-card draw was his game. Simple. Clean. Tough to win unless you were dealt a killer hand. Thanks to his deck-stacking skills, he'd made sure everyone's hands were exceptional.

Oliphant matched the raise.

Ms. Terious was next, twisting the diamond stud in her ear. "Y'all won't be satisfied until I walk outta here broke and bare as the day I was born."

The visual made Huxley shudder. She was his mother's age, with a thick mole on her cheek, enough makeup to sink a ship, and stray chin hairs. Her late-night act involved disappearing objects down her expansive cleavage.

Dazzling Delmar scrubbed a thick hand over his dark beard, considering his cards. A delay tactic. Huxley kept his face blank. He knew Delmar held four of the five cards needed for his full house. He knew because he'd dealt him those cards purposely, just like he'd expertly switched to a new deck of cards last round. Passing Delmar his missing king on the final deal would be child's play.

As a kid, Huxley would stay up all night, his flashlight lighting his *Star Wars* comforter, cards flipping through his fingers. He'd shuffle and reshuffle, stacking decks and picking up cards until blisters formed. In school, he'd play for lunch money. Later he'd play for favors to keep his brothers out of trouble.

Tonight he played for his father's theater.

Delmar slapped his bill onto the pile. "The wife will string me up by my balls if I lose her Louis Vuitton money."

He always commented on "the wife." A ploy to play down his hand, just like Ms. Terious lamented leaving the club broke and battered. They also didn't counter with a raise. Aggressive play would scare others from sweetening the pot. A pot growing ever so nicely.

Horatio Heinzinger was last, the barely twenty-year-old who couldn't disappear a T-bone in a room full of pit bulls. The subpar magician would be lucky to bench press forty pounds, but, thanks to Daddy, the kid could buy and sell half of New Orleans. A welcome addition to their table.

Horatio clacked his teeth, a typical ritual. He scratched his nose next. So predictable, as had been his attempt to drop a card onto his lap when dealing two games ago. Being caught was shameful. It meant your skills lacked finesse. It also meant you had to fold. Horatio folded every round.

Ever the go-getter, he pushed on. He called the bet and raised another fifty. He must like his three deuces. Lucky for him, Huxley had a fourth waiting for him next deal.

Everyone called the kid's bet, growing the pot. All asked for a draw on the last round, swapping their undesirable cards for new ones. Huxley dealt and watched as they scanned their hands. It was a thing of beauty, knowing what you'd dealt, learning the tells that would serve you in future games. How Ms. Terious chewed her left cheek when she was pleased, how Oliphant flared his nostrils.

Now came the fun.

Thinking they had it in the bag, his associates went big, tossing in Benjamins like hundreds grew on trees. The stakes grew. Only Delmar folded, throwing his cards on the table and his hands in the air. The final pot was nearing two grand. Huxley's biggest score in ages. The sum meant he wouldn't have to keep lying to Fox and Axel about the "something else" he had on the go. Plus, if he had to be in a smoky room opposite a tacky dogs-playing-poker poster instead of dating Beatrice, he'd better walk away with a serious score.

The final move was his. He studied his royal flush and blinked a few times too many—his fake tell to make them think he was nervous. "Ms. Terious won't be the only one walking out of here broke. This game is getting too rich for my blood."

Oliphant blew a stream of smoke toward him. "What's the problem? Spent too much on fixing your theater?"

Huxley nearly crushed his cards.

It was the first time Oliphant had mentioned the construction work. Worried he'd punch him in the throat, Huxley had avoided the topic, but he was certain the beady-eyed brat was behind the complaint, thanks to his unrelenting Marlow family vendetta.

There was a time Oliphant had been borderline tolerant. He had apprenticed under Max Marlow, leeching off the great man's knowledge. Although Huxley had never liked Oliphant, his father had enjoyed fostering eager magicians, until Oliphant had given up stage secrets to a competitor. The idiot had let himself be seduced by a blond spy. He'd claimed to be a victim and begged to stay on under Max's tutelage.

Max had told him a good magician would have sensed the scheme a mile off and sent him packing, *after* warning other illusionists to steer clear of the incompetent man.

The incident had damaged Oliphant's reputation. Although he'd tried to regain a portion of his pride through the poker games, losing to Max time and again had only increased Oliphant's Marlow family hatred. He also knew how strapped Huxley was for cash.

"It's funny," Huxley said, tamping the ire in his voice. "I've never heard of the woman who lodged the blight complaint. Odd for it to happen out of the blue."

Oliphant puffed another smoke stream. "Odd, indeed."

"So odd it would make one wonder if someone had a grudge against the Marlow family."

"With a family like yours, I imagine it would be hard to narrow down the suspects."

Huxley clenched and released his jaw. "We are a colorful bunch."

He could call Oliphant out, but there was no point. The theater was an eyesore and had needed fixing. But if Oliphant took his grudge further, he'd learn Fox wasn't the only Marlow who knew more than he let on. Huxley had enough dirt on Oliphant to silence the man for good.

Oliphant stubbed out his cigar and dumped the butt in the ashtray. "Guess you need this win, with all those costs. But if I'm correct, you pulled the last bill from your wallet."

"Seems that way."

"You'll have to get creative."

The others scrutinized the interaction, eyes darting like they were watching an Olympic ping-pong match. They'd been down this block before. Oliphant lived to taunt Huxley, and the others wanted more loot added to the pot.

This was when jewelry came into play, the watches and earrings and rings allowed if money ran tight. But Oliphant wanted something in particular: a T. rex skull he'd lost to Max Marlow in an epic poker match. Oliphant had used the hunk of bones in a special levitation illusion, and he'd win it back over Huxley's rotting body. He was the reason Huxley was playing poker and would never kiss Beatrice again. Watching him choke on this loss would provide a shot of pleasure.

Huxley studied his cards. He blinked four times. "I have a T. rex skull. Would that be allowed?"

Oliphant froze, all but his flaring nostrils. "I'll allow it."

"It's worth a lot," Huxley added, "as you well know." He looked at Oliphant's ruby ring, Ms. Terious's diamond studs, Horatio's gold chain. "You'll need to cover my bet."

Delmar tipped back on his chair's legs, the furniture squeaking under his bulk. "Glad I bowed outta this one. More fun to watch the carnage."

"Y'all are pushing me to my limit." This from Ms. Terious, as she removed her earrings, adding them plus fifty to the pot. She sighed, pretending she didn't think she had the game in the bag.

Horatio hopped on her bluffing train. "Too hard to back out now." His gold chain slinked onto the pile with some cash.

"Guess the best player will win." Oliphant added his stake, trying to sound dejected. He practically frothed at the mouth.

"He will," Huxley said. With the bet called, he laid out his cards, one by one, enjoying the bulging of Oliphant's eyes as he realized Huxley's royal flush had his straight flush beat.

"You stacked the deck." Oliphant forced the accusation through gritted teeth.

Huxley grinned for the first time all night. "You were all too giddy over your hands to notice."

Ms. Terious huffed about losing her earrings. Delmar and Horatio grumbled as they left the room. Oliphant didn't budge. "That skull is mine."

"That skull was my father's, which means it's mine."

"He won it in a sloppy hand."

"If it were sloppy, you would have caught him cheating."

Oliphant jumped to his feet, sending his chair toppling behind him. "You're as arrogant as he ever was. You don't deserve that theater, or that skull. I look forward to the day it goes up for auction."

"Over my worm-infested body."

Huxley didn't tell the man he'd witnessed him picking pockets in Club Crimson. Stealing from drunk customers was as low as low got. Stealing from drunk customers in Vito's club was grounds for insanity. One word to the owner, who made Al Capone look like a teddy bear, and Oliphant would never bother the Marlow family again. But Huxley didn't want to stoop to Oliphant's level. He would deal with things aboveboard, as his father would have wanted.

More drained than pleased, he left Club Crimson with double what he'd made last week. Axel's salacious acts and the current music were bringing in more business, too, and he had eighteen days left to cover what he owed Trevor. The way things were going, he'd have the cash early. He should be overjoyed, thrilled to be upgrading the theater and thwarting Oliphant's schemes. But the constant ache in his chest quelled his pleasure.

He'd relived his kisses with Beatrice on a loop. *Soft. Warm. Watermelon. Woman.* If he could have more of that—a semblance of balance in his life—he'd be able to cope with the rest. Find ways to make it all work. Instead he was Curmudgeonly Smurf, his surly status reaching new heights.

His phone rang, and for one sharp breath he thought it was Beatrice calling, because he'd officially lost his mind.

It was Axel. "Who's that veterinarian you know?"

Huxley didn't often hear worry in Axel's voice. "Something wrong with Stanley?"

"He's not eating, and his gums are red and swollen. He might need antibiotics."

Huxley didn't love that old gopher snake, but Axel treated it like his child. "Have you been cleaning his terrarium? Making sure he has fresh water?"

"I'm not ten, Hux. I know how to take care of my fucking snake. But..."

"But what?"

"I gave you all my extra cash. I know things are tight, but this can't wait. Can you spot me...I don't know, a few hundred? Those vet bills are always insane, and I'll make it up with my next busking gig. I'm just hoping he doesn't need surgery."

"Yeah. Of course. Whatever you need." It was the same answer Huxley had given him when Axel had wanted to attend last year's Vegas magic conference. Huxley had finally saved some cash and hadn't decided if he'd use it to fix a small section of the theater or be selfish and buy himself a much-needed new couch. In the end, he'd sent Axel to the conference. The only thing Huxley hated more than looking at his rundown theater was failing his brothers.

"I'll text you the info and leave an envelope on my kitchen counter." Huxley mentally added another poker game to his roster. One veterinarian visit meant he'd no longer be able to pay for the construction work early, but he'd still make it all work. If surgery was needed, it would hit hard.

He walked toward his theater, needing...something. Hope. The possibility that his life wouldn't always revolve around the stage and family and keeping his head above water. A moment with his father usually helped.

Lights glossed the wet streets. Dark puddles splashed under his sluggish steps as drunk tourists strolled by. Music faded in and out of doors. He stopped outside the Marlow Theater and studied the scaffolding crisscrossing the exterior. His sigh hung in the humid air as he dragged a hand down his face.

Then a loud curse came from the side of his building.

Frowning, he skirted the construction material and peered into the dark alley. Another curse sounded. Snapping his attention higher, he caught sight of shoes as someone slipped into his second-story window.

"Goddamn it." Just what he needed tonight.

He'd had a squatter before. One homeless man who'd snuck in after Axel had left the backdoor open. The bum had been apologetic and vacated with little cajoling. A painless event. Judging by the curse and shoes, this particular trespasser was female. That didn't mean she was harmless.

He unlocked the door and stalked inside. He rummaged around the tools by the front door and found a sturdy wrench, in case a group had trespassed. He also found renewed anger.

He didn't need this headache. He was tired and drained.

Heartsick for someone he couldn't have.

Jaw locked, he paused by the poster on the foyer wall, the first one his father had hung. It showed his father in a top hat, his cape fanning out to the side. *Marvelous Max Marlow* was scrawled at the top. Along the right, where the interior of his cape created a dark background, was his tagline, *Believe in the Impossible.*

Huxley had believed once. He'd thought he could run this theater and support his family with as much panache as his father. He'd thought his shows would wow crowds.

The truth was depressingly stark.

Had he failed because he'd stopped believing? Or had he stopped believing because he had failed? A chicken and egg conundrum, the endless sort that could lead a man to insanity. If he asked Beatrice, he was sure she'd tell him he'd stopped believing. That fate only unfolded favorably for those who smiled and saw partly sunny days. If that were true, then *he* was his own roadblock. The wrench felt heavy in his dangling hand, but his shoulders suddenly lightened.

Could it be that simple? Could reordering his mind change his fate? He assumed his poker nights would be an unclimbable divide, that their timing was wrong, as timing often was.

Unless he believed.

This could be a delay, not an end. A pause in an inevitable romance. *Yes*, his heart said, thudding its rapid reply. "Yes," he whispered to the empty room.

He would believe in them. In the impossible, if that's what they were.

He was sure his father would approve.

A loud *thunk* broke his epiphany. He was raring to tear out of there and find Beatrice, ask her if she'd wait for him and turn their impossible into the possible. First, he had a squatter to contend with.

14

Candy. Bea was sure candy would cure what ailed her. It had prompted her late-night excursion, resulting in a scratched forearm when sneaking back into the theater.

She dumped her spoils by her makeshift mattress—old costumes heaped into a pile on the prop room floor. She'd taken to sleeping by her art project, hoping inspiration would strike. For ten days, she'd woken in the middle of the night, fingers itching to paint a new self-portrait square, but all recent efforts had resembled out-of-focus frames. She'd lost her light. And she knew why.

She'd lost her muse.

No matter her forced smiles, or the goofing around she did with his brothers, something in her had tarnished upon learning Huxley gambled. *I can't expose myself to gambling again*, she'd told herself. *I refuse to paint the self-portrait of a pathetic woman who falls for a man like her father.* But Huxley *did* seem trustworthy, his sweet gestures showing as much: caring for her the night she'd keyed his car, taking her to lunch, helping her conquer her stage fright, kissing her into oblivion, helping her land a job. Still, she kept her distance.

Gambling and its fallout had upended Bea's life once. It had now stolen something else from her: a man who'd zig-zagged her heart.

Her creative drought had returned, worse than after she'd learned her father had squandered her savings. Or maybe the two were linked. A building snowball of bets and losses.

Sitting cross-legged, she ate a handful of Pop Rocks and chased it with a mouthful of cola. Fireworks exploded in her mouth and belly, her intended goal—a simulation of being around Huxley. She hoped it would power her creativity and banish her drizzly thoughts. Her two-by-fours were lined up against the wall, teasing her with unreachable inspiration.

More sugar was needed. She separated her pile of Double Bubble and ate a handful of Skittles. When that didn't work, she unwrapped a red lollipop. She sucked on the cherry candy and rolled it around in her mouth. Nothing. She reached for her cell, wondering if music would open her artistic pores, but a new text caused her to drop the phone.

Big Eddie.

The candy and cola collided in her stomach, twisting into a sugared knot. She hadn't heard a blip from him since blocking his number. She'd been so engrossed in her assistant duties and artistic frustration, she'd almost forgotten her father's problems, and hers by proxy.

Unfortunately, Big Eddie hadn't.

Pay up or your daddy gets it and you'll never eat solid food again. I collect all my debts.

Her mind hurtled back to the time Franklyn Baker had wandered home, scalp bleeding, arm broken, his left eye black and blue. Big Eddie hadn't been the man behind that brutal beating but that didn't mean he wouldn't honor his latest threat.

The twisting in her gut worsened.

Cutting ties with her father had been essential, but she'd always feared getting The Call, the one telling her he'd been hurt *or worse.* Her father was sick, his addiction having sunk its fangs into him. He'd refused to get help. His actions didn't warrant a doting daughter, but that didn't mean he deserved another beating.

Lollipop pressed to the inside of her cheek, she slowed her breath and closed her eyes as her heart rate steadied. This latest message had a hint of desperation behind it, more warnings with little follow through. Big Eddie hadn't mentioned New Orleans, and vague threats about her father probably meant Franklyn hadn't been hurt yet. He had likely gone underground, laying low until the dust settled. His disappearances when growing up had been as reliable as the changing seasons.

Just in case her father hadn't thought to cover his tracks, she wrote a quick reply to Big Eddie: *Your money is coming. If you hurt my father, you won't get it.*

Another lie, this one hopefully stalling the creep long enough to give her father a heads up. She then sent a quick warning to her dad. It was the last thing she wanted to do. Opening communication with Franklyn Baker always invited sweet words and promises, followed by requests for money. The man was a living undertow, inevitably drawing her back in. She wouldn't weaken this time. She'd send one message, then ignore him and Big Eddie, leave her father to handle his own drama, whatever the fallout.

She blocked Big Eddie's number *again* and stared at the screen. She couldn't afford a new phone. At the very least, she should change her number again, but that would mean her father wouldn't be able to reach her this time. She'd lose any trace of him in her life. An odd panic set in. Agitation edged her breaths. The large building felt darker and unsafe, and she didn't understand why she cared if Franklyn Baker evaporated into thin air.

The sound of approaching footsteps had her already rattled nerves jolting.

She whipped her head around to search the space, expecting to see Big Eddie, then scolded her overactive imagination. She needed to get a grip. And hide. No one had slipped into the prop room yet, but the footsteps continued. She should hop to her feet or hide in the zigzag box or cover herself with the nearby red cape. With tonight's continued drama, her lungs and limbs had ceased to function.

They atrophied further when Huxley entered her makeshift bedroom, brandishing a wrench. "This is private prop—" He reared back, startled eyes flitting over Bea.

"It's you," she said breathlessly, relieved to see his familiar face.

His fisted wrench fell to his side. "What are you doing here?" His attention drifted from her lumpy-clothing bed, to the candy pile. It settled on her toiletries, which she normally kept hidden behind old props. "Did something happen with your roommate?"

It took a slow count to ten to calm her nerves and remember that she'd been crashing here illegally the past two weeks. A more immediate problem than a man texting threats from Chicago. She could lie, confirm Huxley's roommate suspicions, but he'd only ever been honest with her, even though it had cost him her affection. Cost them both, in the end. Returning his candor with deception would be cruel.

She removed the lollipop from her mouth. "I'm staying here."

"I gathered that. But why? What happened with your roommate?"

"I never had one."

"What do you mean you never had one?" His tone rose, and the wrench jerked in his hand.

She flinched away from the threatening tool. "Are you going to hit me with that?"

"What?"

"The wrench? You look ready to bash someone."

He blinked at his weapon. Huffing out a breath, he placed the tool down, then sat across from her on the prop room floor. His long legs looked comical folded, his knees sitting high and awkward. He ran his large hands over his dark jeans. "Are you telling me you've been sleeping in my theater for two weeks?"

The words sounded like they pained him. She didn't want to cause him more pain. Her messy past had done enough of that. "I'm sorry," she said, her attention on the lollipop she spun in her hand.

He gripped her wrist, stilling the rhythm. "Don't apologize, Beatrice."

"But I've been lying and you're mad."

"I'm furious...with myself. I haven't paid you, and I've been blind to the fact that you don't have anywhere to live. What kind of man does that make me?"

The best kind, she wanted to say, which didn't make sense, considering his statement. "I still lied. I've been sleeping here without paying rent."

"Are you making money with Della?" He asked the question softly, his hand motionless on her wrist.

Her breaths felt weighted, like the oxygen between them was laced with iron. "I am, but it's tough to find a good apartment at a cheap price, and I like it here." She *had* liked it, at least. Before that unnerving text.

"You like sleeping on the floor?"

"Sleeping in this amazing space. I've been struggling to paint for a while. Then I came here and my creativity flooded back. I didn't want to leave."

His strong cheekbones sharpened as he released her wrist, and her pulse point turned cold. His back was to her painting, but she couldn't control her flicking gaze.

She wasn't ready for him to see it. To see *her* in the unfinished work. He, of course, turned his head and followed her sightline. *Stupid flitting eyes.* He rotated his upper body fully, his knees lifting as he faced the project. And God, she felt naked. Exposed. He was studying her essence, the good and bad that forged her soul.

"It's you." He pushed to his feet and approached the work.

She'd outlined her profile on the wood planks, but only a handful of squares had been filled in. Still, he saw her. He knew. She wondered if he recognized his lighter blue eye or the section of his cape. She sucked on her lollipop, needing to busy herself with something. Cherry sweetness clung to her tongue. Jitters frazzled her further. He kept staring.

"It's far from done," she said around her lollipop.

He kept his back to her. "It's amazing."

Her cheeks probably matched her cherry candy. "I kind of stole the wood planks from a room upstairs, so I owe you for that on top of the car and the squatting. Oh, and the cape dry-cleaning, too. And the toothbrush. And beignets. And lunch." The words *thank* and *you* felt inadequate on her tongue. Instead, she babbled. "I'm racking up quite the tab."

His gray T-shirt clung to his broad back, stretching tightly over his muscles as he crossed his arms. He didn't move after that, only cocked his head.

She sneezed.

"Bless you," he said. Then, "Eighteen days."

She twitched her nose. "What's in eighteen days?"

When he finally faced her, her pulse stuttered. His pupils had blown wide, turning his mismatched eyes the same deep brown. His wavy hair was askew. Ten days ago, she'd dragged her fingers through that soft hair. She'd felt the strong cords of his neck.

She bit through her lollipop and crunched the hard candy.

"Eighteen days," he repeated. "That's how long I have to earn cash for the building. After that, I'll quit gambling."

"Why?" She sucked her cherry-flavored lip and leaned forward. Was he doing this for her? A girl he barely knew?

"Because I plan to take you on a date, in eighteen days."

"Oh." It was a pathetic syllable. It didn't leap like her heart had at his admission, or tumble like her belly. It hung between them, solid and unmoving. She should be thrilled he'd been thinking about her, too, that he'd make room in his life to accommodate her baggage. But she'd heard those words before.

I'm done this time.

Never gambling again.

Doing it for you, Pumpkin.

She wanted to believe Huxley, but her intuition often led her astray. "I don't like the idea of you changing for me. There's pressure with that. We don't even know each other that well."

"I'm not changing my personality, just an extracurricular activity. And not knowing each other is the point. I want to know you better."

"Enough that you'd quit a game you enjoy?"

"I couldn't care less if I never see another deck of cards."

"What about in your routines? You'll have to use them then."

His lips tugged to the side, into an almost smile. "Yes, Beatrice. I'll have to use them in my acts. But there will be no betting of any kind."

"At all?"

"None."

"In eighteen days?"

He nodded, and an idea struck. She wanted that date more than she wanted a lifetime supply of Double Bubble, but fear of getting hurt simmered, threatening to reach a full boil. She needed to ensure Huxley was the good man he seemed, before dating and feelings complicated matters. Her track record proved such espionage was warranted. And espionage was best performed in close quarters.

"I will accept your date offer," she said, "under one condition."

Chin tipped up, he stalked closer. "I'm all ears."

He was all sexy, two-toned eyes, broad chest and slim hips. Factors that could make this stipulation a challenge. She forged on. "I'd like to move in with you."

He froze. "Move in with me?"

"Into your spare room. You mentioned it at that café and said I could crash there. As much as I like it here, the space has felt a bit...uncomfortable lately, and I have nowhere else to go. I'd pay you, of course. And it would only be until I find something else." Until she sussed out if he was date worthy, and the uncomfortable part wasn't a lie.

Living together would exacerbate their sexual tension, but she was still shaken by that text. The notion of sleeping in a cavernous theater, alone, had lost its appeal. A proper bed and room would be a luxury, too. As would the absence of morning construction workers stomping around.

"So just to get this right," Huxley said, a smile spreading, "you'll go on a date with me in eighteen days if we live together?"

She wasn't sure why he was grinning so wide. She never wanted him to stop. "I will."

He passed his hand over his mouth and shifted his weight. "Okay. But I have a stipulation of my own."

"Will there be pimping involved?"

He chuckled, a deep rumbly sound she'd have liked to hear in stereo. "What's with you and the pimping?"

"I saw a program once, on human trafficking. It left an impression." As did the gangster movies and cop shows she enjoyed. For a beat, she contemplated telling Huxley about her father's debt drama, but he had his own money issues, and involving others always made things worse. Case in point: her attempt at helping Franklyn Baker hadn't done her any favors.

Huxley closed the distance between them and crouched in front of her crossed legs. He took her hands in his. "I assure you there will be no pimping, but if I take you on as a roommate, I'd like you to concede something, too."

"I knew you were an even-steven sort."

"Is that a problem?"

"Depends on the concession."

"It's two things, actually."

"Now you're just demanding."

He sunk his thumb into the divot between her knuckles. "You have to set up your art in my living room so you can paint, and I won't charge you rent. If you won't let me pay you, at least let me do this."

She'd never met such a generous man, willing to change his ways to take a woman on a date, refusing rent, encouraging Bea to paint in his place. On paper, he seemed wonderful. But she no longer trusted her instincts, and there was no better way to understand someone's nature than in their natural habitat. The venue change might even alleviate her creative slump.

Her answer to him was easy, but she didn't want to remove her hands from his just yet. "I might agree to your terms, but I forgot to ask some essential questions."

"Such as?"

"What color are your walls?"

He took his time answering. "Robin's-egg blue."

"Do you stock ketchup or green lollipops?"

"No to the lollipops, but ketchup is a must."

She'd have to tape down the lid. She'd also have to find a way to guard her heart and repay Huxley for his generosity. "If we do this, it's just as friends. Nothing happens before our date."

His thumbs drew soft circles over her knuckles. "Just as friends."

"Then I think we're in agreement."

He stood, pulling her upright, and helped her gather her meager belongings. She did her best not to brush against him as they worked. For the next eighteen days, she'd evict all naughty thoughts from her mind. She wouldn't allow herself to get involved with him until ensuring he was nothing like her father.

With the last of her items collected, she said, "Should I change my name to Bellatrix?"

"Why would you change your name?" He shouldered her larger bag, hefted some wood planks under his arm, and walked ahead, leading her toward the stage.

She followed with her candy bag and the remaining wood planks. "Our platonic living arrangement is kind of like we're siblings. To be your sister for a couple weeks I need an X name."

He stopped abruptly, and she nearly slammed into his back. He turned, hovering over her. "You are not my sister, *Beatrice.*"

He sexed up her name again, curling it around his tongue until she felt soft and melty. He continued on his way. She tripped over her feet.

Not siblings, indeed.

15

Breakfast had become Bea's least favorite meal. She didn't love walking past Huxley, who'd offer a gravelly "Good morning" as he'd make them coffee, the rasp in his voice unbearably sexy. She detested the way he sucked on his bottom lip when reading the paper. She hated asking him for plates she couldn't reach, the action forcing his threadbare T-shirts to ride up his back, exposing a sliver of skin.

She'd then sigh. He'd swallow. They'd stare at each other too long.

Breakfast was the worst.

"I'm cooking," she declared, needing a distraction. Not only did he wear thin T-shirts, but he had a collection of adorably nerdy tops he wore around the house.

Today's read: *Talk Nerdy to Me.*

"I thought you liked my omelets," he said.

"I love your omelets." The lightest and fluffiest she'd ever had, but he'd made them the past two mornings, insisting he serve her at his kitchen counter, with a fresh fruit tower on the side. Huxley Marlow was quite the culinary architect. He'd pull his stool next to hers, their thighs touching as they'd eat and discuss the previous evening's performances—which music worked best, ways to mesmerize the audience without increased nudity.

His mid-sized apartment had dark wood floors, high ceilings, and an open living-eating area with a small oak table where they could eat on opposite sides. But they'd sit at the counter, side by side. She'd eat the blueberries from his plate. He'd steal her watermelon. They'd wash dishes together, brushing elbows more than was decent.

They were stellar roommates. With a bad case of *sexualus tensionae.*

It was also her turn to cook.

He sipped his coffee, hip pressed to the counter, hair sexily sleep-mussed. "I thought you preferred sculpting your food over cooking it."

"I may not be a top chef like you, but I can whip up breakfast." Sort of. "Sit down and let me work."

When he didn't move, she woman-handled his hips and forced him to walk around the counter. A dangerous move. Thin sweatpants were all that separated his hipbones from her too-hot hands. She gripped him longer than necessary, standing behind him like a creeper. When he finally sat on his stool, her heavy breaths brushed the back of his neck. A half-sigh, half-groan rumbled from her roommate.

Sexualus tensionae.

Cooking was the perfect distraction.

Her culinary prowess was limited to nuking frozen dinners, opening cans, and raiding candy shops, but she needed something non-Huxley to focus on. She found eggs in the fridge, cheese, and mushrooms. She'd watched Huxley and his big hands closely enough that she could try to mimic his omelet expertise.

Apparently, cracking eggs took skill she didn't possess.

Broken eggshells filled her bowl...and they were the last

eggs they had. Determined to cook for him, she proceeded to pick out the scattered fragments. She felt his eyes on her as she worked, goose bumps shivering up her arms.

Playing the role of sisterly house companion, she'd made sure to wear a bra under her sleepwear, ensuring the white cotton tank top didn't cross any carnal lines. Her watermelon-slice flannel bottoms were definitely roommate quality. Huxley still stared at her like she was a red lollipop, and he had a red lollipop addiction.

Steam curled from his refreshed coffee, malty, toasty scents drifting between them. Shell extraction complete, she cut and sautéed the mushrooms, as he had. Her final product was more a jumbled mess than pretty presentation. At least it was edible.

Huxley accepted his plate. "It looks delicious."

"You're a skilled liar."

"I don't lie. You did an excellent job."

Warmth filled her chest. "This is the fanciest meal I've ever made. Consider yourself lucky I moved in and graced you with my culinary expertise."

Mug in one hand, he leaned his elbows on the counter. "Thank goodness you moved in," he murmured, his rapt attention focused on her, not on his food.

He shifted on his stool.

Her breasts felt heavy.

Sexualus tensionae.

Instead of sitting beside him, she stood across the counter where their arms and legs wouldn't brush, and where she couldn't inhale his soapy, manly scent. She used the space to remind herself there were reasons for their self-imposed roommate scenario, the main one being: believing the best in people often led her to disappointment. This was her chance to understand Huxley's true character before getting in too deep.

She scooped up a forkful of eggs and crunched on something. Mortified, she froze. If Huxley's sour expression was any indication, he'd also chewed eggshell pieces. She managed to swallow, then moved her plate away and waited for him to crack a joke or get annoyed with her awful breakfast. He did neither of those things.

Huxley scooped up another bite and crunched his way further into her heart. "Axel has some new number tonight," he said. "It involves less clothing."

She couldn't touch her eggs or tear her gaze away from this sweet man's face. "It might not be what you imagined for the theater," she said, "but the seats are filling, and I have new flyers. Della lets me take a few breaks at the market to hand them out. The women I target get all giggly when they read them."

Because she'd slapped an image of Axel on the advertisements, one in which he happened to be shirtless. Even two-dimensional, Cocky Smurf charmed the ladies. Bea also spent some post-performance evenings trolling the streets, accosting drunk women with her leaflets.

Along with social media posts, her efforts had more tickets selling nightly. Each show still set off her stage fright, complete with more dressing room panic sessions. Huxley would come in and talk her down as she squeezed the red handkerchief. She'd then remember how his passionate kiss had helped calm her nerves. She'd keep her eyes on his top hat or cape or study his scarred cheek, wishing she could coast her lips over the puckered surface. Her fantasies would distract her initially, her adrenaline rush taking her the last mile.

Last show, she'd only messed up three times, and she hadn't fallen onto any audience members.

Huxley grimaced as he took another bite. "I'm planning a new number. Does fire scare you?"

"Like when it shoots from your sleeves for the dove routine?"

"Yes and no. You'll be more involved this time."

She was pretty sure one touch from Huxley would have her skin bursting into flames. "I can do fire."

"Good." He devoured the rest of his eggs, like they'd been prepared by a five-star chef, not her incapable hands.

She forced her attention to the living room, anywhere but on his handsome self. Her pink pony stood on his coffee table in all its girly glory. It was Bea's favorite thing about the room, especially when she'd catch Huxley looking at Cotton Candy, amusement in his eyes. A few magic magazines and his *Bon Appétit* collection were stacked beside it. Her gaze skimmed the publications and landed on the art supplies she'd set up behind his couch.

Last night had been their weekly free evening. No stage fright or performing. Drop cloth on the ground, she'd lost herself for hours, only to feel Huxley's hand on her back later. So thrilled her inspiration had returned, she'd forgotten she was in his house, on his floor, living with this fascinating man. Her bedroom was next to his. A wall separated them.

"I'm heading to bed," he'd said softly, his deep voice caressing her ear. The intimacy of the moment had sent her swooning so hard she'd nearly face-planted on her paint palette. But the greater joy, the startling reality, was that she didn't need the theater's magical prop room for her creativity to bloom. This new venue had also pumped her full of inspiration.

Even now, while Huxley insisted on cleaning up, two hours before her flea market job began, she filled plastic containers with water and set up her art station. Because she could. Because she was energized. Because with Huxley near, she suddenly had to.

She painted two squares: a section of the queen of hearts and the lip of a martini glass. She wasn't sure when jazz music had begun to play, or when Huxley had sat on the couch behind her. He didn't make conversation or watch her work. Maybe he sensed her need for concentration, or he enjoyed the quiet, too. Either way, his proximity brought with it a soothing contentment.

Needing to shower, she cleaned her brushes and dumped her paint-muddied water. Huxley's attention remained fixed on a small box in his hands. *The* box. The one he'd obsessed over yesterday as well, but she'd been too excited about painting to ask him about it.

She laid out her brushes to dry, ready to find out why he was trying to open an unopenable box, but he put it down and moved to stand in front of her project.

He crossed his arms. "How do you like your martinis?"

"On the sweeter side. I have a thing for lemon drops. But it's a bit early to break into the booze."

He chuckled. "Your painting, I mean. You painted the lip of a glass."

She stood beside him, both observing her work. "I also like Long Island Iced Tea and margaritas, but I didn't paint those. And lemonade. The virgin kind. And some sodas."

"Lemon drops. Virgin lemonade. Sodas. No ketchup." He nodded while cataloguing her preferences. Her wood planks rested on his far wall. He walked toward them, paused, then walked farther back. "It changes completely, depending on the distance. The details get lost from afar, leaving just your profile. I've never seen anything like it."

"It's not totally original," she said, suddenly fidgety as he analyzed her work. "The technique's been done before in lots of ways. It's just my take on it—more personal, I guess."

"And intricate. It must take ages to finish a piece. How do you put a price tag on it?"

She studied the squares, more of them empty than filled, and imagined the hours it would take to complete. More like weeks or months. She'd never considered her time as a commodity. Painting was life. It was oxygen. Selling a piece to someone seemed unthinkable. A notion she'd have to get over if she planned to earn a living with her craft. "I've never sold my work before. The idea of putting it out there for people to judge always freaks me out, and I guess I assumed I'd gain that confidence in art school."

He faced her, fierceness in his penetrating gaze. "You are unbelievably talented. Some people will love your work, and others might dislike it—the same way we can't please everyone with our performances. But that doesn't change how brilliant you are."

His compliment swirled through her in a fizzy rush. She tilted her head back to meet his eyes. "Thank you."

The often stern lines of his brow softened. "How many pieces have you painted?"

"In this style, just this one. I didn't start it until I moved into the theater. My recent paintings before this were awful."

"Impossible."

"No. Like, really bad. They were uninspired."

He searched her face. "What changed?"

His need to know her meant more than he realized, as did their recent time together. So far, living with him, she'd witnessed firsthand the gentleman in her midst. He kept his apartment tidy, blessed her when she sneezed—a nervous tic she'd exhibited less of lately—opened doors and said please and thank you. He'd generally treated her with kindness. Everything she'd expect from a man who planned to date her. This roommate experiment was working in his favor, but this line of questioning chipped at the ugliness keeping them apart.

"I think being around your show and the theater invigorated me. What happened with my father drained my creativity. Something switched off for me after his betrayal." After all of his gambling and lies. Every single time his problems had become hers she had shut down, her inspiration lost.

"Beatrice..." Huxley stepped closer. Their toes touched. The tiny contact sent tingles through her limbs and it was too much. He was still a poker player. For another fifteen days, he was off-limits.

Humming a random tune, she squeezed past him and sat on his couch, but some sort of wire framing poked into her backside. She shifted to a more comfortable spot and picked up his odd box. The small rectangle was black with gold-detailed sides—circles and triangles and filigree woven in symmetrical patterns. "Is there a genie in here?"

He joined her on the couch and stretched his long legs toward her. "It's a puzzle box."

"So it needs to be solved? To open it?"

"It does."

She turned it in her hands. "It doesn't look possible."

"It's designed to be challenging, not impossible. But I've been fiddling with it for nine years and still no luck." He pulled the treasure from her grasp. Their fingers brushed this time, this contact zinging up her arms. She wondered if he felt every connection as acutely as she did. If he fell asleep, picturing her under her sheets, on the other side of their joined wall.

He caressed the box with his thumb. "It was my father's. He left it to me in his will, along with the car and the theater."

"God, that must have been overwhelming. Did it cause friction with your brothers?"

"Because I inherited most of his possessions?"

She nodded.

He rubbed a small scar on his pinky finger, a habit of his when thinking. "It added more strain to an already strained relationship with Xander and Pax, but not with Axel and Fox. They didn't want the headache of the theater, and Dad was old-fashioned like that, handing things down to his eldest son. He also knew I'd be the one to keep it going and keep the family together. Or die trying." Bitterness tainted his tone.

"But you *have* kept it alive. It's getting busier every day, and you three are so close."

"We are, but the past few years have been rough. Axel and Fox even came to me once suggesting I sell the place. So I started lying to them, not letting on how in the hole we were financially."

She didn't like how defeated he sounded, or his Surly Smurf frown. But these weren't problems she could help solve. "So, what's in the box?" she asked, hoping the topic change would distract him.

He sighed and studied the contraption in his hand. "No clue. He took risks with his work and organized his estate before he died. This"—he shook the box—"was an eccentric touch I should have expected. Apparently the key to my future happiness is inside. We've all tried to open it. We've all failed."

"I'd take a hammer to it."

Huxley looked like he'd eaten a green lollipop. "There's a vial of vinegar inside. If it holds a note, something written on parchment, breaking the box will crack and dissolve the paper. Any message inside will be destroyed."

Her throat tightened. Struggling with it for nine years, hoping for a message from his father, must have been some kind of frustrating. She'd have run over it with her car.

She peered at the contraption from the side. "Maybe it has rainbows inside. Or tiny fairies. Or it's like those Harry Potter tents that seem small but are ginormous and filled with every imaginable convenience."

She wasn't expecting to feel his fingers on her cheek, the rough-soft pad of his thumb. "You're wonderful," he murmured.

His voice was impossibly tender, his brushing fingers divine. Swooning was imminent. Smelling salts would be required.

She promptly said, "Fifteen days."

He hesitated, then retracted his hand. "I know, Honeybee. Fifteen days. It's marked on your calendar, circled with a sparkly heart, and highlighted with five colors."

She sat up straight and scowled at him. "When did you see my calendar?" Unless Fox had read her mind when she'd created the silly doodles and blabbed to his brother.

Huxley chuckled. "I noticed it when I put your Minnie Mouse slippers in your room."

She turned her glower up a notch. "I need to shower and go to work." She strutted away but swiveled back. "And for the record, it's six colors, not five."

16

As she reached the French Market, a text came in from Huxley and a traitorous grin split Bea's face. She shouldn't grin, not even when he'd told her she was wonderful, a mere twenty minutes prior. For the next fifteen days they were still platonic roommates. Nothing more. But the sight of his name was enough to make her practically skip to work. His text was more perfunctory than expected. *I'm going shopping for food. What do you want in the house?*

Not only was he refusing rent, now he was paying her way. His guilt over her homelessness had gone too far. *Nothing*, she replied. *I'll hit a late-night shop after the show. It's my turn to buy groceries.*

Don't bother. I have time.

She gave her phone the evil-eye. *You can't pay for everything.*

I'll pay if I want to. We also need more eggs. Ones without shells inside them.

She laughed at his teasing. *I thought you liked my eggs. You ate the whole plate.*

No bouncing balls hinted at a reply. The pause lasted so long she almost pocketed her phone. Then he sent: *I loved your eggs, Beatrice.*

No one used proper names when texting. No one but Huxley Marlow of the Marvelous Marlow Boys. Even in text, her name had an erotic tone. She also wasn't sure they were still talking about breakfast.

What did you like about my eggs?

Her innuendo-laced reply was sent before she thought better of it. Her fingers had a mind of their own, and she was verging on giddy. Not only was the sun shining, but she'd thought more about selling her paintings, making quicker and smaller pieces—fun miniatures for the flea market crowd. Without investing so much of herself in them, sharing them publicly should be less daunting. She would also paint something special for Huxley, a thank-you for his generosity.

The ideas had her buzzing, and flirting with Huxley felt too good on an already good day. They also had data bytes safely between them. And a twenty-minute drive.

She stepped aside. Tourists flooded the market, the bustling chatter and distant swirl of jazz tunes fading as she awaited his response.

It came a beat later: *I loved that they tasted as delicious as they looked.*

She bit her cheek. Those eggs had been far from delicious. Was he talking about her lips? The watermelon gloss? It felt like a hypothetical game—him wanting to taste her, her wanting to be tasted. A game she couldn't resist playing.

She went to reply, but a new text came through, this one from a number she didn't recognize. Although unfamiliar, the one word *help* meant it was from her father, and she stiffened.

He always started with that opener. Simple and to the point. In the past she'd have read his next messages with a pounding pulse, but they were always pleas for money. He'd learned she wouldn't answer calls and had resorted to endless texts. The appeals would involve professions of fatherly love, saying that Beatrice was the only decent thing he'd done in his life, and he was lost without her and was ready to change. He'd tell her this time was different and would ask her to loan him cash.

His intentions weren't always underhanded. He often believed he could change. That never altered the outcome.

With the threats she'd received, she itched to read his latest messages, *just in case*. Make sure he was okay. But if he wasn't, where would that leave her? If she got sucked back into that tornado, she'd spin until she couldn't find her way out. As it stood, she hadn't even changed her phone number yet. He obviously had, but switching hers meant neither of them could reach each other. For some incomprehensible reason, the notion still pained her.

Her souring thoughts were a reminder of why she and Huxley had implemented their waiting-period rule, why she'd asked to move in with him to understand the man better before getting involved. Flirty texts were not part of said plan.

She thumbed to Huxley's message instead of her father's and replied quickly, but her hands were jittery, her nerves rattled. She'd planned to end their flirtatious repartee with the non-sexy text: *I'm menstruating. Buy me whipped cream.* Because whipped cream tasted best when menstruating, and menstruating was non-sexy. Instead autocorrect betrayed her and sent:

I'm masturbating. Buy me whipped cream.

Crap.

Huxley's answering dots bounced. She held her breath.

Then her phone died.

Double crap.

The useless battery prevented her from retracting her words or reading his. At least it kept her from glancing at her father's message, a sign that ignoring him was the right thing to do. Unfortunately, none of it helped with the text she'd sent. She couldn't charge her phone at the flea market, which meant she wouldn't see or speak with the recipient of her dirty text until she was performing with him on stage. Sweat slicked her armpits. Her belly roiled.

Life was not always her friend.

Della sniffed her freak-out a mile away. "What's with the sunburn?"

Bea slipped into their booth and pressed her hands to her overheated cheeks. "You mean the blush I'm sporting because I sent the world's most embarrassing autocorrected text to the man I'm supposed to be sisterly with?"

"Are we talking about Huxley?"

"We are."

"I'm dying to know about the sisterly issue, but the text sounds too juicy to pass up. Start talking."

Aware Della was protective of the Marlow boys, Bea had refrained from gossiping about her new living arrangements. The embarrassing text was the safer topic. "I told him I was masturbating. Then my phone died."

She cackled. "When?"

"When I got here."

"So you were masturbating while walking? With one of those remote devices?"

"They have remote devices?"

Della wiggled her perfectly arched eyebrows. "They do. And let me tell you, they are *fun*. But back to the walking and masturbating."

"I wasn't walking *or* masturbating. I was attempting to stop flirting and told him I was menstruating. While standing still. At the market entrance."

"You actually used the word *menstruating*?"

Bea glowered at her.

Della only looked more amused. "That's adorably old-fashioned. I also love your thigh-highs. You have the funkiest tights."

"Thank you, but we've gone off topic." Though Bea did own an impressive collection of printed tights, today's striped rainbow pair included.

As a kid, she'd shop at second-hand stores, spending hours sifting through tossed treasures. She'd wear fur vests over lace blouses, pink stockings under floral skirts. Kids would tease her and call her homeless and colorblind. She'd pitied their boring shirts and jeans.

Della pinched Bea's hip. "So you sent this dirty text and have no idea how he replied?"

"That sums up my shame."

She smacked her hands together and rubbed them like a criminal mastermind. "Tonight's performance should be interesting."

"So should our slumber party."

Della's protective face snapped in place—full lips flattening, dark eyes hardening. Before she could interrogate Bea, two women approached the table, fussing over the jewelry. Della behaved like the professional she was, closing the sale. Bea, on the other hand, continued her impression of a sunburned lobster.

More customers followed. When a respite hit, Della didn't waste their minutes alone. "Are you sleeping with Huxley?"

As usual, her directness was both refreshing and terrifying. "I'm not sleeping *with* him exactly. I'm sleeping in the room beside his."

When Della's eyes narrowed into twin lasers, Bea relayed her movie-script life: squatting in the theater, her gambling heritage, the blight, the poker games, the fifteen remaining days, and her roommate strategy.

"Let me get this straight," Della said, ticking the listed items on her fingers. "You've both admitted you dig each other, you're living together, you cook together, you eat together, but you're not sampling the goods."

"That sounds accurate."

Instead of replying, Della studied her jewelry table. She selected a green and cream pendant necklace and held it toward Bea. "I'm sorry if I judged you when we met—that whole rebound/relationship thing. I was wrong. I wouldn't have the willpower to live with a man I was interested in without sneaking into his room. Holding back must be brutal."

Bea accepted the offered gift, the swirling crystal beads as beautiful as Della's admission. Della had also hit the proverbial nail on its head. No matter Bea's uncertainty and stress, she very much liked Huxley Marlow. "Thank you, but I'm trying to take this slow. Not get in too deep or get my hopes up. Except I've gone and upped the ante with masturbation imagery. How am I going to work with him tonight?"

"I can come with. Give you moral support…and crack up behind your back."

"I've always wanted a backstabbing best friend."

They smirked at each other.

Bea spun around and held out the necklace for Della to attach. "Do you often attend the theater shows?"

"I used to, but I haven't been in a couple years." She clicked the clasp in place and combed the ends of Bea's hair with her fingers. "It's hard watching Fox."

At Della's melancholy tone, Bea faced her boss and friend. The obvious longing in Della's eyes swamped Bea with guilt. Wanting to avoid topics of dating, which would have led to topics of Huxley, she'd never asked Della about the men in her life. Aside from establishing they were both single, she'd never prodded enough to see what had been in front of her the whole time.

"You like Fox." How could she have missed the signs?

"If 'like' means having an unhealthy obsession that totally derails your life, then, yeah...I like Fox."

"Does he know?"

She shrugged. "He seems to read everyone's mind but mine."

"And you haven't told him?"

"It's complicated." Della spun her bracelet, looking ready to cut their conversation short, but Bea stared her down. She could give good stare when required.

Della huffed out a feeble laugh. "He's best friends with my brother, Rayce, and when Rayce moved away a couple years back, he asked Fox to look out for me, which isn't a new role for him. My father left when we were young. Fox was super overprotective back then. These days, he acts like an overbearing brother."

"And you don't see him as a brother."

Her bracelet fiddling turned agitated. "Not even close. I flirted with him once. Ran into him at a club, and thanks to my buddy vodka, I dragged him onto the dance floor. For a second I was sure he was about to kiss me, but then he got weird and left. He never mentioned it, and I never tried again. He's clearly not interested, and if I tell him how I feel, he might get annoyed or freaked out. I could lose him completely. It's not worth it."

"Oh, Della." Bea pulled her into a tight hug. "He might surprise you. Maybe he has feelings, too. If you tell him, he might admit it or look at you differently."

Sighing, Della shimmied out of Bea's hold. "Trust me, he sees me as a little sister. Nothing more. Which is why I don't watch him perform. He's already at my apartment constantly, helping out with stupid things I can do myself. But there's something about seeing him on stage. It kind of knocks me for a loop. So, like I said, it's complicated." She picked at her cuticles.

Bea could relate to craving a man out of reach. She was currently living with one. But Della had known Fox for years. That kind of unrequited longing put her fifteen-day wait to shame. She also sensed Della wanted a subject change, an opening she'd like to somersault through. Before her text disaster, she'd been contemplating painting more saleable pieces. Della's market stall offered a venue. "If I create some miniature paintings done on natural surfaces, like reclaimed wood and discarded cupboard doors, could I sell them here?"

"Of course," Della said quickly. "I could condense my pieces, or we could hang them on the back divider."

Immediately, Bea wanted to text Huxley, share this news with him and squeal about the images flooding her mind. But her phone was dead, she'd already derailed things with her masturbating comment, and she was wary about how quickly he was becoming her confidant.

Her go-to friend.

Keeping the physical out of their relationship would protect a portion of her heart, but their growing friendship was solidifying him in her life. "Do you think Huxley will keep his word? Not gamble again after he quits?"

Before Della could reply, a bespectacled man barked at a woman, grumbling about her spending too much time at the adjacent booth. He then ranted about cutting up her credit cards. Aggressive hand on her elbow, he led her away.

Della's face puckered. "*That* man is a grade-A asshole who would probably lie about a business meeting to bone his secretary. Huxley is not that kind of subhuman. He's a good guy.

If it were me, I'd believe him. But you've been through a lot. You've got a couple weeks before your date. If you're still not sure, push the deadline. If you rush things before you're ready, it won't work, no matter how trustworthy Huxley is."

If it were up to Bea's body, that deadline would be null and void, but Della's advice felt right. Rushing into something wouldn't do them any favors. As it stood, she'd been flirting with Huxley one minute, putting on the brakes the next. Friendship before *boy*friendship was the safe option, no matter how long it took. They weren't dating yet. He couldn't hurt her irrevocably yet.

She still dreaded seeing him tonight.

"Please come to the show." Bea pressed her hands into prayer. "Knowing you're there will calm me, and you can watch me humiliate myself with Huxley. And maybe Fox will finally read your mind."

Della shifted her jewelry display, lining up already even bracelets. She repeated the unnecessary task with the earrings, her shoulders sitting high and stiff. "Fat chance on the mind reading, but I could video Axel doing his magic-strip number. Post it on YouTube for you guys. I bet it would get some hits and drum up business. I'd also be an idiot to miss you embarrass yourself over that sexy text. Huxley's reaction will be priceless."

She grinned, and Bea groaned.

Her phone was officially public enemy number one.

17

Tormenting Beatrice was wildly entertaining. And she deserved it. Receiving her dirty text this morning had been a new form of torture. Huxley had been forced to take an extra-long shower, imagining whipped cream and his assistant, and several scenarios that ended with them panting and sweaty. By the end of his fantasy, he had one hand braced on the tile wall, his release nowhere near satisfying.

He was still determined to maintain their platonic roommate status, prove to her he could be trusted and would uphold his word. His fantasies, however, couldn't be controlled. He often imagined slipping his hand under her tank top, caging her against the kitchen counter, sneaking into her room to run his tongue along her ear and tell her she was the most spectacularly unique creature he'd ever met.

If a unicorn took human form, Beatrice Baker would be it. Her artistic talent blew him away. Her ability to turn his aggravating puzzle box into an amusement was miraculous. He didn't relish eating her crunchy eggs, but the fact that she'd tried to cook for him had filled him with an unfamiliar joy.

Then that text.

She hadn't looked him in the eye since arriving at the theater, and she'd never replied to his teasing texts. Either her embarrassment was exponential, or her ancient phone had died, as she often lamented. He assumed the latter, which made torturing her all the more enjoyable.

Axel's music blasted into the half-empty auditorium—half-full, he reminded himself. Foreigner's "Urgent" pumped like a sex drug through the room as Axel strutted out in a three-piece suit. The mostly female audience was already whistling, primed for his act. It had been like this since he'd taken to stripping during his routines. He got off on it, flexing and swaggering like the peacock he was. The attending women were vultures dying to feast their eyes on his skin.

The lewd numbers still revolved around their regular magic acts, but they'd been forced to instill an eighteen and over age limit. No one wanted their impressionable teens getting a face full of Axel's gyrating hips as he pulled a dollar bill out of a freshly opened lemon. The change had been good for business and Huxley couldn't complain, but he missed the kids who used to attend. Most had stared at their phones instead of the stage, but some had clapped and gasped like Beatrice had the first time she'd seen their show. It had been a special part of the job.

Beatrice stood beside him now, refusing to glance his way while they watched Axel. "It's his new act," she said, stating the obvious.

Axel's jacket, vest, and shirt hit the floor. Huxley wanted to bleach his eyeballs, but Beatrice tapped her toes and shook her shoulders. She couldn't stand still when music played. She did, however, freeze when Axel gripped his pants and yanked them off. "Definitely new," she said.

"Our father would be horrified." Huxley also wasn't sure where a man purchased Velcro dress pants that could be ripped off.

The women whooped; Axel grinned. He then performed a basic Cups and Balls number, flexing his abs and arms as he shifted upturned martini shakers, his red ball always appearing under the least expected cover. When he asked the audience to guess where the ball would appear next, the most popular reply was *"From your ass!"*

He wore a purple G-string.

Sex sold. It was a twenty-first-century fact. No point swimming against that current, especially when he had a brother who oozed sex. As did the woman beside Huxley, who was conveniently ignoring the dirty-text issue.

"We're up," he said, ready to expose the elephant in their midst. No better place to confront her than on stage.

Beatrice glanced at him, as she always did before they performed. Her shoulders were hitched upward, her teeth lodged into her bottom lip. Her heart probably felt like it would explode. His often did as well, but for a different reason.

Hating that she still battled her fear, he gripped her upper arms and repeated the words he said each night. "Perform for *me*, Beatrice. Not for them. Just for me."

Usually her eyes would glaze, a look of longing eclipsing her face. Tonight she nodded sharply then sashayed on stage, high heels clicking, bodysuit hugging her every curve. Her feathers trailed as she walked a dramatic circle.

He couldn't wait to torment her.

He followed a moment later, pushing his zigzag box. They did their usual act, spinning the box and making a show of banging the metal sheets they'd use. When Beatrice was firmly in the contraption, her hands waving the yellow handkerchiefs, he whispered so only she could hear, "I bought three brands of whipped cream for you. They're in the fridge at home."

Blotches quickly colored her neck. She didn't reply.

He faced the audience and smacked his metal weapons again. Turning his back to the room, he feigned trying to insert one into her chest. She flinched as they'd rehearsed. He repeated the ruse, not shoving the blade all the way through, while he talked to her quietly. "I assumed you'd want full-fat for your purposes, that the real deal would enhance the experience, but since I wasn't sure, I got a couple others." He shoved the first sheet through the box.

The audience gasped.

Bea's cheeks flamed to match her hair.

"I also wondered at which point the whipped cream would be used. Is it best at the start or better when you're worked up? And do you have contortionist skills you haven't shared? If so, we could use them in the show."

Another metal sheet. More gasps. More blushing from Beatrice.

She didn't say a word, but she did make eye contact with Della, who was filming from the audience. Fox's friend seemed to be cracking up. Beatrice mouthed, *Help*.

Della laughed harder.

Huxley went in for the kill. "I also bought a jar of cherries, but those are for me. I can't eat my whipped cream without them." He winked.

"*Menstruating*," she whisper-yelled. "It was supposed to say menstruating." Then her head slumped forward. "I hate my phone."

He liked her phone very much.

Bea's mortification had reached new heights. Huxley was messing with her, and the man was thriving on it. If she hadn't been locked in a zigzag box, she'd have flicked his funny bone.

What she *did* do was refrain from returning his playful innuendo. She couldn't wait for their fifteen days to fly by, as her calendar doodles had confirmed, but Della's advice and Bea's history fortified her anti-flirting plan. She would bottle up all these fizzy feelings for Huxley until she was sure she wouldn't get stuck spinning in another man's tornado.

She joined the boys for the curtain call, bowing with her ensemble. The cheers and whistling were louder than usual, courtesy of Axel, who'd only pulled on a pair of black slacks for the occasion. Normally the crowds would clear, people tapping on their phones or chatting with their cliques as they left. Tonight a bachelorette party lingered, rowdier than usual, coaxing the boys into photos. Axel invited them on stage. Bea stepped aside and fiddled with her feathered costume.

Della appeared at the stage lip, waving her phone at Bea. "I caught you turning fifty shades of red. I only wish I heard what he was saying."

"It was as horrible as you'd imagine."

"Or as awesome."

Several women giggled and gushed over Axel. Bea crouched by Della, happy to have someone to chat with. "Did you capture Fox on video?"

She gazed at her phone like it housed her heart. "He looked amazing up there."

They turned their heads and focused on the boys. Axel was being woman-handled by two of the groupies, their paws all over his snake tattoo. When one of them sidled up to Fox,

Della made a pained sound. The Asian woman placed her hand on Fox's hip. He tilted his head, smirk in place. They moved closer together.

"I shouldn't have come." Della swiveled and headed for the exit before Bea could apologize for dragging her there or offer words of comfort. Fox was certainly blind as a bat, which would make him a member of the flying *fox* family: a megabat from the subtropics of Asia with a four-foot wingspan. Megabats were large enough to be vampires.

Maybe she'd tested the wrong brother for sparkles.

She went to glare at him, only to be stopped short by another bubbly woman flirting with the men—one man in particular. The man who'd made her coffee that morning.

The woman with Huxley was a redhead, like Bea, but not a natural. She wore a fun pinup-style dress, like one Bea would purchase, but she probably didn't have a gambling addict for a father or a tendency to key cars when drunk. The woman pressed a hand to Huxley's stomach and held her phone out for a selfie.

Bea's belly curdled. *He's not mine,* she reminded herself. *He's free to flirt and date and take selfies.* She couldn't tame her body's acute reaction.

Photo done, the woman didn't pull away. She pressed closer to Huxley, winding her other arm around his back. Bea waited for Huxley to excuse himself or create space. He only smiled at something she said.

He didn't smile easily with others. Bea had earned every gratifying grin. Yet here he was, flirting and smiling for a bottled redhead. Bea's eyes stung. Her rapid breaths grated her throat. However hard she'd blushed when he'd teased her earlier, she was sure her skin had turned blotchier.

He glanced at her then, maybe sensing her forlorn stare. All humor drained from his face. Bea didn't wait as he tried to extricate himself from his groupie. She hurried to the dressing room, locked herself inside, and pressed her forehead to the closed door.

Loud steps stopped outside her room. "Beatrice."

She didn't reply.

"It was an act, like in the show. Just to boost business."

"I know," she said, steadying her voice. "I don't care."

"I think you do."

"We're just friends, Huxley. Roommates. You can do whatever you want."

"There's only one woman I want to date, *Beatrice*."

It should be illegal, him using her full name, undoing her with three syllables. Her weakness didn't change the facts, or the fifteen days ahead of them. "I don't think that girl wanted a date." More likely a magic lesson between the sheets.

She couldn't see his expression, judge if he was annoyed with her or himself or the situation. A faint scratching came from his side. "There's only one woman I want to *not-date*, too," he said softly, the subtle suggestiveness filling her mind with images of his hands caressing her body.

She was caught in an undertow, dragged between her growing affections for this man, her jealousy, her past, his gambling, and another fifteen days *or more* of this uncomfortable insecurity. The audience would grow over the coming weeks. More women would attend. More after-show photoshoots would occur. Flirting. Smiling selfies. But entertaining patrons *would* help their word-of-mouth business.

"It's fine," she repeated, lifting her forehead from the door. "I get that it's part of the job." So why was her voice cracking?

She thought she heard a low growl but couldn't be sure. The silence dragged. Maybe she'd missed his retreating footsteps?

"There's a gold bodysuit in the closet," he said, startling her. "Check it for size. I'd like to do a late rehearsal tomorrow, after the show—practice for the fire routine. You'll need to wear it and no fishnets. No additional feathers or added flair, either. I'll see you at home."

His steps echoed away from her, and her body deflated. She didn't want to deflate, to be a marionette, a new man playing her emotional strings. This wasn't Huxley's fault, but her usual Teflon skin had thinned. Her ability to smile and move on proved challenging, which meant she needed to up her effort. She wouldn't care if Huxley slept with a woman while they were roommates. She wouldn't let her jealousy ruin their friendship. She was also curious about the gold bodysuit and what Huxley had in store for her.

She focused on gold and fire, and the new art Della had agreed to let her sell in the booth. She would paint more in the coming days, throw herself into her art. Work on her secret project for Huxley. She'd smile harder.

But the current effort had her cheeks feeling stiff and sore. It was a Kraft-slice smile, when all she wanted was a Cheddar grin. Last time she smiled this hard, she wound up drowning in lemon drops and keying a stranger's car. The Kraft-slice grin slipped from her face. No matter what happened, she couldn't let herself fall apart like that again.

18

The next night, Bea took her bow then slipped offstage, preferring not to witness Huxley in his portrayal of Flirty Smurf. The show had gone well, the seats half-full again. Axel was cocky Axel. Fox was sneaky Fox. Huxley's intensity had been a tangible thing, his hand a brand on her hip, her arm, her back as they'd worked the stage together. His whipped cream chides had been conspicuously absent.

Last night, after she'd walked the New Orleans streets awhile, he'd been asleep when she'd returned home. He'd left before she'd awoken that morning. He'd probably realized he could have any number of women who didn't require a waiting period before they dated. Or not-dated.

She rested in her dressing room now, relaxing on the small bed. The three doves coo-coo-cooed. She'd named them Surly, Sneaky, and Cocky. The cozy red walls comforted her. It was nice having a dressing room. It made her feel like a diva, the sort of woman who'd bark orders and would only drink bottled water from Nepal and eat Japanese strawberries dipped in Belgian chocolate.

Her smile came easier, although still strained.

Her phone buzzed with an incoming text, and her heart migrated to her feet. Huxley could be texting her, explaining their evening rehearsal had been canceled. That he'd like to retract his fourteen-day-from-now date. She shouldn't care. It would be for the best. She wouldn't have to worry about poker games and squandered money and broken hearts.

Then why did her insides feel like they'd been jostled in a martini shaker?

Ignoring her discomfort, she sat up and pulled up the message. It was Huxley, only letting her know he was ready for their rehearsal.

A measure of relief flooded her that he wasn't putting her off, but her father's messages were still on her phone, still unread. She stared at the first one—his one word *help*— and gripped her cell until it bit into her palm. She'd never yelled at Franklyn Baker. Even after he'd emptied her bank account, she'd practiced enough yogic breaths to earn her downward-dog black belt.

Bitterness spun inside her now, a mini storm of repressed anger. The tornado he always inspired. She resented her father. She also loved the man. There was no even ground with him that didn't feel like a fracturing fault line. He was responsible for her current baggage, the reason Huxley was flirting with audience members instead of kissing her. The tornado spun faster, burned hotter. Maybe her history teacher had been right and Bea's unaired grievances were bound to erupt into a mushroom cloud of squelched outrage.

She nearly called her father, opening that puzzle box of awful, so she could finally yell at him through the safety of her phone, but she stopped. And finally blocked his current number. She still hadn't gotten her head around changing hers. If he got another phone, he might reach out again, but this felt like a first step. Plus, she'd warned him about the threats. She'd done her part. He could deal with the rest.

Annoyed with her phone for provoking unpleasant thoughts, and sending a masturbating text, she unhooked it from its charger and stashed it in her purse. She changed into her gold bodysuit. The material was tightly woven, thick and shiny, squeezing her waist like a corset. Her legs were bare, as Huxley had requested. Her heart felt bare, too. Raw and chafed from thinking about her past and present.

She painted on a layer of watermelon gloss and plastered on a Cheez-Whiz smile—better than Kraft slices, but just barely—then went to join Huxley on stage. The earlier loud music, whistles, and raucous cheers had vanished. Only her heels echoed off the wooden floor. She paused at the stage's threshold and gasped.

Candles.

Thirty or forty candles decorated the stage, including two human-sized candelabras and smaller votive-lined pedestals. In the center of the stage was a black table.

"You took a while." Huxley's deep voice made her jump. The low baritone came from behind her. "Everything okay?"

"I lost track of time." Translation: she'd stalled so she wouldn't have to witness his flirting.

"I see."

Did he? Could he sense her swirling turmoil?

He stayed behind her, candles flickering ahead, his warm breaths brushing her hair. The moment felt intimate. Too intimate. She forced her feet forward. "This is quite the setup. I'm once again questioning your vampire status. Do you use makeup to mute your skin sparkles?"

"I thought we decided I wasn't immortal?"

"There's a checklist. It's evenly weighted."

He moved to her side, and the corner of his lips twitched. "Can I see this evaluation?"

That would mean he'd read her Mortal Man column and the bullet point that read: His rare smiles make me melt. They are too tender for an immortal. "It's written in invisible ink. It only appears for women who sing 'The Sound of Music' while wearing a garlic dress and riding a unicycle."

He didn't laugh or roll his eyes. "A unicorn," he murmured.

"Where?" Bea scanned the area.

"Right in front of me."

Before she could process that statement, he stalked by her. He was still in his magician garb, but he'd removed his top hat. His flowing cape was also different—red instead of a velvet galaxy. He picked up a machete from the black table, the weapon looking natural in his large hand.

He sliced it through the air. "Working with fire is dangerous. It involves trust." His blade slashed in an elaborate figure eight. "Do you trust me, Beatrice?"

She was mesmerized, picturing him in a foreign market, stalls teeming with exotic fruits and colorful scarves, snakes performing in time to his swirling sword. One moment he was her sleep-mussed roommate, then a skilled magician flirting with his fans, then this. Majestic. Dazzling. She nodded instead of speaking aloud.

His machete wielding paused. Tension banded his features. "Lie on the table."

It was a brisk command, his surly side surfacing. Surly with a dash of sexy dominance. Although he'd yet to admit he read romance novels, she believed otherwise. She imagined the characters inspired his stage persona. She wondered if he got worked up while enjoying a steamy scene. Her body ignited at the possibility.

She followed his instructions, the cold table a welcome sensation on her too-hot arms and legs. She waited for him to go on.

"Trust," he said again, "is the foundation of a magician's relationship with his assistant. Nothing works without it. If I change something we've rehearsed while performing, and we don't have trust, you might hesitate or freeze, or assume I've forgotten our routine. You could get hurt."

She wasn't sure he was still talking about their performance. She wasn't even sure she remembered how to breathe.

"When I ask if you trust me," he said from somewhere behind her, "I need more than a head nod. I need to hear you say it and know you believe it. So let's try this again." His voice moved lower, closer to her head. "Do you, Beatrice Baker, trust me, Huxley Marlow?"

Instead of remembering the kindnesses he'd offered over the past weeks, or his open admission of his feelings toward her, her mind skittered to how trusting her father had led to dropping out of high school, her depleted bank account, and a loan shark sending her threats. She sneezed once, then again.

"Yes," she said, quieter than intended.

Huxley growled.

She didn't trust him. Huxley heard it in her delayed reply, had seen it in her reaction to last night's stupid photo op, and her quick exit from the stage tonight.

That damn sneeze.

He'd picked up on her nervous habit, hating when she sneezed around him. It told him all he needed to hear: she may have agreed to an eventual date, but she was waiting for him to mess up, hurt her, or lie and cheat. Steal what he wanted, then move on. He'd been on the receiving end of enough of her brilliant smiles to know they'd been forced recently. He also saw them for the cover they were.

She was hurting. She'd probably been hurting for years, believing she could ignore the adult role she'd assumed while her mother had traveled and her father had frittered away rent money, only to lose her dreams to his addictions. Seeing a partly cloudy world through sunny glasses was a gift. It was also a curse. He didn't want her smiles any longer. He wanted her anger. For her to let herself feel all the pain she'd locked away. He wanted to be there for her when she let it out.

For now, he wanted her trust.

Frustration fueling his strides, he moved to the side of the table, backing away just enough. He pulled a small vial from his sleeve and drank the alcohol he'd poured inside. Beatrice's wide eyes watched his every move. Taking a candle in his hand, he held it close to his raised machete and blew a stream toward the flame.

Fire leapt onto the blade, traveling the length of the weapon. Beatrice gasped and gripped the table sides. He widened his stance, slashing the blade through the air, keeping it far enough from his apprehensive assistant. With one aggressive strike toward her abdomen, he created enough wind to extinguish the flames.

Beatrice lay rigid. His lungs worked double-time.

Then she clapped wildly, showering him with a genuine smile. "You breathe fire. You're practically a dragon."

"It's just an act."

"A stupendous one."

He lowered the machete to his side. "Were you afraid?"

She pressed her hand over her chest. "My heart's trying to make a break for it."

"Because you thought I'd burn or cut you?"

"Of course not. It was just new. I got lost in the performance and didn't know what you'd do next. I was nervous. Excited, but nervous. But...what about you?" Her attention drifted to his burned eyebrow. "I'd think fire would make you uncomfortable."

He inhaled the smoky smell, unbidden memories making his fibrous scars itch. "Not when I'm in control. Manipulating fire helped me work through some fears."

Exactly what he was doing for her tonight.

They stared at each other until a *thunk* sounded from above. They glanced up. Likely another chunk of plaster coming loose upstairs. A reminder that fixing the façade was just a drop in the bucket. The real issues were the electrical and plumbing code violations. He still worried another enforcer would stop by to check those infractions and shut him down. But these issues were hidden in the walls, not plastered on the exterior. Oliphant wouldn't know about them, and Huxley would get to it when he could.

His only concern right now was easing Beatrice's mind, proving he was a man of his word. "I'm going to walk you through the routine. Explain everything I'll do before I do it, so you'll know what to expect. No surprises. No unknowns."

He helped her to her feet and described the fuel he'd used on the blade, how the alcohol he poured into his mouth would ignite the flame. They staged the number next, an extravagant lightshow of blades and candles.

Afterward, she lay back on the table. He hovered over her. "For our finale, I'll be lighting fire across your stomach. I'll spread a line of fluid over the area, then slice the enflamed machete toward it. The fire will jump to you, but your midsection will be the only place that catches fire."

She swallowed hard. "How can you be sure?"

"Because I've done it before, and I'd never put you at risk."

She seemed to relax.

He grabbed a brush and the pyrofluid from the pedestal, then painted a line from the left of her waist to her right. "The bodysuit is made of Aramid fibers. It's a fire-resistant material that'll protect you from the flames. Once I light you up, I'll let the fire dance for ten seconds or so, then I'll fan my cape and bring it down on your body. It's a different cape treated with a flame-extinguishing chemical. You'll sit up afterward and prove you're unharmed."

She glanced at the line he'd painted. "It won't melt the fabric?"

"The bodysuit is designed to withstand fire."

"Will it get hot?"

"It'll be uncomfortable, but not unbearable."

She dragged her teeth over her bottom lip. "If I don't like it, is it okay if we leave this part out of the number?"

He wanted to stroke her cheek and erase the worry from her face, but he couldn't touch her after handling the pyrofluid. He also wasn't sure she wanted his touch. "You never have to do anything you don't want to."

Her eyes went soft. "Then light me on fire."

Huxley wanted to light her on fire, from the inside out. Set her body ablaze and turn her world into sparks. For now he had a point to prove.

Stepping back, he painted a fresh layer of fuel on his blade and poured a measure of alcohol into his mouth. He breathed fire, lit his blade anew. "I'll swing the blade now, toward you. I'll stop just above your waist."

"Ready." The determined press of her lips and upward tilt of her chin confirmed she was. Her eyes weren't flitting, either. She wasn't gripping the table or sneezing. She lay beneath Huxley, a fiery sword in his hands, and she wasn't afraid.

He sliced downward, stopping abruptly before nicking her. Fire hopped from his blade to her suit, and a flare lit across her belly, wild yet contained. Exactly how his emotions felt around Beatrice. He wanted to be a raging wildfire with her, not measured and precise. Loose. Untamed. He longed to forget the surly man who spent his time tallying bills and keeping the theater from caving in. But untamed would have to wait. For now, he was responsible for his assistant's safety.

Eight seconds passed, and she twitched her nose.

Nine seconds, and her chest swelled higher.

Ten seconds, and she blinked faster.

He extinguished the flames on his machete and arced his cape over her body, dousing the remaining fire. She was caged beneath him, sharp scents of smoke and alcohol mingling with her watermelon aroma. It heightened his awareness of her. Of *them*.

He should lift up, give her space after their intense rehearsal. Instead he leaned closer. "Were you scared?"

"No." Her soft voiced whispered between them.

"Why?"

"Because I knew what you were going to do."

They were cocooned, covered by his cape, flickering light illuminating the mere inches between them. His muscles unwound for the first time today. "Then know this: I do not want to date any other women. Or *not-date* them. If I smile for pictures and talk to audience members, male or female, I'm doing what I can to help create buzz without stripping. I don't care about playing cards or gambling, and I will happily leave all that behind—which means I'll be taking you out in two weeks. But only if you answer one question for me, now, truthfully."

"If it's a skill-testing question with math, I might not pass."

A laugh rumbled from his chest. It felt good to laugh. He loved that she could lighten intense situations. Still, he schooled his expression and asked the most important question of all: "Do you trust me?"

This time she held eye contact, and gave a firm, "Yes."

———

Twenty minutes later, while waiting for Beatrice to change, Huxley finished tidying the stage. The heat from the fire and her trust still circled him, his heart thumping loudly in his chest.

Except it was more than his heart thumping.

Edna shuffled into the theater, her cane thwacking along the aisle. "This place smells like a urinal."

If Edna wasn't a fixture here, he'd have fired his ticket collector years ago. But she'd helped Max Marlow design his posters and promote the shows from the beginning, even standing in when his assistant had been off. She had babysat Huxley and his brothers occasionally, when they'd been too young to learn magic and too old for daycare. He'd once wondered if she'd been in love with his father, but then she'd insult the theater and lament her stuffy ticket booth.

Why she still worked here was a mystery to Huxley, but he wouldn't let her grumpy tone dim his good mood. "It's late," he told her.

"I can tell time. You, I'm not so sure about. Why are you still here?"

"I should be asking you the same thing. Your husband might slap your face on a milk carton." He crouched and picked up the last candle.

"Unlikely. That would take more effort than using the remote control." Edna clasped both hands over her cane's snake head, hunched shoulders bowing her posture. "Are you here with the girl?"

His spine stiffened. "If by *the girl*, you mean Beatrice, then yes—I'm here with her. We were rehearsing a new routine." While establishing trust and banishing her worries.

Edna harrumphed.

He should walk away, stow the candle, and wait for Beatrice by her dressing room, but Edna's judgmental noise irked him.

He was finally building a life outside the theater, making choices for himself. Selfish maybe, but he deserved it. If Edna was trying to guilt-trip him about neglecting his theater duties, she'd have to find another job that allowed her to grumble at patrons while doing her crosswords. "Beatrice is the best thing to happen to me in a long while. She's kind and fun. She's even helped increase business. So if you're going to mention her, I'd appreciate if you'd use her name."

Another harrumph sounded. Edna pushed her glasses up her prominent nose. "Well then, I hope *Beatrice* is the sticking around sort. Seems to me she's more of a wanderer, showing up here out of the blue. And your ties are in New Orleans."

She turned at a snail's pace, leaving Huxley with a candle in his slackening hand and an uncomfortable tightness in his chest.

Although crudely blunt, Edna could be astute, and he hadn't thought much past finally taking Beatrice out in fourteen days. They'd both admitted anything between them wouldn't be casual, but she'd been cagey lately, second-guessing him at every turn. Her wariness was understandable, and they'd made progress tonight, but she was a free spirit at heart, like her mother who got bored and traveled where the music took her. He could be setting himself up for disappointment.

That uncomfortable ache spread. He dug his fingernail into the melted candlewax and watched Edna's slow procession out.

19

"If you're making your seafood pesto pasta, there better be enough for me." Axel barged into Huxley's apartment and invaded his kitchen. He sat his intrusive ass on the counter. Beside the cleaned shrimp.

Fox strolled in behind him and snatched a trimmed green bean. "Count me in."

Still gripping his chef's knife, Huxley stopped chopping his onion. "I don't remember inviting either of you."

Axel pulled his phone from his pocket. He grinned at the screen and began typing while talking to Huxley. "It's Monday Funday. You used to cook for us on Mondays."

"I used to cook for you every day. Then we grew up."

Their mother could burn water. Max Marlow's kitchen skills hadn't been half bad, but he hadn't been home enough to use them. Out of necessity, Huxley had learned how to make lasagna at thirteen, burritos shortly after. Melted cheese made all the Marlow boys happy.

"I miss it, big bro," Axel drawled. "I miss our family time." So engrossed in his phone, he wasn't even looking at Huxley.

Family time, my ass. But Huxley gentled his tone. "How's Stanley doing? The antibiotics work?"

"Like a charm." He glanced up from his cell, relief etched in his face. "Your vet was awesome. No surgery needed."

Thank God for that.

Fox moved to the living room and paused to study Bea's art. The smaller paintings she'd been working on were as brilliant as her ongoing self-portrait. Less personal, but skillfully crafted. He hadn't asked her why she'd painted his burned eyebrow in her larger portrait, or a section of his cape. He wasn't sure if it had been planned or had been a spur-of-the-moment decision. All that mattered was that she'd done it.

"She's talented," Fox said, nearing one of her miniatures.

Huxley smiled. "Very."

She'd gushed when describing her new apple series, how each fruit was built from tiny squares, like her portrait, these focused on insects and animals that fed on the produce. Close up, you could make out the armor of a flathead borer beetle, the wings of a codling moth, a horse's powerful thigh. From afar, the three-dimensional fruit took shape. Like his world was taking shape around her.

"But you're still not sleeping with her," Fox said.

Huxley almost lost control of his knife. "What business is that of yours?"

He hadn't explained the details of his relationship with Beatrice, only telling his brothers she couldn't afford rent and was crashing there. Too much information turned Fox into a psychoanalyst and Axel into his worst nightmare.

Axel actually put his phone down. "You're not sleeping with her?"

Huxley chopped faster, mutilating the poor onion. "Again, not your business."

"But she's hot…unless she doesn't dig you. Is it the stripping? Have I ruined her for other men by strutting around shirtless?"

"The only thing you've ruined is my appetite."

"Is it the size of my wand? She did say she'd like to make it shoot sparks."

Huxley breathed through his flaring nose. "I'm the oldest brother. I have the Elder wand. There's no competition."

"Is she saving herself for marriage?" Axel barely maintained a straight face.

Huxley should never have given his brothers emergency apartment keys. At least Beatrice hadn't come home from work yet. "Why are you taunting a man holding a knife?"

Axel returned his attention to his phone.

Fox sunk into the couch and picked up the pink pony. "You have the most uncomfortable couch, and I'm scared to ask about this."

"The sofa sucks. And if you value your life, you'll put that down." Huxley wasn't sure when he'd gotten possessive over the plastic pink toy.

Fox shrugged and swapped the pony for the puzzle box. "I screwed things up with Beatrice for you."

The comment stopped him short. "First of all, nothing's screwed up. Second, how is any of it your fault?"

Fox pushed at the sides of the box, trying different orders and sequences. It, of course, didn't open. "The night you finally kissed her, I gave you that ring and watch. Mentioned the poker game. She looked ready to faint and things changed after. Does she have a gambling issue?"

Releasing the knife, Huxley planted both hands on the white counter. "Understatement."

"Which is why I screwed up. But she's been different recently. Seems to be all smiles again."

Since the fire rehearsal. Since he'd worked to gain her trust.

The past four days had been better and worse. Aside from the moments he'd catch her lost in thought, a frown puckering her brow, her reservations seemed to have vanished, leaving only a coquettish woman who tormented his soul. If keeping his hands to himself had been a challenge before, it was downright tortuous now. She hadn't even worn a bra under her tank top this morning. He'd bit his fist at the sight, claiming a stubbed toe.

"We've reached an understanding," he said.

"Which doesn't include sex?" Axel hopped off the counter and opened Huxley's fridge.

Huxley crossed his arms. It was either that or slam the fridge door into Axel's head. "Our sex, or lack thereof, is none of your concern."

"I beg to differ."

"And why is that?"

Axel emerged from the fridge with leftover chicken salad. He opened the lid and proceeded to eat it with his fingers. "I have to work with you. You've been surlier than usual. You also spend a ridiculous amount of time staring at Bea."

"Staring at her when?"

"Whenever she's in the room," Fox interjected.

Jesus. Am I that far gone? Edna's comment still sat with him, the heaviness of it often prompting his surliness, worries about investing too much emotion in a woman who might not be here for the long haul. When Beatrice was around, he shut those concerns out. He'd remind himself she'd painted pieces of him in her portrait. He'd marvel at how attuned to her he'd become, verging on obsessed for a guy who didn't obsess over women. It could be the forced waiting period— the longing and imagining. The kiss that had given him a taste of how sweet she would be.

Most likely, it was the Beatrice Baker Effect: her unicorn essence that drew people into her orbit.

Axel licked his fingers and went to return the remaining chicken salad to the fridge.

Huxley kicked the door shut. "Don't even think about putting that back."

"Why?" He examined the salad, perplexed.

"You don't see me coming into your place and sticking my hands in your food."

"That's because I only have beer and salami in my fridge."

"Are you still nineteen?"

"Stop with the compliments. You're making me blush." Axel put the Tupperware on the counter and petted the top. "I'll take it home. After we enjoy our family dinner."

They hadn't shared a meal in ages. Axel was always busy with his street magic, Fox with whatever Fox did. Irritating inquisition aside, he missed the ritual of the Marlow men stuffing their faces while talking smack. It made him think of his youngest brothers, wondering if Xander still hated raw tomatoes, if Paxton had graduated past the pig food group. He should try to locate his brothers, but he wasn't sure they wanted to hear from him.

To the two siblings who had forgiven him for their father's death, he said, "Is there an actual reason you came by, besides mooching food and annoying me?"

Fox glanced up from the puzzle box. "To get your car keys. We met a guy who knows a guy. We're getting it repainted."

"How much will it cost?"

"Nothing."

He squinted at them. "How does repairing a car cost nothing?"

Fox stared at Huxley without speaking. Axel studied the floor.

Huxley grumbled. He could berate them for whatever suspicious activities led to his Mustang's makeover, but he was tired of driving the defiled car. If one more person called him *Assface* or *Isopod*, he'd get arrested.

Instead of giving them hell, he pulled more shrimp and mussels from the freezer. "Beatrice will be home soon. Don't bring up the gambling. Or the sex."

Axel grabbed a couple beers and joined Fox on the couch. "This sofa really is shit, and what's the deal with Bea? How long is she staying here? And why exactly did you say you weren't having sex?"

"If you're looking to get uninvited to dinner," Huxley said as he placed the frozen seafood in tepid water, "you're making excellent headway."

Fox took a lengthy pull on his beer. "I'm curious about the lack of coitus as well."

Axel snorted.

Huxley narrowed his eyes at Fox. "You usually know this stuff before I do. You losing your touch?"

Fox shrugged.

"No. Seriously. Let's hear more about the coitus." Axel was having way too much fun.

Tired of dodging their inquiries, Huxley wiped his hands on a cloth and faced his obnoxious brothers. "Bea's father is a gambling addict who screwed up her life. She's sensitive to anything gaming related, my poker games included, so I suggested a waiting period. I'll have enough cash to pay Trevor for his construction work after the next two games, then I'll quit. Beatrice has agreed to go on a date after that."

"And *then* there will be coitus?" Axel smiled around his beer bottle.

Huxley flipped him off.

Fox was less amused. "You sure that's smart?"

"I'm sure it's brilliant."

Fox dragged a hand through his hair. Instead of his usual ponytail, the loose strands hit his shoulders. "Oliphant won't let it go. If you walk out on a win and don't let him challenge you, he'll retaliate."

"I can handle him."

The hard lines of Fox's face didn't budge. "Isn't that what Dad said before Oliphant defaced all his posters around town?"

That infuriating stunt had involved Oliphant printing mini penises and sticking them in their father's two-dimensional hands. It had been childish and stupid. Oliphant had done it after losing his prized T. rex skull in that fated poker hand. As petty as the man was, he was in his forties now, not his twenties. He was a bratty coward, not a wannabe frat boy. Plus, Huxley had leverage. "He's not a concern. I'm cutting ties with the group in two weeks."

"And then there will be coitus!" Axel shouted his prediction...as Beatrice walked in.

Huxley swore under his breath.

She studied the trio. "Who's having coitus?"

"*Don't*," he told Axel, seething.

Axel held up his hands in surrender, while cracking up.

Fox continued his unforgiving stare. His stern regard rankled Huxley. Fox's mind reading wasn't a mystical sixth sense. He excelled at deciphering tics and quirks, watching more than talking, which allowed him to sense moods and understand behaviors. His ability to predict action and reaction was uncanny. He still refused to enter the fortune-telling racket, due to their mother's seedy business, but he was right more often than he was wrong.

This time he was wrong. Oliphant wouldn't be a problem.

Huxley wouldn't let the degenerate derail the tentative steps he'd taken with Beatrice. He'd promised her a date in ten days, and a date they would have. If he hadn't been so intent on finding a middle ground with her, he'd have considered adding an extra game to lose his poker title. Losing meant he'd walk away from their games clean, no unwritten rule broken. To go to Beatrice now and explain he'd acted rashly and had forgotten to tack on another week, that he had to play *another game*, would be a deal breaker. The trust he'd gradually earned would disintegrate. It also didn't matter. He had Oliphant by his proverbial balls and the man didn't even know it.

He met Fox's ticking jaw with a scowl of his own. Huxley looked at Beatrice, forced a smile, and said, "Axel was just bragging about all the women texting him now that he's an exotic dancer."

"Be jealous," Axel said.

Huxley wasn't remotely jealous. Not when Beatrice stood in his kitchen wearing heart-printed thigh-highs, a black skirt, and an off-the-shoulder pink top. Her exposed collarbones had him licking his lips. "How was the market?"

"Crazy busy." She eyed the food and their uninvited guests. "Are we having a party?"

Axel kicked his booted feet onto the coffee table. "I'm the guest of honor. Feel free to spoil me."

"Or kick him out," Huxley suggested.

She glanced at the still-open front door. "Do we have room for one more?"

"Did you bring a date?" Axel asked, a second from earning a black eye.

But she responded, "I did."

The tendons in Huxley's neck snapped tight. They hadn't discussed their promised date since the fire rehearsal, but she'd been going out of her way to touch him since—small brushes whenever they were near, just as he did her. The lack of bra this morning had been too blatant to be accidental. He'd assumed her coy behavior meant she wanted the next ten days to fly as quickly as he did. Unless she'd actually begun thinking of him as a brotherly roommate and didn't care that her flirtations had him in a constant state of arousal.

Or maybe Edna was right, and this was the start of her losing interest, looking for someone who didn't play poker and wasn't tied to a theater that would keep him in New Orleans. *Or* his imagination was working overtime, and Beatrice was messing with him.

Assuming the latter, he said, "If you bring a date, you'll have to help me cook."

She moved to his side and lined up her hip with his upper thigh. "My date is Della, and I'd love to help you cook."

He relaxed at her admission but winced slightly. He would eat her food any day of the week. Subjecting others to her cooking, however, was cruel. "I was teasing. I've got everything under control."

She turned so her breast grazed his arm. His thighs stiffened. *Every* part of him stiffened. She tipped up her chin and met his hooded eyes. "But we're so good together. In the kitchen," she added.

A rush of air left his lungs. "You're playing with fire, Beatrice."

"You're the one who plays with fire," she said, matching his low tone. "I'm the one who gets burned."

He didn't like that implication, regardless how innocently made. He also wasn't fooled. She knew she was riling him up, assaulting him with undercover flirtations. The overtness of her new affections was both excruciating and exciting. He just hoped it wasn't another version of her smiles—beautiful on the outside, covering whatever pain she couldn't face.

"Torture me again," he said, choosing to follow her lead, "and ten days becomes twenty."

She pursed her lips, then shrugged a shoulder. "You're bluffing."

Of course he was. Lasting another ten days was already pushing his boundaries, but her use of the poker term had her dropping her gaze.

She tried to step away, but he moved to block her. "Good thing you can read my tells, then."

Avoiding gambling jargon would make the subject taboo, and taboo subjects became noxious weeds, sprouting where least expected, taking over perfectly landscaped yards.

Taking a breath, she clicked her heels together and closed the final inch between them. "I was bluffing, too," she said.

She stared up at him. He stared down at her red lips.

Ten days, he reminded himself.

"You guys know we're still here, right?" Axel's intrusion was, sadly, welcome.

Bea put more than a hair's distance between Huxley and her overworked body, unsure when she'd become a flirty femme fatale. The old Beatrice Baker had no fatale or femme qualities. She was bubbly and fun, little snark or coquetry in her arsenal. Since Huxley's impassioned fire rehearsal, she'd embodied the hip-sway of a belly dancer, the feminine confidence of a burlesque babe. All because he'd earned her trust.

A niggling unease still lingered when Huxley wasn't around, but the more time she spent with him, the surer she became. She even went braless this morning, unwilling to pretend they were platonic roommates or chaste siblings.

Della's entrance helped diffuse their *sexualus tensionae* further. "I got caught behind a garbage truck, then 'Single

Ladies' came on the radio. I had to wait until it finished."
She dumped her purse on the bench by the door. "I wasn't
expecting a dinner party."

Huxley grimaced at his brothers. "Neither was I."

Della's braids were piled in an intricate knot on her head.
She eyed the group. "I came to check out Bea's art, but I can
go."

Huxley jutted his chin toward Della. "*You* should stay. It's
them I'm not so sure about. In fact, I'd like to adopt you as
my sister and disown these two clowns."

Axel was sprawled on Huxley's couch, careless boots
planted on the coffee table. He laced his hands behind his
head. "I'm too hungry to be insulted, and she's family anyway.
Aren't you, sis?"

Della's attention shifted to Fox, who sat very still. Statue
still. His facial expressions were often on lockdown, but he
was more unreadable than usual.

"Della," he said in greeting.

"Fox," she replied. "You left your toolbox in my bathroom."

"I did."

"You plan on picking it up?"

"Yes."

"When?"

"Tomorrow."

"What time?"

"Not sure."

Della nibbled her bottom lip.

It was an easy exchange. Normal, by all accounts. But Fox
was being a foxier version of himself: motionless, shorter on
verbiage and longer on unblinking stares. The only part of
him that moved was his right middle finger, which tapped
against his thigh. If Bea didn't know better, she'd say he was
trying to read Della. She'd also guess he was failing.

Della rubbed her breastbone and focused on Axel. "If I'm your sister, let me be the first to give you sisterly advice. Don't taunt the chef. He'll spit in your food."

Axel didn't flinch. "If he does I'll tell Bea he thought he was a cat as a kid."

Bea hurried into the living area and sat on the loveseat perpendicular to Axel. She placed her chin on her hands. "Tell me more."

"You really must shut up."

They ignored Huxley, and Axel's grin grew. "He followed our cat, Houdini, around for months. He licked his arms instead of taking a bath. He ate on the floor beside her."

"No."

"Yes."

Bea clutched her chest and laughed until her sides ached. She didn't have siblings. She'd see her cousins from time to time, but they'd spend their visits watching *Duck Dynasty* or arm wrestling, while occasionally lobbing spit balls at their grandmother, whose own spit would drool down her drunken cheek. Reminiscing wasn't in their repartee. "Please go on."

Axel didn't need her cajoling. He looked positively gleeful. "He also stole our mother's romance novels and hid them under his bed instead of *Playboy*. He thought they were dating self-help books."

"Lies," Huxley mumbled. When Bea's renewed cackling shook her chair, he jabbed his knife at Axel. "Why don't you tell her about the time you swallowed an entire GI Joe platoon to impress Lisa Hedgecroft with your supposed disappearing magic?"

Axel rubbed his stomach. "Not my finest moment."

Fox quit tapping his thigh and relaxed into the cushions. "I still remember the pained sounds coming from the bathroom. Then he'd shout, 'Got another one out.'"

She and Della shared a horrified look and dissolved into laughter again.

Huxley paused in his cooking, his attention on Bea as she swiped tears from her eyes. His Adam's apple dragged a slow line down his neck and his two-tone gaze fastened on her face, his fixated stare pebbling her skin. He then gathered fresh herbs and Parmesan cheese from the fridge, always at ease in the kitchen. More guests didn't faze him. Teasing brothers didn't break his stride. He chopped and blended and sliced, happy to feed his family.

A family she felt a part of.

Twenty-eight years with her parents, and she'd always felt more castaway than crewmate: friend to her mother and mother to her father, forced to fight for her survival. Three weeks after being thrust into the Marvelous Marlow Boys' world, and she *belonged*.

20

Once the dishes were cleaned up, and their lively guests departed, Bea changed into her PJs and joined Huxley on the couch. They'd learned to sit in the center where no framing poked their thighs, while leaving "appropriate" space between their bodies. Even without the contact, she felt like a root beer float, delicious and floaty. Full of bubbles and teasing laughter.

He switched on the TV, landing on a *CSI* rerun. They'd discovered their joint love of *CSI* recently. Huxley enjoyed puzzling out the crimes, while she loved the endings, knowing the bad guys would be caught. Wishing life imitated that art.

Ten minutes in, she narrowed her eyes at the screen. "The sister. It has to be the sister."

"No way. The brother is dodgy. His best friend seeing him at a bike rally is as weak as alibis get."

They made a game of it, playing Guess the Villain, listing why it had to be the brother or sister or shady waitress. Bea was usually right. "But the sister is being super helpful. It's always the nice one."

"That means if Mrs. Yarrow is killed, you'll be the prime suspect."

It wouldn't be a stretch. Mrs. Yarrow lived next door and spent an inordinate amount of time tending her garden. While in hot pants. Sixty-year-old women shouldn't wear hot pants. Mrs. Yarrow, in particular, shouldn't use them to flirt with Huxley. "I may have the odd nefarious thought toward her, but it would be self-defense. Her garden attracts an abnormal number of bees."

His face clouded. "Should we spike her spray-tan bottles with poison?"

"Nope. Tint them blue. That would teach her to keep such lovely flowers. And you're going down on the brother call. You may as well add a point to my scoresheet now."

Their scorekeeping mainly served Bea, who would dance around Huxley, waving the writing pad, rubbing her success in his face.

Unperturbed, he slung his arm over the back of the couch. His hand rested by her shoulder, and all thoughts of beating him vanished. Bea tried to follow the show, but Huxley's hand was in her peripheral vision, close to her body. Her eyes strained from sneaking peeks. She didn't even taunt him when the sister was exposed.

Huxley seemed distracted, too, barely glancing at the TV. "Thank you," he said.

"For what?"

"For tonight."

She angled toward him, away from the show. "But I didn't do anything. You cooked. It's your family. I'm just an interloper."

"We haven't had a family dinner in a while. They were here to pick up the Mustang, which means they showed up because you keyed my car. The jokes and general assholery were because of you, too. To make me look bad in the loving way brothers torment each other." He fingered a lock of her hair, rolling the loose strands between his fingers. "Having you here makes everything more fun."

She leaned farther back, hoping his busy fingers would graze her skin. Because...*this*. His admission. The contact. The touching. When she was with Huxley everything felt so incredibly right. "I've always been on the periphery of groups, friendly with everyone or the outcast, but not part of the inner circle. Being here, with you—I can't describe how it makes me feel."

Real.

Important.

Content.

"That makes me happier than you know." He drew lazy circles on her shoulder, and shivers swept across her skin.

They didn't talk again. Another episode aired. The TV flashed scenes of dead bodies and arid desert. They didn't guess who shot whom or who was lying. Their gazes strayed from the screen and the space between their thighs diminished.

"How long have you had this couch?" she asked as she avoided a poky part.

He shifted with her, tugging her closer to his side. More contact. More him. He latched his arm firmly around her until she nestled under his chin. "Too long," he said softly. "I've been meaning to replace it, but I helped Fox furnish his apartment, then I sent Axel to a Vegas conference. And there's always theater expenses. I'll get something soon."

"Your brothers are lucky to have you."

He shrugged and stroked her hair. For ten, twenty, thirty minutes, they breathed in time, nuzzling closer. She nosed the exposed skin above his collar, inhaling his manly scent. His fingers glided up and down her arm. They didn't take things further, but there was an intimacy to the cuddling that felt incredibly good. And an unexpected thought hit her exposed nerves: *What if this is* too good *to last?*

God, she was tired of nurturing this fear, but what if Huxley wasn't being honest with *himself* about the role poker played in his life?

He was an honorable man who valued family. He believed a promise was as binding as Axel's straitjacket. He shouldered the responsibility of the theater to make his late father proud. He also read romance novels. The pastime may have begun as a guilty pleasure, or a how-to in the ways of women, but the way he'd fought to break her walls, earn her trust in a trial by fire, deny his desires to prove his worth—he was a romantic through and through. He wouldn't hurt her on purpose.

That didn't mean he wouldn't do so accidentally.

She sneezed once. Twice.

"Bless you." He leaned back, studying her. "Everything okay?"

"Perfect. Great." It was great. He was great.

Get it together, Bea.

She flattened her hand on his abdomen. The solid shape of him grounded her and curbed her crazy. She reminded herself how good she'd felt around him recently, how in tune to each other they were. She focused on the heat of him against her and nothing else. His body was scalding through his *Property of Starfleet* T-shirt. A body she wanted to see. She often thought about the scars Della had mentioned, the hidden ones on his torso—where they were, what they looked like. What had happened the night his father died that had landed him in the hospital.

Her awareness of the past he'd endured and the masculine firmness below her hand banished her ridiculous worries. Her nose twitched, but she didn't sneeze. His breaths grew more ragged, matching hers.

His hand drifted under her loose hair, grazing her sensitive ear. He cupped her neck. "Beatrice."

She purred at the sound of her name and shifted against him, tilting her head to see every scar and line that shaped his handsome face. Fierce hunger sharpened his cheekbones. Barely-contained wildness lit his eyes. He leaned closer, and her desire spiked. When he finally angled his mouth toward hers, she couldn't resist.

She closed her eyes, and *oh*—the feel of his lips finally brushing hers was intoxicating. They both moaned. His kiss started soft and delicate, then his lips pressed harder. His fingers dug into her scalp. She answered with equal voracity, tugging him closer, letting her tongue tangle wildly with his. The kiss was hot and demanding, the type that broke ancient curses and turned frogs into dashing princes.

She tried to drag him closer, but he pulled away. Too close to gauge his expression, she whimpered her disapproval and moved to kiss him again.

He held her firm and whispered, "Ten days."

She fisted his cotton shirt. "Who's playing with fire now?"

"We have an agreement, Honeybee. One I intend to keep."

Deep down, she knew this was the smart thing. Her heart believed Huxley was as honest as they came, but her head had mutinied only minutes ago. That didn't change how charged her body was. "It's not what a romance hero would do."

"I wouldn't know."

He was full of it. "He'd ravage me. Turn my world inside out."

He brushed his nose against hers. "Do you want this hero to break his promise?"

She released her punishing hold on his shirt. "No."

"Do you want him to give in to his desire, knowing it will ruin things in the long run? Or do you want him to torture himself by holding back, because the woman in his arms is worth the torment?"

"It's not fair," she said on a sigh. *She* was the reason he'd pulled away. *Her* issues had undermined them this whole time.

And he'd totally read a bunch of Harlequin novels.

He pulled her head to his chest. "No. It's not. But my last poker game is Saturday. If I keep kissing you, stopping will be even harder. And if we sleep together, you'll resent me going. We'll start this relationship with doubts. After the game and next week's revenue, I'll have enough to cover the construction, which means I'm taking you out Thursday night. And after I take you out, I'll perform the type of magic trick that will turn you boneless."

That dirty promise exacerbated her arousal. Based on the thick line stretching his denim-clad crotch, his anatomy was as mutinous as hers. His willpower was also astounding. Maybe it was his superpower: kryptonite-resistant self-control.

Her phone buzzed from the coffee table, providing her a welcomed distraction, unless it was her father from a new number, or Big Eddie. She never welcomed those distractions.

She extricated herself from Huxley's hold and picked up her cell, just in case it was Della about work or her mother texting a new selfie. Last Bea heard, Molly Baker was in Japan, living it up with a band called Crispy Caterpillars.

The text wasn't from her mother or Della.

It was her father, from a new number, with his usual ruse: *help*.

She groaned. "I should finally change my number. He'll never give up."

"Who won't give up? Is a guy bothering you?" Huxley's dark tone matched his darkening eyes.

"Not a guy. Well, yes—*a guy*. Just not that kind of a guy. My father." She tucked her feet under her, the phone heavy in her hand.

Huxley, now a healthy distance away, hooked his ankle over his knee. "He's been contacting you?"

"He knows I want nothing to do with him, and that I never answer his calls, so he texts the word *help*, which usually breaks my resolve. Then he asks for money and I picture him dead in a ditch somewhere and cave in. I blocked his last number, but he must have a new phone. His persistence is impressive."

She stopped herself before she explained about Big Eddie and the drama chasing her. She'd mentioned the loan shark offhandedly a while back, when Huxley had taken her for lunch and asked about her lack of mug shot. Going into detail now might make her feel better, but she didn't want to be a *CSI* character, predictably sucking people into her troubles, dragging them all down. Those characters were as bad as the horror movie girls who wandered into the dark alone.

"Then why *haven't* you changed your number?" Huxley asked.

She flipped the phone in her hand. It was nothing but a metal box. It didn't tease her or make her laugh, or feed her belly and soul, but it connected her to the two people responsible for her existence. "I don't like my father, but I love him. I like my mother, but I don't love her. I didn't choose my parents, but my mother left some guy she cared about to be with my dad, which means they were once in love. They chose to have me. Not knowing where they are, or if they're okay, would be worse than seeing their texts, especially my father's."

Molly Baker had been fun growing up. She'd encouraged Bea's art and had taught her that if music played, the Baker girls must dance. She believed positivity was contagious and made people around her happier. She was an entertaining friend, but she hadn't been there when Bea had dropped out of high school to work full-time, or on the days Bea had cleaned up her father's puke. She hadn't earned Bea's love, just like her father hadn't earned Bea's respect. But they were still her parents.

She eyed her phone warily, worried the latest messages weren't a scheme. Big Eddie could have made good on his threat to hurt Franklyn Baker.

"I admire you," Huxley said.

"Because I come from a dysfunctional family?"

"Because you come from a dysfunctional family and you've found it in your heart to forgive them. None of us speak with our mother. She cheated on my father often and didn't follow his wishes from his will, squandering his insurance money instead of helping with the theater. I have no idea why he trusted her, or why he even married her. The woman didn't even cry at his funeral. Not that any of it matters. He's gone, and I'll never speak with her again."

"Why?"

His matter-of-fact tone turned somber. "I'm afraid of what I'll say."

"Because she didn't give you money?"

He shook his head vehemently. "Sure, I was pissed about that. She knew Dad wanted some of her payout to go to the theater. But her inability to mother is what tipped the scale. Fox and Axel were rough after Dad died. *I* was rough, but Paxton and Xander were worse. They had issues with our father. I think they maybe had a fight with him before he died, and our mother should have been there for them after. Helped them through it. But she did nothing."

He rubbed the scar on his pinky finger—short, agitated strokes. "They eventually moved away, and I haven't spoken to them in years. Right or wrong, I blame her for a lot of that. She also knowingly ruins people's lives, just to earn a buck. So, yeah, I don't want to know her, or be anything like her."

Just like Bea didn't want to be like her father. It was why she strived to make people happy and brighten their world. Huxley, on the other hand, kept his promises to a fault. "You could hate your mother," she said, "*or* you could thank her."

"For not loving her kids?"

"For turning you into a loyal, caring man."

The tense lines around his mouth softened. "You certainly enjoy torturing this hero in your romantic tale, don't you?"

He wasn't the only one facing painful torment. Her skin still sparked from his gentle stroking of her arm. Her lips were parched from not tasting his. "Do you want to kiss me again?"

His familiar growl rumbled between them. "I want to kiss you many places." Instead of fulfilling his delicious promise, he held out his hand. "Right now, I'd rather you pass me your phone."

"Why?"

"I think you want to know your father's okay, but you don't want to look. You're worried reading his words will suck you into his problems. If I tell you what it says, it'll be easier."

She hesitated handing over her phone, still worried those texts would embroil them both in a nastiness she'd hoped to avoid, but she suddenly craved Huxley's support. The fact that he understood her fear of becoming a tornado was a testament to how well he knew her, the simple gesture intuitive and sweet. If Fox ever gave up his mentalist duties, Huxley could fill his sneaky shoes.

She held out her phone. "If he's going on about something schemey, I don't want to know. If he's asking for money, don't tell me. I just want to hear he's okay."

That a loan shark hadn't sent him to the hospital.

The possibility had guilt constricting her chest, but she squashed that nonsense. She wasn't the one who'd gambled beyond her means or tangled with the wrong men. She was tired of feeling responsible. After confirming her father wasn't hurt, she would do what she'd avoided until now. She'd switch her number and lose contact with him for good.

Come to think of it, she should do it now, before Huxley read his messages. Quit being such a pushover.

She reached for the phone, ready to erase Franklyn Baker from her life, but Huxley was clutching it tightly, squinting at her messages. He stood and paced. His angular jaw hardened into stone, his lips thinning into a grim line. "Is there a man who's threatened your life?"

His question was so low, so wound tight with bridled anger, she held her breath.

"Beatrice..." He scrubbed a hand down his face and crouched in front of her. "Did you promise to pay off one of your father's lenders? Or is he fabricating stories?"

She suddenly felt small on the uncomfortable couch, the larger world too big to contemplate. "I did."

"Christ." Huxley was back to pacing, wearing an angry path on the hardwood floor. "I need to know everything: who the guy is, what he threatened, how much he thinks you owe." Why the hell she hadn't shared the minor fact that she was in danger. He'd missed the signs when she was homeless, squatting in his theater. Now this.

"He's a loan shark, but there's no way for him to find me. I don't use credit cards or anything, and I turned off my phone's GPS."

He glared at her cell, unsure why she thought the GPS was her solution. "A phone can be tracked without activating its GPS."

Her eyes widened. "Really?"

"Yes, really. What did he threaten?"

Instead of replying, she shrunk smaller, like his anger was compressing her. He couldn't control the rage rushing through him, the barking timbre of his voice. All he could picture was Beatrice hurt. "I don't mean to get mad," he said more evenly, "but this is important. What did the man threaten?"

She tucked her knees to her chest. "He said he'd remove one of my fingers for every day my payment was late. That was a month ago."

"A *month*? Why didn't you say anything? Did you even call the cops?" So much for controlling his temper.

"Calling the cops would get my father in trouble. I know he deserves it, but it goes back to that whole love-hate thing. I can't be the one to do that to him. And I did tell you about the threat."

"I think I'd remember learning your life was in danger."

"At our first lunch—at the breakfast café. You asked about my lack of mug shot and if any dodgy sorts would follow me to New Orleans. I told you there was a man who wanted to sever my fingers. There's been other stuff since, but this is my problem—my *father's* problem—and I didn't want to involve you."

Now he wanted to punch the wall. She *had* told him. He'd shrugged it off, assuming she'd been playing around, acting like her fun, silly self. Was there no end to the ways he'd failed her? "I thought you were joking at lunch, and what other stuff has happened?"

"Nothing but empty threats, and it doesn't matter. I don't think he's a high-tech loan shark. If he could track my phone, he'd have shown up here by now. And I've been sleeping with scissors in my bed."

He wanted her sleeping in *his* bed. Tucked into his side, safe and protected. He also wasn't so sure her location was secret. He scrolled through the messages again. "You texted your father a picture of crocodile heads."

She scrunched her face. "The Caught in the Wild one? From the market?"

He checked the phone. "I think so. The photo's not here, but one of his messages thanked you for sending it. He said you should pose with the crocodile heads next time."

"But I sent that to my mom."

He double-checked the text. "You must have sent it to your father accidentally. If he tells someone, or someone has his old phone and puts two and two together, they'll realize it was taken in New Orleans." Someone could be here now, stalking her. Planning to do her harm. He could barely think over the loud pound of his heart. "I need specifics. Debt details. Anything else you know."

He wasn't sure how he'd broken off their kiss earlier, how he'd kept from pinning her to his couch and exploring her every dip and curve. It could have been Edna's warning not to get attached to his assistant, or his need to retain Beatrice's trust. She fit into his family with ease and slotted into his life seamlessly. Her body had molded to his just now like an extension of his own. If something happened to Beatrice Baker, it would unhinge him.

She told him the little she knew, each bit of information twisting his insides. "I'll discuss it all with Fox and Axel," he said. "We'll figure things out together. But I don't want you walking around alone at night anymore. No handing out pamphlets to drunk women."

She worried her lip. "Do you really think that's necessary? It's been a month, and nothing's happened."

"This is serious, Beatrice. Men like this don't mess around." He didn't tell her Big Eddie was likely working for someone even scarier. The last thing he wanted was to worry her more.

She finally nodded. "I guess that makes sense. What else do the texts say?"

He scanned them again but was too agitated to think clearly. He slowed his thumb and started over. "Some are more of the same you wanted to avoid, but two of them warn you a man named Big Eddie is looking for you. That he's tossing around threats."

She stared blankly a moment. "Has he hurt my dad?"

Franklyn Baker's texts ranged from moaning about unpaid bills and how much he missed his "Pumpkin" to claiming he'd be sleeping on the streets without a loan. He wrote that Beatrice was the only good thing in his life. The man wielded his parental guilt expertly. "He doesn't mention being hurt, and I'd guess he's capable of looking out for himself. The messages are yours to read, if you want."

She studied her knees a moment. "I think I'll head to bed." She stood and looked up at Huxley. Her brow was puckered, hinting at worry, but the edges of her lips tugged upward. "Thanks for a great night."

In the face of a degenerate's threats, she still focused on the positive part of the evening, ignoring the bad, seeing the silver lining. He didn't buy it. "If you're having a rough night, my door will be open. Use it."

She curled her bare toes and glanced at their bedroom doors. She swallowed visibly. "I appreciate your concern, but I'll be fine."

That made one of them.

21

Saturdays at the market were crazy. Bea and Della alternated who stole bathroom breaks, barely finding time to eat. Della bedazzled customers with her cute jean shorts and stunning jewelry, while Bea packed purchases and made change. Customers even smiled and pointed at Bea's paintings.

It was the third day her art had been showcased on their dividing wall. The first day, after Huxley had helped hang the pieces over red batik fabric, he'd whispered, "You have the nicest apples I've ever seen."

The charmer hadn't been talking about fruit, but he must have been a good-luck charmer. She'd sold a piece that afternoon.

Two older women were pointing at the four remaining apple paintings now, talking to each other. The only words she caught were *funky* and *unique* and *bold*, enough to have pleasure crowding her chest, and her nerves over sharing her art diminished. They were gushing over *her* creations, *her* strange imaginings. It felt like she'd showered in sparkles.

Della grabbed Bea's elbow. "You need to negotiate this time. Your work takes a lot of hours. Don't sell yourself short."

Her first sale had lasted all of three seconds. The woman had offered forty dollars for her eighty-dollar painting, and Bea had to keep from jumping for joy. "I got too excited the other day. I would've sold it for a penny."

Della snorted. "I get it. I couldn't believe people were willing to spend cash on my jewelry at first, but it's a business. Don't undervalue your product. If you charge more, people will think it's worth more."

Bea pictured herself falling in love with a sculpture or painting and being denied purchase. "What if they can't afford it?"

"Someone else will come along."

"What if they really, *really* love it?"

"It's a commodity, Bea. Not a cure for cancer."

Right. Commodity.

Donning her best negotiator face, Bea approached the women. The shorter one wore a canary yellow chemise and loose, floral pants, the ensemble as colorful as Bea's flower-print halter dress. The taller woman had the shiniest black hair she'd ever seen and an onyx necklace to match. The stones looped around her neck so many times they overtook her collarbones. It looked like she might have trouble breathing.

Exactly how Bea felt. But she could do this.

"The paintings are originals." Bea deepened her voice to match her negotiator face.

The canary woman whispered something to her companion, then she planted a manicured hand on her hip. "Are you the artist?"

"I am."

Eyes on Bea, the canary woman lifted her pointed chin. "Do you do larger pieces?"

"As a matter of fact, I do." Just like that, her naturally higher-pitched voice returned. "I'm working on a self-portrait now. The concept is the same, exploring all the layers that make an apple an apple, or a person unique. I painted a dandelion in my portrait yesterday, because I used to collect them as a kid and made necklaces for all the local dogs. I wasn't allowed a dog, which was probably for the best, considering we could barely feed ourselves, but I always wanted an Irish wolfhound. They're big enough to ride."

Della rolled her eyes at Bea's verbal deluge, and Bea clamped her mouth shut. The babbling was part nerves and part enthusiasm, but if she wanted to close this sale for more than forty dollars, she needed to rein herself in.

"Larger pieces are very time consuming," Bea said.

"I imagine. Can I see the purple one up close?"

She handed her the piece and managed not to gush about her favorite detail. If she started waxing on about the mouse's tail she'd painted, it would lead to blabbing about the rodent she'd found in her kitchen at age twelve. She'd kept Princess Tiny for a year.

Bea gave the woman space and watched Della, who was in deep discussion with the onyx necklace woman. Della swept her long braids over her right shoulder, then spun her bracelet absentmindedly, a habit when bargaining with customers or deciding how to display new jewelry. Whatever they were discussing, Della was in entrepreneur mode. The woman passed her a business card.

"I'd like to commission a painting."

The canary customer's statement almost caused Bea whiplash as she looked away from Della. "You want something specific?"

"I have a special project in mind, a much larger piece, assuming you accept contract work."

Someone liking her style enough to trust that Bea could take a new concept and run with it was way bigger than selling a premade piece. She wanted to crow and shout, *Yes! Where do I sign?* But that wasn't what a serious business woman would do. "I don't use taupe," she said.

"That's not a problem."

"And I'd need an advance."

"Quite understandable."

"It would have to be in cash. I'd also need to see where you plan to hang the painting. If it's a portrait, we'll have to spend an afternoon together. I'd need unlimited access to your home and photos." One couldn't immortalize a person's face without assessing their world, but Bea worried she'd gone too far. One taste of action and she was a madwoman, negotiating excessive demands. It must have been the diva dressing room. It was bound to affect her.

The woman didn't balk at Bea's extravagant list. She pulled her phone from her shoulder bag and showed Bea a photo of the world's cutest poodle. "You'll be painting Maude. She's getting older, and we'd like a portrait for our parlor. We'll fly you to New York. You can spend the day with her. How much of an advance would you need?"

Bea had never been on a plane or painted commissioned work. She'd never even negotiated successfully. Sweat studded her cleavage and her mouth dried. When she remembered how to inflate her lungs, she said, "Can you excuse me a minute?"

She then worsened her whiplash by using her tipping head and mouth to silently beg Della to join her at the back of the booth. Huddled together, Bea exhaled. "She wants a large portrait of her poodle."

"So why do you look like you swallowed a cup of Joe's hot sauce?"

If ketchup was the worst condiment, Joe's hot sauce was the best. No matter how profusely she sweated, she always loaded it onto her po'boys. "Because I demanded an advance."

"Look at you, being all sassy."

They discreetly low-fived. "Now she wants to know how much. She's also flying me to New York so I can meet Maude the Dog and see their home."

"Jesus." Della shook her head, grinning. "Maybe we should swap jobs. I'll make change while you sell my work."

"Only if it comes with a po'boy raise, extra hot sauce, please."

"Done."

They assessed the sharp couple. Both women were polished enough to recognize a true Chanel from a knockoff blindfolded. Negotiating would take finesse.

"The one I spoke with is Jacqueline Berry," Della said. "She's a sick jewelry designer. They're on vacation, but she came here to see my work. She's looking to expand her lines."

"Della, that's amazing!"

She waved off Bea's excitement. "Working with her would mean moving to New York. I love New Orleans." She fingered her bracelet again. Agitated about the prospect of leaving Fox? "Regardless, I know a bit about her, and the lady is one hell of an eccentric, so a dog portrait isn't surprising. They also have buckets of cash."

Bea was about to rewind to Della brushing off an incredible job opportunity when a bee flew by her head. She froze.

Della went on to strategize negotiation tactics, but Bea's eyes darted uncontrollably, searching for her buzzing adversary. "Purse," she told Della.

"What?"

"I need my purse. My EpiPen's inside."

"Are you allergic to bargaining?"

"Yes. But also bee stings. I almost died when I was eight." Her near-death had involved a game of Pin the Tail on the Donkey and a very unhappy Melanie Swank, who'd gotten pinned when Bea had been stung. It had been her last birthday party invite. She wasn't about to let another bee sabotage her life. "The EpiPen's just a precaution."

Della was off and rummaging under their table before Bea finished talking. Jewelry boxes flew as she dragged out Bea's beaded rainbow purse. "Did it sting you? What do I do?" Her eyes were wild.

The bee had begun circling Della's head. She swatted at it with the purse. Bea ducked and twirled. The eccentric ladies watched them, eyebrows raised. By the time the bee absconded, Della was disheveled, and Bea's hair resembled a bearded vulture's nest.

Della slumped. "I think I'm allergic to you being allergic to bees. Now, tell me what you're thinking about this advance."

Half an hour later, Bea's first commission client, Arabella Grieves, returned from a bank with an envelope filled with hundred-dollar bills. Twenty-five, to be exact. Bea would receive the other half upon completion and would fly to New York in a week. Her feet barely touched the ground for the rest of the day.

Except when her spine tingled like someone was watching her.

She listened for familiar buzzing, worried the bee had set up surveillance, waiting to catch her unaware. No noise assaulted her ears. She studied the market crowd next, scanning for a tall man with a goatee, but Big Eddie was nowhere to be seen.

Then she cursed Huxley.

It was because of him she glanced over her shoulder more often, that she drove down random side streets on her way home, like an undercover cop shaking a tail. Another fake job added to her résumé, after expert negotiator and diva extraordinaire.

They'd had a Marvelous Marlow meeting the other day, during which the brothers had informed Bea about their sleuthing. Turns out, Big Eddie was a low-level thug in a larger organization. Since he hadn't turned up in New Orleans, they surmised her location was still secret. That didn't stop Huxley from flying into overprotective mode. He walked her to her car morning and night. He texted her regularly to check in. He'd also removed one of Della's YouTube posts, the one titled, *Beatrice Baker and the Marvelous Marlow Boys.* Bea had hated to see that post removed. Huxley only worried about how long it had been live.

He was partly smothering friend and all domineering male, the domineering part surprisingly sweet. No one had ever worried after Bea.

She held in her commission news for the length of the evening's show. Performing took focus. If she let out her glee, she'd have spent her time dancing rather than assisting.

After the curtain call and annoying girl fandom, she dragged Huxley into her dressing room. "I made a sale today."

"Of course you did. I told you your apples are the nicest I've ever seen." His gaze dropped to her chest.

If she weren't busting to share her news, she'd ask him if he had a banana she could paint next. Instead she bounced her knees. "I didn't sell an apple. I was commissioned to paint a portrait."

"No way."

"Yes way. I negotiated like a boss." Now she was bouncing on her toes. Then she was in the air. Huxley lifted her up by her armpits and spun her in a circle. His cape flared as they twirled. She tipped her head back and laughed.

He lowered her in front of him. "I'm proud of you."

She clutched his forearms. "I'm proud of me, too. And check out what's on the makeup table."

He glanced at the red handkerchief she hadn't used. "You didn't take it on stage?"

"Nope. I believe I've *mostly* conquered my stage fright, thanks in large part to you."

His attention shifted to her lips, as it often did. His hands moved to her waist. "That's all you, Beatrice, which means we have more to celebrate. But back to this portrait—who's the subject of the painting?"

The question was quiet, and he didn't let her go. She swayed slightly, as though music played. He mirrored her moves. He did that often lately, dancing absentmindedly when she'd turn swing music up at home, as they'd navigate around each other in the kitchen. Her surly man finding his fun.

She wanted to toss her arms around his neck and dance fully, celebrate with a kiss. She settled on enjoying the view of his scruffy jaw. "Maude the Dog. The client is flying me to New York next Monday."

"Next Monday," he repeated, his grip tightening on her hips. It was only nine days away, but their first date was also approaching. So much would change by then. After Thursday, they wouldn't have to stand like this, touching with reserve, eyeing each other's lips instead of licking them.

When Huxley said, "I should get going," she remembered why there would be no licking or dancing or celebratory kissing.

"Right." She moved out of his reach. "Have a good night."

Her stomach turned over, an involuntary reaction. There were no lies here. This was his last poker night. He'd made that clear. Still, she pictured him in a smoky room, betting, winning, losing. The outcome didn't matter. His honesty didn't ease her anxiety reflex, either. Any and all betting wound her internal clock back to finding her rent money stolen from her secret Cookie Monster jar as a teen, to her zero balance in her adult savings account.

Huxley pulled off his top hat and raked his hand through his soft curls. She diverted her attention to Surly, Sneaky, and Cocky, cooing in their cage.

"Fox will walk you to your car," Huxley said eventually. "Congratulations, again."

His receding footsteps hurt her heart, but she didn't dwell on the dull ache. For the first time, she felt like a bona fide artist, not a doodler or food sculptor. She was living in a colorful city with colorful friends and would soon be dating a colorful man, who no longer gambled. She didn't need a fancy art college to be happy. She could take art classes on her own or draw Huxley in the privacy of their apartment. They could do a reverse *Titanic*, with him lounging on the couch, au natural, while she sketched the grooves of his hip bones and gave him sexy eyes.

She smiled at that reverie as she drove home. She ate a late-night Pop-Tarts snack. Her *Titanic* fantasies continued as she brushed her teeth and crawled into bed. They thwarted her sleep efforts until the front door opened and closed.

Huxley returning from his last poker game.

She listened as the kitchen tap turned on, then off. She pictured him leaning against the counter, his long neck tipped back as he drank his fill. He'd still be in his black slacks and gold button-down, looking ever the delectable magician. She wondered if he was wearing his cape.

His footsteps neared her door. He stopped. As did her heart. Then it revved.

He was so close. *They* were so close to finally erasing the distance between them. She sat up, and the covers pooled at her waist. Her thin tank top brushed her sensitive nipples, each drag echoing between her thighs.

The softest *thump* sounded. His forehead resting on their barrier?

She padded to the door and pressed her forehead against the wood. It was like they were in the theater again, together but apart, while she'd listened to his private confessional. Two people whose thoughts were connected, their bodies divided by uncertainties. She could easily open the door, lift her top and unbutton his. If she pushed, he wouldn't deny her this. But she'd smell the cigar smoke on his clothes and remember where he'd been and why they'd waited.

Even now, odd memories thwarted her. She'd often celebrate New Year's with her father, just the two of them with bags of candy and streamers galore. Every year he'd tell her he was joining Gamblers Anonymous, that he'd get help and quit. He would say it with gummy bears in his mouth and streamers in his copper hair. She'd believe him, because he hadn't been lying. He'd truly thought the next year would be different. And the next. And the next.

He'd wanted to change, but he'd been too weak to follow through.

This thing with Huxley could be history repeating itself. He might falsely believe he didn't need the poker games, but she trusted otherwise. Their time as roommates—cooking together, laughing, sharing his living room while she painted and he read or fiddled with his puzzle box—had proven just how wonderful Huxley was. She wouldn't doubt him again. Their date would unfold as planned. In just five days.

She stood still, breathing hard. She heard him exhale, followed by a soft scratching. She imagined him writing her a love letter on the door, a note worthy of an epic romance. A pledge to be faithful. A promise to rock her world. A vow to use his magic hands on her body until she levitated.

She drew a heart on her side. Then a castle.

Then a prince with a large *sword*.

She groaned too loudly and his scratching ceased. Her fantasies didn't. She imagined unzipping Huxley's pants and touching the length of him, how hard yet silky he'd feel. Would his familiar growl fill the air? Was he the type of lover who would kneel above her to watch her every move, or would he press his chest to hers, skin-to-skin, heart-to-heart? She couldn't decide which she'd prefer. She wanted it all.

He moved, his footsteps traveling toward his room. Sighing, she tossed her overheated body on her bed, more wound up than before. She wouldn't sleep tonight. Or for the next five days. Not until their promised date, and his promise to turn her boneless under his skilled touch.

But steps neared her door again, then stopped. She pushed up to her elbows, entranced. His shadow spilled under her door and into her room, a folded paper sailing over the floor. She scrambled to her hands and knees and crawled over the hardwood toward the gift. Maybe he'd sent her a note asking her to rate him from one to ten. Or a "Which Disney Prince Would You Bang?" questionnaire. *Tangled*'s Flynn Rider, please and thank you.

What she got was so much better.

> *Dearest Beatrice,*
> *You may not think I've touched you yet, but I have. Every time I close my eyes, I drag my hands over your hips and down your thighs. I press wet kisses to every inch of your skin. I'm not sure how I ever stood still when music played, but those days are done. Thursday night is just the start.*
>
> *Yours,*
> *Huxley*

Mine. He is mine. He was the scorching oxygen searing her chest, the wet heat pooling between her thighs. He was better than Flynn Rider or Prince Charming, or that swoony cartoon man who kissed Snow White. He was flesh and bone. Too good to be true. A magic man who penned one hell of a love letter.

22

Huxley guided Beatrice into the packed club, his hand on her lower back as they navigated the crowd. He hadn't been sure where to take her for their first official date, only wanting to be somewhere he could touch her at will and feel her dancing body against his.

Brimstone didn't disappoint.

The alcohol and perfume-scented air swelled with the band's sensual beats, gold lights highlighting the crimson couches they passed. Whispering couples ignored them. He followed close behind Beatrice, guiding her to the bar.

Her gray eyes twinkled as she took in the mass of arms and legs on the dance floor. "This place is amazing."

"Axel suggested it." Huxley couldn't remove his hand from the dip of her spine or keep from glancing at the curves displayed in her red dress. The fabric cinched her waist and flared at her hips, teasing him to what lay beneath. He waved the bartender down, needing something for his parched throat. "Manhattan for me, with an extra cherry, and a lemon drop for the lady."

The bartender nodded, and Bea pressed closer to his side. "You ordered for me."

"Is that okay?"

Instead of confirming or denying her feelings on the matter, she said, "You know what I like."

He did know. He had quite the mental file on Beatrice Baker, every nuance catalogued and saved for future reference. She liked lemon drops and Long Island Iced Tea and learning odd animal facts. She hated ketchup and green lollipops. She loved foiling *CSI* criminals and taunting him with her wins. He hoped she adored dancing in this club with him, too, and falling into *their* apartment later.

Already, Huxley considered his place theirs. He liked being in the small space with her and had no intention of letting her move out. Lately, he'd stressed less over the building repairs, not even donning his plumber or carpenter hat on his one day off. It wasn't easy, stepping back from the theater, but reading on the couch while Beatrice painted and they both tapped their feet to swing or jazz settled his soul in an inexplicable way.

Tonight they would do more than tap their feet.

If he wasn't worried about Big Eddie's threats, he'd already be lost to the heady atmosphere and their impending night. As it stood, he scanned the inebriated crowd, searching for a tall man, as Beatrice had described: goatee, slight paunch, dark hair. He didn't find the seedy character, but his sights locked on another unsavory sort.

"I know that mustache..." Beatrice said, squinting at Oliphant, then her eyes widened. "That guy was at the bar the night we met."

Huxley would never forget that night, but he'd rather not have his nemesis here as a reminder. He tried to focus on his date, who skimmed her hand down the side of his dress shirt.

She wetted her lips. "I don't think I mentioned how dashing you look."

He'd taken a page from Fox's book when dressing tonight, finding a black button-down and slacks he hadn't worn in ages. If it made Beatrice look at him like he was an ice cream cone, he'd have to dress like this more often. "All eyes are on you, Honeybee. Your red lips and dress make it hard for a man to focus."

"All men?"

"This man has forgotten if the world is round or square." But he couldn't forget the twitchy mustache eyeing him and his date. He didn't want to leave her side. Not for a second. But Oliphant hadn't wandered into Brimstone coincidentally.

When Huxley had announced he wouldn't play poker again, Oliphant had nearly choked on his cigar. He'd launched a slew of insults, but Huxley had barely flinched. Name-calling and ranting were nothing compared to the notion of disappointing Beatrice, and playing another poker game would do more than disappoint the woman on his arm.

Battling the guitar solo and boisterous crowd, he raised his voice. "I need to speak with that mustache. I'll be right back."

"Don't be long." She pressed her lips to his neck, a soft kiss that echoed through him.

He wouldn't be long. He also wasn't going to be kind to Oliphant for interrupting his long-awaited date. After another quick glance around to confirm Big Eddie's absence, he pushed his way to Oliphant.

"I'd say it's fancy meeting you here, but there's nothing fancy about it." Huxley moved so he was facing Beatrice. Her upper body swayed to the music.

Oliphant hooked his thumbs on his suspenders. "Is enjoying a night of jazz a crime?"

Getting between him and his date was a federal offense. "Quit pretending like you aren't stalking me."

"Just thought I'd check to see if you changed your mind about a rematch."

"I'm not sure what part of 'I'm quitting the poker scene' wasn't clear to you, but I'll dumb it down a notch." A head taller than Oliphant, he loomed over the older man. "Nothing you do or say will bring me back. You lost fair and square. Give it up. Move on. It won't happen in this lifetime. I'd also appreciate you fessing up about the blight complaint. I wasn't proud of the theater's appearance, and it'll be good as new before the hearing, but that was a dick move."

A bearded man approached Beatrice, and Huxley cut his tirade short. She smiled at the uninvited guest. She smiled at everyone. The asshole took it as his cue to plant his elbow on the bar behind her. Huxley ground his molars.

He was about to blow past Oliphant, but the swine opened his slimy mouth. "She's a sweet-looking dame. The trusting sort. Wouldn't want her to trust the wrong person."

Huxley curled his hands into fists. "You look at her, you talk to her, or you breathe in her general direction, and I swear to God..."

The older man waved off Huxley's implied threat. "No need to get physical. I've just noticed shady sorts eyeing her."

Unease spilled down Huxley's spine. It wasn't Oliphant's style to issue threats. He was underhanded, a coward who lurked in the shadows and used false names to lodge complaints. If he had seen a man watching her, it could have been Big Eddie. He glared at his nemesis. "Did you see a tall man with a goatee?"

Oliphant smoothed his shirt, a sudden glint in his dark eyes. "I did not. But there's a bearded man intent on your date. And I'm glad to hear the theater construction is done. I'm sure it was expensive and stressful."

Stressful didn't begin to describe the past month, but he'd be handing over Trevor's final payment next week. Axel's snake hadn't needed surgery. The theater was looking great. Closing this aggravating chapter of his life was a huge milestone. But he didn't understand why Oliphant looked pleased. Gleeful, even. Assuming Oliphant had placed the blight complaint, he'd be itching for Huxley to fail. Fox's warning that the scum would retaliate if not given a rematch reared its ugly head.

Time to set him straight. "I've pawned everything I've won to pay for that work. There's nothing left—nothing for you to win back in another game. I'll stay out of your face if you stay out of mine, but mark my words...if you mess with me, or anyone I care about, you won't be able to lift a deck of cards for the rest of your life."

Oliphant's mustache twitched. "False threats don't intimidate me."

There was plenty of wind behind this particular sail, but Huxley wouldn't show his final cards and lose the upper hand. If the idiot thought picking pockets in Vito's club was smart, it was his funeral. Vito's glare alone could snap a man's neck. If the Italian giant knew Oliphant was ripping off his customers, they'd need dental records to identify Oliphant's body, and Huxley would do almost anything to protect his own. Including snitching to Vito about Oliphant's activities.

"It's been lovely seeing you, as always." Huxley stepped away, not bothering to hide his contempt.

"Just like your father," Oliphant said, desperate for the last word. "Always thinking you're better than everyone else. Not an ounce of class in either of you."

Huxley swiveled back. "You need to learn when to shut up. And that stupid dinosaur skull you've been lusting after since my father won it? I pawned that, too."

Oliphant's beady eyes narrowed into evil slits. He could scowl as much as he wanted. Huxley's leverage wouldn't change, or the fact that their conversation should have ended five minutes ago.

He turned to stride back to Beatrice and his stomach bottomed out.

She was gone. Their drinks were on the bar, but she wasn't there. Neither was the bearded man, a man who could be working for Big Eddie.

The room spun, the romantic light now too dark and claustrophobic. Dread winded his chest. Bile built in his throat. Huxley shoved his way toward where she'd been, ready to bulldoze the place to find her. Then she popped up, studying something in her hand, unconcerned, like he hadn't just been picturing her drugged and dragged from the club.

The second he reached her, he crushed her to his chest.

She hugged him back. "I missed you, too."

Fuck. He couldn't slow his pulse or let her go. He also didn't want to scare her. She'd already complained that his vigilance was making her crazy. "Five minutes away from you is too long."

"I found a good-luck penny," she said, too adorably sweet for him to stay stressed. "And I ate your extra cherry."

He slowed his breath and stretched his neck, gradually easing his hold on her. "That's why I got the cherry, and I hope you made a wish."

"I did." They settled against the bar, her shoulder nestled into his side. She sipped her lemon drop and swayed her hips. "A man asked me to dance."

"Did you find this man handsome?"

"Ugly as a star-nosed mole."

Her ridiculous animal knowledge relaxed him further, and he forced himself to quit scanning the room. She was safe.

Nothing would happen to her with him around. He couldn't ruin this night with his overreactions. "He didn't look so bad from where I stood," he said, focusing his attention on the prettiest woman in the club. "A bit hipster, but no star-nosed mole."

She lifted a hand and traced his burned eyebrow, then the scar on his cheek. "He was boring. Bland as every man in here. Except you."

"I have scars on my body." He blurted that truth before the thought had even crossed his mind. He couldn't understand how a woman as fascinating as Beatrice Baker found his ugly mug attractive. He also didn't want her to be surprised when they got home.

Her eyes drifted to his chest. "Della mentioned it."

"Does it bother you?"

"I have a birthmark above my belly button. It's shaped like a wilting daisy. Will that bother you?"

Heat sped his blood. "I can't wait to meet this wilting birthmark of yours."

She tipped up her chin, her eyes so full of emotion he was sure an illusion had vanished every other person in the club. "I can't wait to meet your scars."

Where did I find this woman? Except he knew the truth. He hadn't found her. She'd keyed her way into his life and heart. Because of her, he'd been spending more time with his brothers and less obsessing over the theater. The Marvelous Marlow Boys were performing to a full audience. He'd still like to find a way to entertain kids again, not just horny women, but he'd finally found some balance. Beatrice was the magic ingredient.

She shifted her hips, subtle moves timed to the slide guitar. They ordered another round. His worry dissipated. They talked. She danced against him, her body matching his subtle cadence until he was leading her to the dance floor, every step fueled by Brimstone's sultry mood and his need to have his hands on his woman.

Bea was entranced. Bodies filled the dance floor, wrapping them in the club's heady rhythm, like they were part of a vital organ, writhing, pounding, pumping. This music was lust incarnate. The air reeked of it, the smoky sounds an aphrodisiac of the highest order. Bea was high on the sexy atmosphere. She was even higher on Huxley Marlow, a very marvelous Marlow boy.

His muscular thigh was between hers, one of his large hands branding her lower back. The other stole feels of her ribs, the outer swells of her breast. His hips hit every beat as he led, guiding her body like she was a guitar and he was a guitar master. She twined her fingers through his hair. He snuck tastes of her neck, her ear. She ground herself against him, daring and dirty. Forget femme fatale. She was a siren seductress intent on hypnotizing her man.

Huxley's body replied, his thigh wedging more firmly against her. Pressure built in her core. His own arousal was thick and hot against her hip. The feel of him—excited and hard for her—sent her to the moon. Her high heels positioned her perfectly, allowing her to trail wet kisses across his collarbone. She dipped her tongue into the groove at the base of his neck, tasting salt from his sweat-glazed skin. An approving rumble vibrated against her lips.

The tempo changed. It turned more provocative, faster, inebriating. She closed her eyes, sure she'd disappear into the notes, get lost between the steely drag of the slide guitar and steady pulse of the bass. Tipping her head back, she arched with the movement, curving her spine over Huxley's forearm.

He followed her flow, like they were connected, his heart drawn to hers. He kissed her jaw, her neck. The cleavage swelling from her dress.

Then he kissed her mouth.

It wasn't a tentative taste that grew as they moved. The sensual dancing had made sure of that. This was a rocket-blast kiss, scorching from the first touch.

Their tongues made up for weeks of neglect, curling around each other as their hands clutched and bodies rippled. Even when they came up for air, their lips wouldn't disengage. They shared each other's oxygen, breaths tinged with the sweetness of alcohol, laden with desire. His tongue darted into her mouth, a quick flick that grazed her upper lip. She nibbled on his lower one. They pressed their foreheads together, teasing tastes stolen as they rocked.

Bea had folk danced and belly danced and breakdanced, but she'd never *become* the music, lost her mind in a sweeping of lips and limbs.

One song bled into two, then three. She was slick between her thighs. Huxley was a steel rod against her hip. When she couldn't handle the foreplay any longer, she clutched his shirt and said, "If you don't take me home right now, I'll get arrested for indecent exposure and that mug shot I've avoided for twenty-eight years will become a reality."

23

Bea's feet were floating off the ground, figuratively and literally. Huxley had her pinned against his chest as he kissed her and kicked the apartment door closed.

"You're skilled at multitasking," she said while her lips traveled across his scarred cheek. She tongued the edges of his damaged ear. He groaned in reply.

She'd heard his vulnerability earlier, when mentioning his scarred body. His tentativeness had pained her. She wished he could see himself through her eyes, how his imperfections were the very things she adored. This man was beautiful, inside and out, but telling him wasn't enough. She'd have to show him.

He, however, had other plans.

"You're mine tonight," he said as he carried her into his room and laid her on his bed. "I plan to kiss you senseless, use my tongue and fingers until your spasms shake the walls. But that's not all." He knelt in front of her and lifted her left leg, his two-toned eyes wild with need. He unbuckled her high-heel strap, then kissed her foot and the knot of her ankle as he slid off her red shoe.

"What else will you do?" Her breathy voice sounded desperate.

"Oh, Beatrice. What *won't* I do?"

She squeaked at his gravelly promise. Her breasts felt fuller, the ache between her thighs heavy. She squirmed on his navy duvet. "I want details."

She wanted to listen to his rumbly voice all night.

Not complying, he repeated the reverent treatment to her other foot, finishing by caressing her calves and lifting her dress until his fingers skimmed the edges of her black thigh-highs, the lacy ones she'd purchased from the vampire shop. "I do love these stockings of yours. You tortured me that day in the store with them. I've imagined slipping them off of you for weeks."

"What else?" She needed specifics. She wanted to read his mind and learn what depraved thoughts had kept him up at night.

He smiled indulgently. "I plan to kiss every inch of your legs while I spread your thighs and feel how wet you are. Would you like that, Beatrice?"

"Is the sky blue?"

He chuckled. "But that won't be enough, will it?"

She shook her head, words no longer an option. But God, she loved hearing her name tumble from his lips in a velvet slide. Watching him wasn't half bad, either. Light filtered in from the living area, casting enough color to illuminate his aquiline nose, the elegant cut of his jaw. His burns. His scars. There was nothing unhandsome about Huxley Marlow.

He rolled one of her stockings down, eyes hooded, long fingers adept. "I plan to bury my face between your legs, get drunk on the taste of you." Everything inside her clenched, but he didn't stop there. "I'll feast on the swells of your breasts, learn every flick and lick that turns you on. Then, and only then, will I bury my aching cock inside you. And make no mistake, Beatrice, it is aching."

Dear God. It's me, Beatrice. Thank you for inventing dirty talk.

"Are you sure you only *read* romance novels? Or do you write them under a pen name, too?"

Smirking, he rolled down her other stocking. "I'll never tell."

He lavished her legs with attention, tracing her calves with his nose, marking her with his teeth. He neared the hem of her dress, then ghosted away. Tempting her. Teasing her. Driving her mad. She wasn't the only one. If Huxley's effusive moans were any indication, the fancy five-bladed razor she'd purchased had indeed made her legs silky smooth.

When he had her writhing, he stood and held out a hand. "As stunning as that dress is, it needs to come off."

Weak with need, she eased her fingers into his palm and tried to stand, but wound up stumbling into his arms. "You've made me clumsy."

Intensity sharpened his features. "I'll always catch you."

Her heart pressed against her breastbone.

A fresh make-out session later, her lips were bruised and he wrenched away. Color suffused his cheeks. He spun her around and brushed her hair over her shoulder.

"Stunning," he murmured as he unhooked the clasp at her neck. The top half of her halter dress fell to her ribs, revealing her strapless bra. Cool air brushed her exposed skin, his warm breath caressing her nape. His arms circled her from behind, and he cupped her lace-covered breasts. "You should always wear red."

She let the back of her head fall onto his chest and arched into his large hands. "I'll paint my body red if you keep touching me like this."

"We'll paint each other. But not tonight." He massaged her breasts with such reverence she mewled. "Tonight, I see only you. No forced smiles. No bravado. No colors to hide behind. Just you."

Her languid body stiffened. Had he sensed her reservations the past week? How nerves had flooded her one moment, desire the next? She didn't think her cheery outlook was a bad way to navigate life. It kept her moving forward and stopped her from dwelling on unchangeable things. It had helped her quit worrying Huxley might gamble again and derail their fragile footing. Yet here he was, asking her to look deeper, be vulnerable. Acknowledge her hint of reservation that still lingered: once they slept together he would own a part of her heart.

He released her and gripped the zipper at her back. Shivers descended her spine as he dragged it down. When the dress pooled at her bare feet, he whispered, "Turn around."

She didn't move. Her pulse rattled in her neck.

"Beatrice." The tenderness in his voice washed over her. "Turn around, Honeybee."

Honeybee. Beatrice. The name he called her didn't matter. The yearning in his plea mattered. His patience the past month mattered. *He* mattered.

She turned around, embracing this moment, their future, whatever it held.

His jaw slackened. "Look at you."

Haziness softened his eyes as his gaze raked over her red lace panties and strapless bra. Every inch of her skin. He almost appeared drugged. An expression Huxley never wore. He was the planner. The thinker. The surly brother who plowed through whatever life tossed at him.

"Do you need to lie down?" she asked.

He shook his head. "I just need a minute."

"You can touch me."

Instead he touched himself. "Fucking *aching*." His words grated out.

He still wore his pants, but he gripped his erection through the straining fabric and gave himself a few rough strokes. The sight immediately made her feel drugged, too. Aroused to the point of delirium. She did this to him. She reduced him to pleasurable pain. Releasing himself, he blew out a harsh breath and stepped toward her.

Her body responded with throbbing need, but she held up her hand. "I want to see you first."

Eyelids heavy, he licked his lips. "...Don't you want me to kiss that wilting daisy?"

The lust in his steamy gaze hadn't changed, but a hint of hesitation delayed his reply. *Her* birthmark. *His* scars. He was worried she wouldn't want that kiss once he bared himself.

An impossibility.

"Take off your shirt." She donned her diva personality again, making demands for her pleasure alone.

He blinked three times and fisted his hands briefly. Never breaking eye contact, he toed off his black oxfords and removed his socks, working methodically. She enjoyed the show and his current state of dress. There was something about a man in bare feet, the casual ease of it—all black slacks and stylish shirt up top, unfussed repose below.

He untucked his shirt next, then slipped the top button through its hole. Then the next, and the next. By the end, the edges of his black shirt hung open, exposing a column of skin and smattering of chest hair. It wasn't enough. "All the way."

"Demanding."

"It's the dressing room. You've turned me into a diva."

"I've been meaning to talk to you about your temperamental nature." Smirking, he let his shirt drift to the ground, and her knees liquefied. Not because puckered skin covered a football-sized section of his left ribs or most of his abdomen. Not because of the angry scar slicing from his right pec to his waist. He was showing her his battle wounds, the pain he'd endured, the colors that had shaped the man he'd become.

This was his self-portrait and she wanted to kneel at its beauty. *Honored* didn't describe how his vulnerability weakened her in the very best way.

She closed the distance between them and touched the wrinkled skin over his ribs. "A burn?"

"Yes." The reply came out like a whispered secret.

She traced the long scar down his midsection. "And this?"

"A stab wound." The soft light articulated his muscles as his abs tensed under her explorations. "Can I touch you now?" he asked.

"I'm not done yet."

His fingers twitched. "I can't wait."

He grabbed her hips and pulled her against him. "Unless you want the rest of my skin to burn, I suggest you let me grab that glorious ass of yours." He took handfuls of her behind, his head tipping forward as he ground against her. "Glorious," he murmured.

His reaction to her curves made her happy she'd never swapped bodies with Emma Stone or anyone else. It also shattered her composure. Studying his self-portrait could wait until later. She was flammable. She needed his skin on hers, his hands kneading her flesh like he'd never felt a woman before. They had weeks of pent-up longing to obliterate.

They kissed and moaned, hands groping, teeth nipping.

"Pants," she said as she dug her nails into his shoulders.

Unwilling to stop kissing his neck and chest, removing his pants involved some laughs and hopping. Then he was against her again, his boxer briefs barely containing his magical *sword*. It was as large as she'd drawn on her door. She tried to climb his body.

Chuckling, he walked them to his bed. "The bee is also a monkey."

"Do you think now is a good time for bee jokes?"

"Anytime is a good time for bee jokes." Manhandling her hips, he tossed her onto his mattress. But she wasn't having it. She needed to feel him. Touch him. She pushed to her knees and dipped her hand into his boxers. She sighed as he groaned.

He swayed on his feet. "Stop."

"No." The silk-hard feel of him shredded her sense.

He growled and pulled away, then shucked his boxers, giving her the view she'd imagined on repeat. Curls of blond hair dusted the unburned sections of his chest—the same hair that trailed toward the sword her prince wore proudly. His length twitched. Wet heat pooled between her thighs, and she couldn't look away. Huxley wasn't a bulky man. He was the naturally trim sort with broad shoulders and a narrow waist. He stood with unabashed confidence, his strong thighs flexed, no longer hesitant to let her see his body. That alone turned her molten.

He joined her on the bed, his purposeful movements forcing her to lie back. Kneeling between her legs, he spent his promised time nosing and kissing her ugly birthmark before removing her bra and easing her red panties down. He hovered over her, proud cock twitching. Every inch of her pale skin was exposed.

He traced circles around her nipples, then lazy shapes downward. He palmed her center. "Red really is my new favorite color."

She wasn't sure if he was referring to her discarded lingerie or the curls he was toying with. She didn't care. "Touch me."

"I am touching you."

"*Please.*" She wasn't above begging.

Her knees fell wider, and he caught his breath. "So wet for me." He stroked her, reverent glides that drove her mad. Kneeling fully, he gripped the base of his shaft as he worked her, like he was stemming his desire. When he pressed his thumb where she ached most, her hips spasmed. "Stop teasing me."

"I can't."

"Huxley..."

"*Beatrice...*"

Her hips jerked again, everything inside her coiled tight. She'd never been so responsive to someone in bed. She'd never felt like she had family, until this prince of a man had welcomed her into his. She never wanted to please someone so badly, to be the reason he cried out in pleasure. But it was she who cried out. He pushed two fingers inside her, his thumb working overtime, all teasing gone. Like on the dance floor, he directed her body, controlled her moves. He kept his distance, though. He watched as a twist of his fingers made her gasp.

His eyes flared. "My expressive Honeybee."

His crooning undid her, and her belly furled into a feverish knot, tingles blooming at the edges. She bit her lip. His magic fingers worked her over until she dissolved under him, because of him, his rapt attention stretching out her pleasure.

If she painted her self-portrait now, she'd be a vivid rainbow.

She trembled. "You've done that before."

"No." He pulled out his fingers and stroked her swollen flesh. "Never that."

Her heart squeezed. She understood what he meant. They weren't virgins. Nothing they would do tonight would be a first, but it would be new. It would be earthshattering, because it was them.

She reached for him, needing more. "I'm desperate to feel you inside me."

24

Huxley didn't think he could want Beatrice more, but the need in her breathy voice blinded him. Which was unacceptable. He needed to see every shudder of her body, every arch of her back. He licked the fingers he'd had inside her, stealing a taste, a meager tease that would have to suffice. As much as he wanted to feast on Beatrice Baker, his willpower was waning.

He grabbed a condom from his dresser and dropped it beside her. "If you're desperate, I'm a lost cause. But I still have some business to attend to."

Business that included worshipping her spectacular breasts. Everything about Beatrice was soft and lush—her glorious ass, the generous swells he now cupped. He had large hands, and she was more than a handful, pale pink nipples puckered just for him. He rolled his tongue around them. He sucked and kissed and squeezed until his vision blurred.

Her frenzied hands tugged his hair. "Now," she begged.

A demand he couldn't deny. Condom in hand, he fitted himself between her thighs and tore the packet with his teeth. "You're mine, Beatrice. All mine."

She scratched her nails down his thighs. "My magic man."

His throat burned at the declaration. "Yours alone."

She'd owned him since the day he'd sat in her car, inhaling her watermelon scent, marveling at her eccentric paintings. He'd be hers as long as she would have him.

He rolled down the condom and positioned himself at her entrance, holding still for a beat. Her red hair was haphazard, her creamy skin a vision on his dark sheets. She wasn't looking at his burned flesh or the gnarly stab wound cleaving his torso. Her rainstorm eyes were locked on where they were about to join. She was panting for him, disfigured body and all.

"Yours," he repeated. A decree. A law he'd like to pass.

Then he pushed in.

Her hot pressure wrapped around him, inch by glorious inch. They both groaned, potent sighs they'd waited weeks to unleash. Sighs of pleasure. Sighs of rightness.

Sighs of *fucking* perfection.

Her face tightened then softened. He stroked her cheek. "Okay?"

She nodded. "Deeper."

The vixen read his thoughts. He lifted her hips and seated himself to the hilt. She released a small cry. His rough grunt chafed his throat. Their hips were flush, but it wasn't enough contact. Nothing would ever be enough. He dropped to his elbows and caged this fascinating woman. He rolled his pelvis.

"God, Huxley." She rocked, meeting his languid strokes.

"You feel so good. So perfect."

Each rotation got better, hotter, *wetter*. Her breasts were crushed to his chest, her knees hitched high. He dragged in and out of her, again and again. The same steady rhythm, but there was nothing stable about his spiking pulse or the heat fisting his gut.

Heaven had nothing on Beatrice Baker.

She clutched the back of his head and claimed his mouth in a blistering kiss. "Faster."

"No."

"*Yes.*"

"Not if you want this to last." Sweat gathered along his spine, each rolling thrust intensifying his pleasure. He was strung taut, a minute from exploding, desperate for their connection to be earthshaking for her.

She ground against him, urging him on. "Next round can be slow."

He was so intent on enjoying every second with her, he'd forgotten this was just the beginning. They'd have endless days to explore each other and eat her awful breakfasts and watch reruns on TV. To perform at night, then come home and make more magic between the sheets.

She clenched around him, an internal squeeze that lacerated his resolve. Slow was no longer an option. Lifting to his knees, he canted her hips and gave her all he had. All his angst in the past years. All his fear that someone wanted to do her harm. All his gratitude for her appearance in his life. Nothing had ever felt this *right*.

"God, Huxley. Yes. Like that. *Yes!*" She came on a cry, incoherent sounds that shot his ego to cloud nine.

His body tensed, more pleasure than he'd ever felt barreling up his thighs in a mind-numbing rush, the strength of it flooring him. His release came in shuddering waves. His arms shook. His body spasmed. The last snap of his hips winded him, and he barely kept from collapsing on her.

Soft kisses on his face returned him to reality, as did the gentle strokes on his back. "That was a whole lotta *wow.*"

He nipped her neck. "You read my mind."

"Be my valentine," she whispered.

He chuckled, fighting not to slip out of her yet. "Valentine's Day isn't for nine months."

She hugged him tighter. "I know."

Ah.

Beatrice wanted to be his, not just for tonight or a few months. She wouldn't take off because the mood struck her, like he'd worried. She was his zigzag girl. His watermelon woman. She was looking ahead, seeing him in her future, and he'd be an idiot to mess this up.

He felt himself thickening again, his lust growing with the swell of his heart. "I'd love to be your valentine."

Round Two involved him burying his face between her legs until she begged him to stop. Round Three was so slow and tortuous sweat slicked their skin and the room temperature shot to scorching.

They lay latched together now—legs threaded, fingers tangled, the morning hours creeping closer. His room smelled of Beatrice and sex.

Each time she blinked, her lashes brushed his chest. "What happened," she asked softly, "the night your father died?"

If she'd asked the question before tonight, he might have simplified the truth. Left out details and given her generalities. But she was his valentine now. If he wanted her to drop her guard and not hide behind her smiles, he'd have to offer the same.

A streetlight filtered through his window, lighting the top hat on his dresser, the Max Marlow poster on his wall, the cape he'd carelessly tossed on his floor when changing tonight. All memories of his father. "I was the only Marlow who went to his last show. Fox and Axel were tired of the same routine. Xander and Paxton hated the magic scene. But I loved watching my dad. He did this yearly number where he lowered himself into a water-filled barrel, handcuffed. The crowd always went nuts for it and applauded like mad when he popped out of the top. The last time didn't go as planned."

Beatrice ran her nose back and forth along his chest. Such a simple gesture. So much affection in it. It made him wish he *could* write a romance novel and base every heroine on her—captivating, strong, full of life.

"He was in the barrel too long," he went on. "I knew it, but if there was one thing my dad drilled into me growing up, it was to never lose the illusion. Don't break character or let the audience see your tricks. But there was a dent in the side of the barrel he hadn't noticed. It didn't give him the room he needed to release the handcuffs. He was locked inside, drowning, and I stood and watched." Bitterness coated his throat. Nine years of regret.

"It wasn't your fault."

He'd heard the same before, but not from everyone. "Tell that to my brothers."

"Fox and Axel?"

"No. They love the theater and were as obsessed with magic as me. They knew the drill when it came to performing. But Paxton and Xander resented everything magic-related, and it caused a rift between them and our father. Dad neglected them and focused on us. There was a lot of bad blood, but that didn't stop Pax and Xander from losing it after Dad died. They were furious I didn't do something sooner, blamed me for caring more about the illusion than our father. They weren't wrong."

"No, no. They *were*."

He didn't answer. Max Marlow had taken risks with his routines. It was why his father had organized life insurance and planned a detailed will, down to an infuriating puzzle box Huxley would probably never open. But Huxley had known something had been wrong that night. No matter his father's teachings and the audience watching, he'd known, and he hadn't acted. He'd lost his father because of it, and he'd alienated Paxton and Xander in the process.

"And the scars?" She traced his burns. "How'd they happen?"

It was another bedtime story he wished he didn't have to tell, but she needed to hear it all. He tucked loose hairs behind her ear and breathed her in. "When I realized Dad was gone, I stumbled into the first bar I found and drank my body weight in vodka. They eventually stopped serving me, so I hit another bar, where I wound up picking a fight with the wrong guys."

A lot of that night was a blur, but not his fury. His absolute *rage*. "I could barely see, but my mouth worked just fine, and I mouthed off. I wanted to punch something or someone. Or maybe I wanted to get punched. Whatever I said was enough to have several guys hauling me into an alley."

"Baby," she murmured, stroking his scarred chest.

His face and body were a constant reminder of how he'd failed his father, the choices he'd made, but he didn't remember the last time he'd spoken about that night. Nine years ago, probably. Tonight, in his valentine's arms, in a dark room, the words tumbled out. "As far as anyone figures, I got stabbed with something rusty that wasn't a knife. My ear got mangled in the process, as did my face, probably while I fought back. Then some guys held me down while others poured alcohol on me. They lit me up."

Beatrice sucked in a sharp breath. She kissed his mutilated ear, then the scars within her reach.

"It's okay, Honeybee. It was nine years ago."

She fussed over him some more. "If I told you about someone dousing me in alcohol and lighting me on fire, would you be okay right now?"

He stiffened. No. He would not. It made him think about Big Eddie and threats and his sweet girl fighting for her life. "Point taken."

She pushed onto her elbow. "Who found you?"

"Fox," he said, swallowing through his tension. "He followed my trail, dragged our other brothers with him. They got there shortly after the flames caught. Much longer, and the burns would have been way worse. But it was the stab wound that had me laid up awhile. Whatever they used tore up my insides and left a nasty infection."

Fierce determination sparked in her startling gray eyes. "Don't you ever get drunk and pick a fight again. I won't allow it."

Since he made it a habit not to lie, he said, "Promise you won't, either."

"I'm more likely to vandalize property than start a fight."

That she was. And he couldn't promise he'd never succumb to that level of violent despair again. One thing that night had taught him was that he had a dark side. He wasn't above lashing out when life turned on him. The past month, Beatrice Baker had become an integral part of his world. If something happened to her, his anger would raze the earth.

25

The last thing Bea wanted was to leave her love nest and fly to New York, even for a night. Being Huxley's valentine was better than building Skittles castles. She'd rather lie in bed with him than paint over all the taupe in the world. But here she was, packing a bag to meet Maude the Dog, while Huxley lounged on her bed in nothing but black briefs, flipping through a *Bon Appétit* issue, pretending like he wasn't distracting her.

He stopped flipping and studied a page. "I need to make this snapper."

Such a comment shouldn't be considered seductive, but Huxley was half-naked, his hair still askew from her busy fingers. Everything out of his mouth was foreplay.

"I like fish," she said distractedly.

His teeth scraped his bottom lip, an adorable move that made him look more boy than man. "The smoked paprika is a cool touch."

"Yeah...cool." What was cool? All she saw was the red mark she'd left on his shoulder.

He scratched his chest. "We'll have taco night when you get back."

Yep. Nibbling. Scratching. This was some serious foreplay, and talking tacos was definitely a euphemism. She stopped packing. "Why are you torturing me?"

He cocked his head. "With fish tacos?"

She gestured in his general direction. "With that."

He looked down at his bare chest. "This?"

"All of you. It's too much."

The devil smirked. "Tell me more."

If she started gushing about her obsession with him, she'd never stop. She thought about him constantly while working the market and couldn't wait to perform with him on stage. The sex they'd had in her diva dressing room (all three times) had blown her mind. More of her self-portrait squares were being painted with Huxley as her muse, and waking next to him made smiling all day as natural as breathing. He'd cut gambling out of his life to make her feel secure and give their relationship a chance. His brothers felt like family. New Orleans felt like home.

She didn't want to fly to New York.

"I should delay my trip," she said. "I can start the commission later. It's too soon to leave our nest. Lightning could strike the apartment while I'm gone, or you could get swallowed by an earthquake."

He tossed his magazine aside and patted the spot in front of him. She was already dressed in her lucky polka dot top and pink pedal pushers. She shouldn't wrinkle her clothes or muss her makeup by lying anywhere near Huxley Marlow. Her body, however, was beyond her control. He was the due north to her fluttering heart.

Once she lay on her side, facing him, he placed his palm on her hip. "You'll only be gone one night. Nothing will change. The apartment will still be here. I'll be here. There will be fish tacos and *CSI* reruns when you get back. But I'll miss you."

He was right. She was being silly. One night away was nothing. Yet unease prickled her neck. The last time she'd been this excited about something was for art school. That happy ending had resembled more of an oil spill.

She shook off the memory. "I'll miss you, too, but it'll allow us to have a prodigiously fabulous reunion. You can surprise me at the airport. We'll run into each other's arms."

"Prodigiously?"

"The most prodigious."

He did that thing where he looked at her like she was a unicorn. He kissed her cheeks, her forehead, her nose. Anywhere but her Cherry-Bomb lips. "Will you manage to act surprised?"

"Seeing that look in your eyes always surprises me."

This time his pupils flared. He claimed her lips, not a care to her lipstick or her impending flight. He kissed her deeper, and she gave as good as she got. In seconds, Cherry Bomb was smeared on them both. "We look like sex-crazed clowns."

He smacked her behind. "Best get you cleaned up, then."

Before she got up, she pulled an envelope from under her pillow. She'd removed spending cash from her commission advance and hadn't bothered with a deposit yet. With all Huxley had done for her—offering her a home, cooking beautiful meals, paying for more than he should—she wanted to contribute.

She toyed with the edge of the envelope. "There's eighteen hundred dollars in here. I want you to put some toward rent and food and use the rest to help fix the car."

He didn't move to accept it. "No."

"Yes."

"Your diva attitude doesn't work with me."

She scowled at him. "Aren't I intimidating?"

He swiped some rogue Cherry Bomb staining her upper lip. She sighed. Messy lipstick wasn't intimidating.

"My car has been fixed free of charge—some favor owed to Fox and Axel, and now that I've paid for the construction work and our shows are packed, money is less of an issue. You'll also be receiving a weekly paycheck for your assistant services. If you want to help with rent or groceries down the line, that's fine. But you're just starting your business. I'd rather you save what you earn. Take art classes and buy painting supplies."

She almost launched a rebuttal, claiming she didn't want his charity, that performing with him and conquering her stage fright were reward enough. But saving for more art supplies was important, and he was wearing his lie-detector face. He meant business. At least her surprise gift for him was almost done. A thank-you painting he wouldn't be able to refuse.

She pressed the envelope to his bare chest. "Hold this for me, then. Until I have time to set up a new account. Use it for our fancy fish tacos. But if you're in a tight spot and can't make rent, or you need help with the theater, you have to promise to tell me. I want to contribute."

He snatched the envelope from her hand and planted a kiss in the center of her palm. "It's a deal. Now get up and pack before I strip you out of those sinful pink pants."

———

Huxley hated watching Beatrice pack. He despised the notion of sleeping without her. The thought of her traveling alone made him itch. He'd never felt so protective of a woman. He wasn't sure if it was Big Eddie's threats, or the way he sometimes danced with her on a whim, in the living room or on the sidewalk, or that he pretended to fiddle with his puzzle box while she painted. He barely noticed the box those days. He wasn't sure she knew she hummed while she painted, soft and soothing. What he did know was that he was in deep with her.

They ate a non-crunchy-egg breakfast, then he pulled on his boots, happy-to-wear jeans, and a Gryffindor T-shirt on his day off. Not happy to say goodbye to Beatrice.

He'd surprise her with something for her return. Maybe paint her a unicorn. A grand scene with arching rainbows. His artistic creativity was limited to stage performing, but he was pretty sure she'd enjoy his lame efforts. First he had to visit the theater and pay Trevor the last of what he owed.

He escorted her to her car and kissed her nose. Anything else and he'd wind up covered in her lipstick again. "Text me when you get there."

She ran her hand through his hair. "Text me when you think of me."

"I'll blow up your phone."

She smiled his favorite smile—loose and carefree. "Maybe not *every* time."

"Morning, Huxley!" Mrs. Yarrow waved from her front garden, flanked by her colorful flowers. Her yellow top barely contained her spray-tanned cleavage.

He averted his eyes. "Garden's looking great."

"I got that mulch I told you about. It's done wonders. Come by later—I'll show you my azaleas."

An irritated grunt sounded from Beatrice. "I bet she wants to show you her *azaleas*."

Chuckling, he brushed his thumb between her brows, erasing the puckered line wrinkling her forehead. "Are you jealous of a sixty-year-old woman?"

They eyed their neighbor in all her over-tanned glory. If the leathery skin didn't turn him off, the blond bouffant and bloated lips would do the trick. As would her marital status. Mrs. Yarrow's grin slipped as she swatted something by her face. A bee, likely.

Beatrice was unamused. "Injuring her would be self-defense."

He couldn't argue. If he saw more bees, he might have to torch the garden.

"Have fun with Maude the Dog." He walked backward to his Mustang parked across the street, not wanting to take his eyes off Beatrice.

Instead of smiling at the sight of his restored car, she pouted. "I kind of miss my chicken scratches. They reminded me of meeting you."

As thankful as he was for that night, he'd rather walk around in Ugg boots than continue driving a defaced car. He smoothed his hand over the midnight blue side, caressing his other beauty. His father would no longer be turning in his grave. "You misspelled part of it, anyway."

She opened her door and stepped one foot inside. "I could do it again. Get it right."

"I'll pass. But if you want to text me more about masturbating with whipped cream, don't hesitate."

She scrunched her face in an adorable scowl.

He winked. The whipped cream gave him ideas.

They slipped into their respective cars. They closed their doors and started their engines, but he suddenly felt lost, like when he walked into a room and forgot what had taken him there. As though there was something he should have done before leaving. Frowning, he ran a mental tally of his morning: the oven hadn't been turned on, no taps were left running. He'd made sure to turn off all the lights. He frowned harder, and a strange ache spread through his chest.

Beatrice drove off first, but he met her at the second stoplight. They idled, side-by-side, and that odd sensation returned, stronger this time. Her windows were rolled up, but he could tell she was listening to music: she bopped her head and drummed her *SMILE* steering wheel.

Lost in the moment, she didn't notice him, but he was entranced. Cast under her unicorn spell. She was so full of life. Of fun. Of laughter. Her silliness filled the growing cavity in his chest. It swamped him with something new, a deeper affection that had him looking at the mostly cloudy sky above and seeing only shafts of light.

Love. Pure, unadulterated love poured into him.

That's what he forgot, what he should have said as they'd stood outside the apartment, at their cars, joking about long-distance texts.

He should have told Beatrice Baker he was in love with her.

He honked, and she jumped. Unlike most people caught singing in their car, she didn't get embarrassed and stop. She sang harder. She shook her shoulders and bobbed her head, making a perfect fool of herself. He fucking loved her for it, and he needed to tell her. Now. Before she left. Before this strange cavity in his chest widened.

He lowered his window, palms turning slippery, but the light changed. She blew him a kiss and drove ahead. He edged forward and waited to make his left turn. He waited for the hollow in his gut to shrink.

Trevor was waiting for him at the theater, paint-splattered workpants on. "Wasn't sure we'd get it done in time, but the guys hauled ass."

Huxley stepped back to take in his theater. The second story windows weren't streaked with cracks. The columns and cornices gleamed red, white, and gold in the partly sunny light, no chips visible. The brick exterior was freshly painted. New exterior lights hung over the Marlow Theater sign, and the gutters ran in a straight line. Max Marlow would be proud.

Huxley was proud.

As frustrated as he'd been with his inability to fund this restoration until now, he hadn't realized how much he'd needed this. Beatrice wasn't the only reason he'd been happier and sleeping better, seeing sun through the gray. For the first time in years, he felt worthy of wearing his father's top hat and cape. Never again would he let his theater fall into such disrepair.

The interior still needed major TLC, but he'd finish it slowly, as money came in. He'd keep introducing new routines. New music. Find ways to entertain crowds and fill seats.

He'd keep Max Marlow's legacy going strong.

He handed Trevor his final payment. "Can't thank you enough. Anytime you want to attend a show, let me know."

The big man massaged his dark beard. "Can't say magic shows are my thing, but I have a twenty-year-old stepdaughter who just about fainted when I told her I was working on a project here."

That kind of female fanfare had Axel written all over it. Huxley shuddered. He'd never strip on stage, but Axel was apparently born to strut his stuff. "Tell her to mention your name when she calls for tickets. She can bring a few guests."

Trevor clapped him on the back. "She'll go nuts for that. Gotta run to a big job. Don't you dare scratch the paint."

He'd bubble wrap the building if he could. As it stood, he'd oversee ongoing upkeep instead of winding back here again.

Edna shuffled past him to her ticket booth, pausing briefly to scowl at Trevor's back. "Those hooligans done making a racket? It's hard to work with all that hammering and yattering."

By "work," Edna meant solving her crossword puzzles.

Unfazed by her ornery attitude, Huxley admired his repaired building. He pictured his father at his side, proud arm slung over his shoulder. Maybe he'd visit him tonight, a quiet theater evening while Beatrice was away. "Dad would love it," he said to Edna.

She scoffed. "You Marlow boys aren't the brightest lot."

He scratched his cheek, unsure where that zinger had come from. "Then why do you still work for us?"

"I believe in charity work."

He was too pleased with the completed façade to unpack that riddle. He lifted his phone to snap photos of Trevor's work. His court date was in two days, and the session would be cut and dry. He'd reinstate the Marlows good name. It was smooth sailing from here.

Except it wasn't.

Huxley was determined to surprise Beatrice with a gift, but he painted about as well as he knitted, which was pitifully. His afternoon was spent huddled in front of a large canvas, unsure how the purple he'd intended had turned brown.

"Stupid paints," he mumbled as he fisted his brush.

His painting was supposed to depict a wild unicorn leaping from one rainbow to another. Free and colorful, like his watermelon girl. He'd used his pink pony as the model but the painted version resembled more of a mutant-horse with a penis attached to its head. He still couldn't wait to see her reaction to his efforts.

Evening had come and gone and he hadn't eaten dinner. He hadn't even tackled the background yet. The only times he'd stopped were when his phone had buzzed with texts.

Like now.

It was past two a.m. He wasn't expecting Beatrice to still be up, but he wasn't complaining. This time there were no funny quips about wishing she could roller skate on her client's marble floors or about Maude crushing on a neighbor's Chihuahua. Instead she sent a selfie of herself with her new favorite poodle, cuddled together on a plush dog bed.

He grinned. Trying to capture her delight in a painting was a fool's errand. That kind of sunlight couldn't be bottled. She couldn't and shouldn't be tamed.

Leaving the background for tomorrow, he grabbed his keys and drove to the theater. He may have lost the chance to tell Beatrice he loved her before she left, but he would tell her the second she returned. He would tell his father now. It may be silly, sitting in a darkened theater, speaking to no one. Maybe Max Marlow heard him on those lonely nights. Maybe not. But this wouldn't be the sad confessions of a lost son. This would be the declarations of someone finally found.

He parked across the street. His rumbling engine faded—an engine he and his father had rebuilt. The timing was perfect, having the car fixed along with the theater. Everything was falling into place. He closed the door and traced the hood's pinstripe. Good thing it was a thin detail, not a bold design. Any larger, and Beatrice might not have mistaken it for her ex's car. She wouldn't have upended his life.

Shoving his hands in his pockets, he crossed the street, a faint smile tugging at his lips. Just thinking about his zigzag girl made him smile. So simple yet astounding, how love could transform your world. Turn half-empty glasses half full. If he wasn't careful, he'd start skipping down the street.

The area was quiet and peaceful at this hour, the perfect backdrop to his pleasant musings. Then he heard the unmistakable hiss of spray paint and the clattering of a can hitting cement.

The direction of the noise could only mean one thing, a possibility that had Huxley's heart pounding in his ears as he raced toward his immaculate building. His gut lurched at the sight. His half-full grin slipped from his face.

Goddamn Oliphant.

26

Some punk blew past him, running like his ass was on fire, but Huxley didn't chase the kid or call after him. He stood frozen, the cement feeling unstable below his feet. All he could do was stare at the male genitalia scrawled over his newly refurbished theater.

There were several images spread around, but the largest was drawn with an artistic flair, of the comic book sort, with wings allowing this particular erection flight. It put Huxley's penis-mutant-unicorn to shame. It also brought bile to his throat. He'd exhausted every option but burglary to fix the theater. Repainting would cost another few *thousand*, and his court date was just over a day away. Spots flashed behind his eyes.

Considering Oliphant's history with defacing Max Marlow's posters with dick pics, this stunt had that mustache's germs all over it. It must be why Oliphant had been smug when Huxley had admitted he'd used his last dime upgrading his theater. Oliphant knew a blow right before his hearing would cripple him. It was an attempt to force him back to the poker table.

No fucking way.

Oliphant clearly hadn't thought through his sabotage. Huxley had his photos from earlier and Trevor's corroboration that the work had been done. He'd call the cops and make sure Oliphant paid for this.

His phone buzzed, and Huxley jumped. Oliphant's name and message enraged him further:

Return to the poker table tomorrow morning at eleven. If you don't show or if you call the cops, I'll send a note to the code enforcer about your shoddy electrical wiring.

Huxley nearly crushed his phone. How the hell had he discovered the electrical issues? Not that the *how* of it mattered. If the City learned about the faulty wiring, they might shut the theater down completely. Without the performances, he couldn't afford the repainting or electrical upgrades. It wouldn't just be the wiring, either. They'd see the lead pipes he needed to replace, the crumbling plaster.

They could label the building condemned.

How the fuck had he let this happen? After all his progress, how had he worsened his situation?

If Beatrice were here, she'd call Oliphant a spiny lumpsucker or feral warthog. Huxley considered him a conniving miscreant who belonged in Axel's straitjacket. Sadly, that didn't change this clusterfuck.

Instead of sinking to his haunches and pulling out his hair like he wanted, Huxley paced. He turned over his options. Calling the cops was out. Playing poker was a one-way ticket to losing Beatrice. That left unleashing Vito.

Huxley tapped out a message on his phone, each aggressive thumb punch vibrating up his wrists. *One word about the wiring and I tell Vito you've been stealing from Club Crimson's customers.*

Oliphant's reply came fast. Too fast, like he'd been expecting the threat. *Good thing Vito takes a cut of what I earn. Seems to me your only option is a poker game.*

Huxley's lungs ceased to function. He stared at the message like it had been sent to someone else. Like someone else's life was falling apart. Vito had been his ace. His backup plan. Without that, he was screwed.

Instead of picturing Max Marlow, proud arm slung over Huxley's shoulder, all he saw was his father glaring down at him, counting the ways his son had messed up. The theater was his brothers' livelihood. It was his father's legacy. Huxley couldn't let his family down like this. Again. Over and over: not saving his father when he should have, ruining Max Marlow's pride and joy, possibly losing the theater.

Huxley's mind drifted to Beatrice and their conversation before she'd left. She'd trusted him with her cash advance, saying she wanted to help with the rent, or future theater bills if help was needed. *Fuck*, he needed a miracle, and her eighteen hundred could be a start. The stake for a game. Just one more to squash Oliphant's threat. It would keep the street urchin from leaking the information in the short term. He'd have to figure out something else, a way to shake the man's vendetta for good, but this would buy him time.

Huxley paced. He waffled. He pictured Beatrice encouraging him to accept her money earlier, take her help. She'd wanted to contribute. She'd said it herself. Then he imagined explaining about *another* final poker game. Her perfect red lips would likely curl in disgust. She'd probably pack her bags and move out. Gambling her savings is exactly what her father had done. Exactly what Huxley promised he'd never do.

But if he didn't borrow that money, he'd have to tell his brothers they were out of work and watch as someone else took over their birthright.

He needed to speak with her. Explain what happened. Convince her there was no other option. Even with the late hour, he called her cell. The phone clicked over to voicemail.

"*Goddamn it.*" Of course it was switched off. Or the battery was dead.

He paced more. His jaw ached from grinding his teeth.

Instead of going home, he returned to his car and sat there, staring at nothing. He wasn't sure when he nodded off, but the squeal and hiss of a stopping bus jarred him awake. It was morning already. Hip-hop blared from a passing car. People hurried by on their way to work, some pausing to laugh at his building or snap a photo. His saliva turned rancid.

Tearing his gaze away, he tried Beatrice again. Voicemail, again.

A boisterous laugh drew his attention. Some bike messenger in spandex shorts was cackling at the theater. At Huxley. More shame heaped onto his shoulders. It was seven a.m., four hours before Oliphant's deadline. With no options left, he texted Beatrice.

You said I could use your money if the theater was in trouble.
It's in trouble.
I'm sorry. I hate to ask this.
But I need your money to stake one final poker game.
Oliphant had some kid graffiti the building.
He's threatened the theater as well.
I have no choice.

He stared at the texts he'd sent, wondering if he should follow with more of an explanation, pleas for help, but the ache he'd felt when she'd driven away before he'd confessed his love spread through him at an alarming rate. He felt gutted. A shadow of the partly sunny man he thought he'd become. He wasn't sure he was making the right choice. He wasn't sure the choices had ever been his to make.

Plunking his forehead onto his steering wheel, he closed his eyes. He still had to contact Oliphant and organize the poker game. He'd probably already primed the others, dangling bait for an impromptu match. Even the thought of besting Oliphant didn't fill a millimeter of the emptiness overtaking him. A bottle of vodka might do the trick.

Before he could pick up his phone or hit a liquor store, sharp rapping rattled his window.

Edna's snake-headed cane glared at him. He rolled down his window and kept his head a healthy distance away. "The theater's been vandalized," he said.

"I'm old, not blind. I know a flying johnson when I see one."

He sank into his seat. "I bet Dad wishes he sold the place off. Better than seeing all of this." He waved a defeated hand toward the snickering crowd.

Edna snorted. "Your father loved the theater, but he built it for you boys. To see you happy. So if you wanna keep disappointing him, then go ahead and toss away your life for that stack of bricks."

He nearly slammed his palms into his steering wheel. Edna didn't have a clue. She hadn't been there when Max Marlow had sat with Huxley in the darkened theater, telling his kids magic was in the Marlow blood, how performing brought joy to the world. "The theater was his life."

Her wrinkled mouth shriveled to half its size, and she jabbed her venomous cane at his face. "You *boys* were that man's life. He built his reputation for you. He died wanting to impress *you*. Which is exactly what you're doing—killing yourself to impress a ghost. If you wanna see a dead man happy, give him grandchildren, for heaven's sake. With the girl. She's not all bad."

Muttering about ungrateful kids, she hobbled toward her box office, brandishing her cane. The gawkers hurried away. Huxley pinched the bridge of his nose.

Edna Lisowsky was a crotchety old lady, but she'd known Max Marlow better than any of his children had. She'd spent her waking hours with the man. A fact that still befuddled him, as did the mystery of why she'd stuck around after his death. Unless she *had* been in love with the younger man, choosing nearness to his family over letting go, doling out snippy wisdoms and blunt advice instead of leaving. Max Marlow had been a handsome man, charismatic and charming. And love was a limitless thing, too big to end with death.

Vast. Immeasurable. Unflinching.

It was why heroes risked it all for their heroines even if it meant losing in the end. *Not* that he read romance novels or anything. But he had spent the past day reliving how Beatrice had danced with his cape while he'd fought their connection. He'd planned the perfect dinner for her return, excited to cook for her. He'd painted a deformed unicorn to make her smile, even though it had driven him nuts, and he'd do it again.

He loved her. He knew it. Yet instead of risking everything for her, he'd risked *her* for a goddamn piece of real estate.

"You look like hell." Fox slid into his passenger seat.

Huxley didn't reply. Nausea churned his gut. He couldn't play poker again, no matter the reason. Not if it meant losing Beatrice. Except he'd already texted her that he'd planned to play.

Like an idiot.

Axel shoved Fox's seat forward, earning him a few curses, and squeezed into the back. "If I see Oliphant, I will cut off his dick, attach wings to it, and fly it into his mouth."

It would be an amusing visual if Huxley wasn't a minute from puking. "Which is why I'd planned to call Vito, but he's working with Oliphant."

Fox, for once, wasn't thinking ten steps ahead. "What's Vito got to do with this?"

"Doesn't matter," Huxley mumbled. He should have listened to Fox's warning that Oliphant would retaliate with some sort of nefarious activity. Nothing to be done about that now, but the word *nefarious* winded him.

It made him ache for Beatrice even more.

Fox didn't push the issue. "What about the graffiti?" he asked. "Isn't the hearing tomorrow?"

Huxley sighed. "When the enforcer checks the building, he'll either extend our deadline because of the graffiti, or he'll assume we did it ourselves to delay the proceedings. If it's the latter, the court will find us in violation of the City order, we'll get slapped with a fine *and* have to repaint. They'll probably give us one last deadline, but it'll cost us. Either way, we need cash to fix this. And as much as that all sucks, the blight issue was only ever about the exterior. We have bigger problems now."

He went on to describe Oliphant's threat and the possibility of losing the theater if the City discovered the extent of their building's interior shortcomings. "Basically, we need more cash to fix the graffiti and I need to stop Oliphant from leaking our electrical issues, but I'll figure it out."

"You're an idiot."

Huxley reared back at Fox's insult, not that it was off the mark. He'd already surmised as much. "Tell me something I don't know."

"Okay. It's like you don't know you have family."

"Bullshit." All Huxley did was work to keep his brothers happy. Pay for their furniture, vet bills, magic conferences. Keep them employed.

Fox gestured aggressively between Axel and himself. "Us two guys, your brothers—remember us? We care about the theater, too. And I'm tired of you thinking you have to do everything alone. So, *I'll* call Trevor and a couple other guys about repainting. We'll scrape together cash for a fine if it comes to that and raise more for the work, but the operating word here is *we*. This isn't your burden alone, and I'm tired of you thinking it is. And when I'm done making those calls, I'll deal with Oliphant. I have something on him that will shut him up."

Huxley narrowed his eyes at his brother. "What exactly is this something?"

Fox's face was as unreadable as usual. "Don't ask me about it, like I won't ask you about the Vito angle that went bust. But if you'd called me right away instead of facing everything on your own, you wouldn't be sitting here, wallowing."

Axel said something about helping out, too, but the words barely registered. Huxley was too busy breathing through the dread suffocating him. He really was an idiot. He should have leaned on Fox and Axel, worked together instead of always trying to take care of them. He wasn't their father, and they were all older now. He no longer had to do the heavy lifting for the family. If Huxley had called Fox first thing he wouldn't have panicked. He wouldn't have asked Beatrice for a gambling loan.

She could be reading his texts now. Cursing him. Writing him off. He couldn't shake the fear that he'd screwed things up with her, no matter his next move.

Edna's advice was there, too. The soundtrack to his anxiety. "Do you think Dad regrets leaving me the theater? Seeing it like this?"

Axel leaned over the center console. "What was his other option, leave it to me?"

Huxley almost laughed. "I mean the choices I made. I know he wanted to see his legacy go on, but I could have sold it from the start. Split the profits. It would have left us cash. Maybe Xander and Paxton wouldn't have taken off. Or I could have sold it when you guys asked me to, when business started getting worse. Then Dad wouldn't have to look down and watch it all fall apart."

A teenager in basketball shorts rode his bike past the theater. Abruptly, he did a one-eighty and stopped in front of it. The kid proceeded to crack up.

Fox mumbled, "Asshole," then said, "Dad didn't leave you the theater because he couldn't stand the idea of losing it. He left you the theater to keep us together." When Huxley didn't reply, Fox shook his head. "Without the theater, we would have drifted apart. Xander and Paxton had no intention of sticking around, even if the accident never happened. Their issues with Dad and our family drama ran deeper than that. And we never should have asked you to sell the building. We did that because we were worried about the stress it was putting on you. We should have pushed harder to be involved instead."

"But if I sold it, you guys wouldn't be living paycheck-to-paycheck."

"You're right. I'd probably be picking pockets in my spare time, and Magic Mike here"—Fox jutted a thumb toward Axel—"would be working the porn circuit. We'd barely see one another, let alone work together."

Axel smacked Huxley's shoulder. "If that's what I would've been doing, then hell yeah—he'd be pissed. *I'm* pissed. You should've sold the theater." Always the comedian.

Fox held Huxley's eyes, both of them ignoring Axel as Fox's reasoning sank into Huxley's thick skull. Without the theater, they wouldn't be as close as they were. A flying penis didn't change that. It couldn't take away joking and laughing over bowls of his seafood pesto pasta. It couldn't replace two brothers who did God knew what to fix his vandalized car. Busting his ass to save the theater was about keeping the remains of his family together. That would make his father proud, and finding love was the standing ovation to that performance. The best natural high there was.

Love he might have lost. "I screwed up," he told his brothers, then explained about texting Beatrice for help and betraying her trust. He may not have actually agreed to the game with Oliphant, but asking for the money was as low as he could have sunk.

"You're an ass." Axel's glare could cut ice. "You don't meet girls like Bea every day. You said yourself, poker is a deal breaker for her."

He was lucky to *ever* have met a girl like Beatrice. "It was a knee-jerk reaction. With the blackmail and everything, my head was spinning. I wasn't thinking clearly."

Fox upped his volume a notch. "So why are you talking to us instead of groveling to her?"

"She's away."

"Call her!"

He wasn't sure why Fox was yelling. Fox didn't lose his cool. He barely ever cracked a smile. "Her phone's probably dead," Huxley said defensively. "The battery sucks."

Fox shoved his door open. "I'm heading to get some graffiti remover to Band-Aid that catastrophe, while you get ahold of Bea and figure out how to get her back. Don't fuck up. She's your match. Letting someone like that walk out of your life will be the biggest mistake you ever make."

Huxley was well aware of his idiocy. Didn't make hearing it any easier. "What do you know about love? You haven't dated in ages." Even after their recent shows, Fox would flirt with women who'd stay behind, then leave by himself.

The fight drained out of Fox. "I know plenty. Not fighting for your soulmate will destroy you. Which is something else I need to take care of." He closed the door behind him, leaving Huxley speechless.

Axel stared at Fox's empty seat. "What just happened?"

"Don't ask me." Something was up with his brother, or *someone*, but all that mattered right now was Beatrice. Not fighting for her and begging for her forgiveness would destroy Huxley. It would turn him into the surliest version of himself. Asking to use her cash for another poker game had been unacceptable, all because he'd put the building first and believed he was disappointing a man who'd died nine years ago.

Huxley kicked Axel out of his car, then spent the next twenty minutes texting Beatrice. Each apology made him sicker. Clammy sweat coated his palms. He left a few voicemails, too, while praying Fox's contact would eliminate Oliphant as a threat.

Now he could only wait.

Beatrice's plane would arrive at four p.m. He'd have to spend the morning with his brothers, doing what they could to scrub a portion of the graffiti off, then he'd meet her at the airport, heart and bag of Skittles in hand, ready to beg and plead for his woman.

27

Painting Maude the Dog's portrait was going to be a blast. The standard poodle was the peacock sort who strutted down the street walking her master, not the other way around. She was sly and mischievous, hiding the remote control when ignored and opening door handles with a press of her paw. She had the hots for the next-door Chihuahua, and her choice of crystal-studded collars put Bea's wardrobe to shame. The purples, pinks, and blues she'd use to paint her likeness in tiny squares was sure to brighten up Arabella and her wife's polished home.

Armed with photos and a few rough sketches, Bea had switched to an earlier flight, eager to return home and get started. She would gather supplies today and wake up tomorrow, ready to paint. Arabella sent her off, thrilled with the plan, air-kisses offered to both cheeks. All Bea needed to perfect this perfect day was a working phone.

She'd fallen asleep after sending Huxley a dog-bed selfie and had woken up late to a dark screen. Too busy rushing to get organized and hail a cab, she hadn't had time to charge her phone, and she felt antsy. She never imagined herself a cyber addict, but she liked being connected to her magic man, even electronically.

She bounced her heel as she plugged her cell into the airport outlet. She needed to tell Huxley about her flight change, in case he planned to surprise her with a prodigiously fabulous reunion. The possibility had her fingers tapping in time to her jouncing heel.

Two boys stood across from her, one with buckteeth and a handful of cards, the other, a younger version of the older blond, in a *Transformers* T-shirt. The *Transformers* child picked a card from the fanned deck and peeked at his choice. Bea watched with glee, imagining a young Huxley playing cards with Fox or Axel. Wowing his siblings with a sneaky trick.

The older boy fanned his hand over the cards. The *Transformers* child stood rapt, studying the movement, searching for the trick behind the illusion. When the bucktoothed boy pulled a nine of hearts from the deck, his brother's jaw nearly hit the floor.

Bea clapped, unable to help herself. She'd never thought much about having kids, but she considered it now. She pictured Huxley falling asleep with their baby nestled against his chest, entertaining tykes with card tricks and disappearing coins. Cooking family meals. Making mashed potato sculptures and peanut butter paintings with her and their child.

She couldn't imagine a more colorful world.

She wasn't about to ambush him with talks of babies and forever, but the heartwarming fantasy made her realize her Huxley obsession was more of a Huxley love craze. Yep. She was fully, completely in love with her dashing magic man. She needed to tell him now. Share her growing glow before she erupted from the pure joy of it.

Giddy from her successful trip and her racing heart, she checked her phone for life. A bright screen glowed. She curled on her seat, unconcerned about wrinkling her polka dot dress. Not when she was about to tell Huxley she loved him more than all the candy in the world. He'd also do a fine job of rumpling her dress later, something she should suggest before takeoff.

But when she swiped to her home screen and saw forty-one missed texts from him, her playful mood plummeted.

Forty-one texts couldn't be good. Something might have happened to Fox. Or Axel. Or Della. A fire could have torn through the theater. Maybe Big Eddie had come looking for her and Huxley had gone all caveman on him and landed in jail. Or *maybe* Huxley had texted her every time he'd thought of her and blew up her phone after all.

Hoping for the latter, but expecting the worst, she tapped on his name.

You said I could use your money if the theater was in trouble.
It's in trouble.
I'm sorry. I hate to ask this.
But I need your money to stake one final poker game.
Oliphant had some kid graffiti the building.

She slapped a hand over her mouth and flipped her phone over, unable to read more. The white sash around her waist felt too tight. The stale terminal air lodged in her throat. *I read it wrong. I must have read it wrong.*

She reread the first four texts, eyes burning with each pass, ending with: *One final poker game.* The words glared at her, flashing like a neon sign, warning her of danger ahead. She flipped the phone back over, her vision clouding. The walls seemed to spin. The idea of someone vandalizing the theater pained Bea, but there was always one more. Then another *one more.*

A never-ending cycle of *one mores.*

But Huxley wasn't her father. He didn't drink excessively. He cared for his family. He was responsible in his surly responsible way, always putting others before himself. When in bed, he loved on her body with such devotion it blew her mind. He was also the man who'd returned inspiration to her dry creative well, and all he wanted was *just one more* poker game.

She reached for her phone, hands shaking, desperate to reply. *Of course,* she pictured herself writing. *I understand.* It was only money and she'd hate to see the theater damaged, but the sting behind her eyes worsened. She'd lived this life already. She swore she'd never do it again. Yet here she was, trying to convince herself he was different. That this time was different.

It was never different.

There were more messages, but she couldn't read them. There was no point. It was a page from her father's book, asking for money, then burying her indecision under a barrage of sentimental texts. She couldn't walk that road again. Not with a man who owned her heart. The breaking of it would hurt that much more.

Fingers trembling, she deleted his texts and powered off her phone. She boarded the plane and stared out the window.

Her trip to New York had been her first flight. She'd spent those two hours playing with her seat recliner and stowaway tray, chatting with the woman beside her about the magic of air travel and zooming across the skies. Her return trip, she saw nothing but the taupe interior.

A stocky man settled into the seat beside her and clicked his seatbelt on. "You headin' to New Orleans on vacation?"

She offered a flat, "Yes," then returned to her window perch. Her signature smile had gone AWOL, as had the bounce in her voice.

Living in New Orleans *had* been a vacation. An exhilarating rush. For a spell, she'd been a zigzag girl with a zigzag life and zigzag friends. For a spell, New Orleans had been home.

But home was permanent. Vacations always ended.

She wasn't sure where she'd go or what she'd do. Maybe buy a map and close her eyes, see where her finger landed. Drive to a new state. Be like her mother and travel where the mood took her. She could paint anywhere, live from the back of her Beetle. With tomorrow's court deadline, Huxley had likely already organized a poker game and spent her advance, but she'd have more cash coming in when Maude the Dog's portrait was complete.

She would find her smile and move on, like always. Except her chin trembled, and her chin never trembled. A traitorous tear pushed from her blinking eyes.

The flight home sped by too fast. She had to bite her cheek to avoid a full-on ugly cry as she grabbed her bag, but she thanked her lucky stars she'd switched flights. Seeing Huxley now would breach the wobbly dam stemming her tears.

The scenery blurred on her drive home. She didn't become her undercover cop persona, taking odd side streets in case Big Eddie was hot on her trail. She barely glanced in her rearview mirror. When she reached Huxley's street, her heart had become a battering ram intent on cracking her ribs. She drove by twice, ensuring his car wasn't there. She may not be an undercover cop, but she was a Navy SEAL, one who would slip into his apartment and out before he got home.

A polka-dotted Navy SEAL.

But five steps into the apartment, she froze. She dropped her bag and clutched her chest. A massive canvas leaned against the coffee table. Paints were strewn over her drop cloth, as were dirty brushes and muddied water. The makeshift studio

resembled a toddler's playroom, but it was the painting itself
that had those blasted tears finally breaking free.

Her marvelous Marlow boy had painted her a mutant
unicorn. There was a star on the animal's flank, a rainbow
below its hooves. Although the shape looked more giraffe
than horse, the phallic cone attached to its head gave its
unicorn-ness away. She didn't bother swiping at her tears or
biting her cheek. She dropped to her knees and released her
anguish in gushing sobs.

Dormant pain from her father's betrayal blasted out. Pain
from her mother's lack of mothering, from Nick the Prick,
from Tanya Fry's mean hair-dye stunt. The birthday parties
she'd never been invited to. Dropping out of school. Every
just one more she'd ever heard.

This was the mushroom cloud of squelched outrage she'd
been warned about. It was the ugliest of ugly cries. Snotty.
Hiccupy. *Loud.*

The anger wasn't directed solely at her past, though. It was
also aimed at herself. She'd been ready to sneak away without
confronting Huxley. Without telling him how hurtful those
texts had been. The same way she'd never told her father his
actions had shredded her heart.

Huxley had shown her how beautiful love could be. He'd
helped cure her stage fright and had lit her on fire to earn her
trust. He'd eaten her awful eggs and made love like a super-
hero. He had inspired her to paint. He didn't deserve to be
deserted, no explanation as to why she'd left. She owed it to
herself to unleash her pain. She owed him a chance to explain.
The idea of the confrontation made her feel sick, but leaving
was walking the path of least resistance.

That was her father's path.

Her tears diminished. Her gasping sobs lessened. She'd
been so distraught, she hadn't heard the front door open, or

the approaching footsteps. It wasn't until Adidas sneakers stood in front of her that she jumped and fell backward.

"Hello, Beatrice."

Holy crap.

Big Eddie was as tall as she remembered, his Hawaiian shirt tented slightly over his paunch. A gold chain hung around his neck, and the thick, bejeweled fingers of his right hand held a gun. This was not a drill. The thug who'd threatened to remove her fingers loomed over her, snarly grimace contorting his goatee.

He raised the weapon, and fear blasted through her.

She should scream or run, or headbutt him in his nuts since she was sitting at nut height. Instead she cried harder, unsure how she wound up at gunpoint, with the best-worst unicorn painting painted by the best man.

Another sob burst from her chest.

"Enough!" Big Eddie glowered at her, the barrel of his gun aimed at her face. "Shut the fuck up, already."

"But you're going to shoot me."

He waved his gun, like he was using it to paint the air. "Give me my cash, and you don't gotta worry about getting shot."

"I don't have the money." The reality of her situation had her scanning the room for a nearby kitchen knife or screwdriver, fruitlessly. Only a magic wand could lure a distant weapon to her spot on the floor.

"Fucking Franklyn Baker," he muttered. "Worthless piece of shit."

"I can't disagree. And I'd rather not die for him." She took one breath, then another. She had to think. Convince Big Eddie she'd pay him. Distract him long enough to get away.

"You should've thought about that before taking on his debt." Sweat ringed the large man's armpits. Something odd flickered in his eyes, a hint of hesitation?

She wiped her snotty nose and hoped to God that hesitation meant he didn't like the idea of hurting her. "You could lie. Say you couldn't find me." She tried to lean back and reach for her purse. Find her phone. Call for help.

His look of hesitation fled and his jaw hardened. "This ends one of two ways, girl. It's the cash or a bullet. You decide."

Terror gripped her chest. "Please. I'll get the money. It'll take time, but I'll find a way. Please, *please*...don't do this."

His sweating worsened, beads of moisture gathering along his neck. He adjusted his grip on the gun, pointed it at her heart, and she squeezed her eyes so tightly she saw spots. She prayed for it to be quick and painless as her pulse pounded in her ears. Her body quaked uncontrollably.

But nothing happened.

She cracked an eye open to find Big Eddie slumped slightly, his gun aimed at the ground. "You look so much like her," he said, the lines of his face slack.

"Like who?" She didn't know why he was waffling. She was breathing so fast she might pass out.

He scrubbed his free hand down his face and laughed bitterly. "Your mother lit up a room when she walked into it. Made me feel like I was fucking invincible. Then she left me for that asshole father of yours. I should kill you just for that. Teach 'em both what it's like to lose what you love."

Big Eddie? *This* was the guy her mother had been dating when she'd fallen for Franklyn Baker? That would explain his shock when Bea had entered the bar to negotiate with him, his hesitation now. If she didn't know better, she'd say Big Eddie liked the idea of shooting Bea—the daughter of the woman he once loved—as much as she liked the idea of being shot.

This was something she could work with. She was a performer now. Huxley had taught her the art of staging illusions. She'd learned from the best.

"My mother talked about you," she told Big Eddie, fisting her hands to control her shaking. "She said there was a guy she loved when she met my dad. I think she regretted her choices." A partial lie, but he wouldn't know, and Bea needed to play to his emotions. "If you hurt me, you'll be hurting her."

He shook his head and muttered under his breath. Then he glared at Bea. "If I don't get the cash I'm owed, it's my neck on the line. You gotta answer to me, and I gotta answer to folks worse than me."

Bea took a fortifying breath and said, "I have a suggestion about that."

28

Huxley's shoulder throbbed from scrubbing the graffiti, he had a headache from inhaling chemical fumes, and they'd barely made a dent. There were still penises. That were flying. He kept glancing at his watch, willing the time to fly instead.

Beatrice would be landing in three hours. That gave him one hundred and eighty minutes to review his apology and perfect his groveling. She had to give him a chance. Listen to him. He'd let her key fresh insults into his Mustang, if that's what it took. He'd eat her crunchy eggs every day. He would beg endlessly.

For now, he and his brothers dripped with sweat and frustration. Their fingers were red from the harsh chemicals. Huxley's worn jeans and stormtrooper T-shirt reeked of the stuff. That and guilt. He was the reason they were covered in grime. He'd poked Oliphant, had taunted him about that stupid dinosaur skull. He'd refused to let the man have a rematch because he'd made promises that he'd then broken.

Yet his brothers were still here.

Fox dropped his scrub brush in a bucket and wiped his hands on his jeans. His black T-shirt read, *This Shirt is Yellow*. "Break time."

Axel climbed down their stepladder. His T-shirt read, *World's Okayest Brother.* "My face has been next to a penis for the last hour. I need a shot of Jack."

Huxley passed him a Coke. "This'll have to do."

They stood in a semicircle, drinking Cokes, swiping their brows, glaring at the passing assholes laughing at their theater. At least they were together. Fox's mysterious contact had come through, forcing Oliphant to rescind his blackmail. Huxley had never hugged Fox so tightly, Axel joining in on their family moment. If Beatrice couldn't forgive him, if he'd really screwed things up, he'd always have them.

Somehow, he knew that fact wouldn't ease the sting.

Fox dropped his empty can in their garbage and picked up his phone from the ground. He tapped on the screen and frowned. His thumb moved quickly as his frown deepened. "We have a problem."

Axel belched. "Bigger than flying penises on our theater?"

Fox's tense eyes locked on Huxley. His brother's ticking jaw and unnerving stare filled Huxley with dread. "Did Oliphant do something else?"

"It's about Beatrice."

A strange buzzing filled Huxley's ears. Fox was the one who'd gathered intel on Big Eddie, a Chicago connection who knew a guy, who knew a guy, who worked with the loan shark's boss. "Is he in New Orleans?"

"He's at your apartment. Now. With her."

What the fuck? He shook his head, unwilling to process that horrifying fact. "Her flight doesn't land for another three hours."

"She must have switched flights."

No. No. Christ, *no.*

They flew into action as they spoke, all three jogging toward his car.

"She would have called." Huxley was still in denial.

"She didn't," Fox said.

Because he'd texted her, asking to use her money, telling her he needed to play poker. Because he'd won the Dumbest Man Alive contest. Now she was in trouble, hurt, or worse.

Axel held up a hand. "Toss me your keys."

He lobbed them over awkwardly while tripping on a pothole. It was like he couldn't coordinate his limbs or see the road. He could barely think, let alone drive. This was his fault. All of it. If she walked out of his life, couldn't forgive or trust him again, he'd have to deal eventually. Accept his fate and trudge forward. The notion devastated him, but if something bad happened to Beatrice Baker, the sun would never shine again, his heart would shrivel up inside his chest. The Marlow Theater he thought he needed could crumble to the ground. Nothing would lessen that blow.

"She'll be fine," Axel said as they piled into the Mustang.

Huxley slammed the passenger door behind him and repeated the mantra. *She will be fine. She will be fine.* He white-knuckled the door handle as he asked his father for the biggest favor of his life. He promised every god in existence a repentant life, if only Beatrice would be okay.

"She'll be fine," Fox repeated from the backseat.

Not even his farsighted brother's prediction could calm his jackhammering heart.

⸻

Bea wrinkled her nose but otherwise remained still. "Take the shot before I throw up."

Big Eddie hovered over her prostrate body, gun in hand. "You sure about this?"

"Positive."

He scratched his neck. Red splotches flared under his irate rubbing. "If it don't work, I'll be fed my balls. Look worse than you do now."

She hoped she looked bad. Awful. Dead as the deadest doornail. She had ketchup splattered on her polka dot dress, dripping from her neck and mouth. A circle of red paint extended over the drop cloth from her ribs, more ketchup pooling over it to give a 3D effect.

If Big Eddie's boss thought she was dead, she wouldn't need to be killed. Big Eddie could save face without doing the deed. It might cause more trouble for her father, but Franklyn Baker had made his bed. A bed she'd rather not die in.

"A bit more ketchup," Big Eddie said and grabbed the bottle.

As it stood, Bea was suppressing dry heaves. Ketchup was the worst. "Fine. But open the window. And hurry up. If it crusts over, it won't look as real."

He splattered more of the nauseating condiment by her fake bullet wound. They'd decided on a classic shot to the heart. Big Eddie had claimed he was a skilled marksman, that anything else wouldn't be believable. A fact that only increased her panic. He also hadn't released the gun since breaking in. He may have been going along with her fake-death plan, that didn't mean he wouldn't get fed up and change his mind. She was still fighting for her life. And fighting to breathe through the ketchup stench.

"Window," she said again.

He opened the bedroom windows, not that it helped. Ketchup smelled like a tomato urinated in condensed milk. Trying not to inhale through her nose, she lay as still as possible. Big Eddie fiddled with the kitchen window for an eternity, only to curse after his efforts. "Sorry. I broke the window screen."

Laughter bubbled up her throat, the straitjacket kind of manic giggles. He'd stalked her, had broken into her home, threatened her at gunpoint, but he was sorry he broke the window screen. She bit her cheek to tamp her crazy giggles. This was not a time to lose her mind. This was do or die, literally.

"The ketchup is drying," she said.

"Oh, yeah. Right." Letting the gun dangle from a finger, he raised his phone and snapped a couple shots. He changed angles and snapped a few more. Then he spent an excruciating length of time studying the results. "Needs more chest blood."

She squinched her face to keep from inhaling. "Are you sure? There's lots of ketchup on me already."

"I'm sure."

The ketchup bottle farted out its last dribbles. Big Eddie even used one of her paintbrushes to apply an extra dab to her neck. She'd created a fake-crime-scene monster. Now she'd have to burn that brush. And God, the ketchup stench! "I'm sure that's enough," she said, on the verge of losing her mind.

"Yeah, yeah, yeah." He aimed the gun at her head while taking one-handed photos. "Just remember who's in charge here. You don't go nowhere till the boss tells me the job is done."

Translation: if she didn't sell this death tableau, reeking of ketchup would be the least of her worries.

Amping up her mortuary face, she played the best dead Bea there ever was. Until she heard an actual bee. Her eyes popped wide.

"Fucking hell." Big Eddie waved his hands around his head, swatting at the evil insect. He dropped his phone. His gun sliced through the air with jerky movements. "Fucking *hell*."

Fucking hell was right. Not only had he broken the window screen. He'd invited in an Anthophila: deadly poison in a compact, winged package.

Mrs. Yarrow's garden would kill her after all.

Bea wanted to run away from Big Eddie and the bee, but the thrashing gun kept her rooted. Her purse was on the floor behind him, her EpiPen tucked safely inside. Not far. If the worst happened, she could get to it and administer a shot. Staying still was the smarter option.

Big Eddie, however, was far from still.

The loan shark whirled his gun in frantic arcs, spryer than she'd expect for a man his size. He cursed. He punched the air. He apparently hated bees as much as she did. Maybe this was what happened when you faked your death. Karmic consequences that worsened at breakneck speed. He flailed, and his hip slammed into the counter. It was an opportunity, a chance to slip past him and dash for the door, but a deafening *bang* nearly shattered her eardrums.

She squeezed her eyes and screamed. An image of Huxley flashed in her mind, a fleeting snapshot of her man in his cape. A still of him dancing at Brimstone, love in his eyes. It twisted her heart as much as the sound.

She shook her ringing head as reality sunk in.

Gun. Shot. Big Eddie *shot a gun.* The gun aimed at her.

Trembling, she assessed her limbs, messing up her death tableau to test for injury and search for actual blood. She found none, but the bee had found her. And the ketchup.

It stung her neck.

Axel drove like a bat out of hell. It wasn't fast enough for Huxley. *She will be okay. She will be okay.* He'd never felt so helpless or enraged. More livid than after his father's death. If

Big Eddie damaged a single red hair on Beatrice's beautiful head, Huxley would eviscerate the man.

They careened around the last corner, screeching to a halt outside his place. He was halfway out the door before the car stopped, rage crackling through his veins. Two strides away from his Mustang, a loud *pop* blasted from the direction of his apartment.

The horrifying sound was followed by a scream. Beatrice. His girl. *Screaming.*

His legs pumped under him, no longer part of him. His heart wasn't his either, slashing around in his chest. He was adrenaline. He was fear. He slammed his shoulder into the door, only to bounce off it. Fuck. *Key.* He grabbed it from his pocket. Before he fumbled too long, Fox snatched it. The second he opened the door, Huxley rushed past him into the most gruesome scene he'd ever seen.

Blood. Too much blood. It was everywhere, and Beatrice was at the center of the horror. She clutched her throat as though struggling to breathe. *He* was struggling to breathe.

"Beatrice." Panic shredded his voice.

A man who must have been Big Eddie was panting like he'd run a marathon, gun clenched in his hand. As much as Huxley wanted to sink his fist into the bastard's face, he rushed to Beatrice, sliding to his knees at her side. He padded his pockets on the way. He didn't have his phone. Where was his phone? "Call nine-one-one!"

"On it."

He didn't know which brother answered. All he could see was red.

"Baby. Where are you hurt?" He barely choked out the words, gently touching her body, searching for the wound. He couldn't contemplate the blood, *this much blood.*

Her life spilling onto his floor.

"No," she slurred. She opened and closed her mouth. Her pupils were dilated. Blotches covered her neck. "The pen."

The pen. What pen? "I got you. You'll be fine." But his hands shook. He couldn't tell where she was hurt. He didn't know why she smelled like the Decatur fish and chips shop.

"I didn't do nothing. Lay off."

Huxley glared at Big Eddie. Fox and Axel had him on the ground, the gun kicked from his hands. Axel dug his knee into the loan shark's spine. "You call shooting her doing nothing?"

Big Eddie writhed like a beached whale. "She's not shot! It's ketchup."

Ketchup? Huxley's nose twitched, identifying the sweetly pungent scent. It's why she smelled like fish and chips. It didn't explain why she couldn't breathe.

"Pen," Beatrice said again. Her lips had swelled. She clawed at her throat. Then, "Bee."

Oh, fuck. Pen. The pen. Her EpiPen. "Where's her purse? Find her purse!"

Fox snatched a small bag from the floor, colorful enough to light a cave. Definitely hers.

"*EpiPen*," Huxley yelled. He didn't know why he was yelling. He couldn't stop. "There's one inside!"

Her purse contents went flying as Fox pulled out the pen and dove toward them. Fox then pulled off the cap and jabbed it into her thigh. "Get some pillows," he said, firm and even. No hint of wobble or worry. "Raise her legs. It'll kick in soon."

Huxley wasn't sure when his brother had learned first aid. He didn't give a shit. He snatched a couple couch pillows and elevated Beatrice's legs. When she was adequately reclined, he lay beside her, propped on his elbow. He watched her chest rise and fall. The blotches gradually receded. Fox brought over a cloth and bowl of water. Huxley went to work, wetting the cloth and cleaning her neck. Hot needles stabbed at the backs of his eyes. "Can you talk, Honeybee? Are you hurt?"

She rolled her tongue around her mouth and swallowed. "Just dizzy and nauseous. And I smell pretty bad."

"You've smelled better." But she was alive. She was talking. Still, the stabbing needles worsened, clogging up his throat, too. "You almost scared the magic out of me."

"The magic?"

"If I lost you, there wouldn't have been any left."

If he'd watched her die, he'd probably never perform again. All he'd ever see was her pulling faces in his zigzag box, twirling in her feathered costume. Aflame on stage. It would have been too much. "I'm sorry. So, so sorry."

Tears welled in her gray eyes and spilled over. "You should be."

There. *Right there.* Her words hit the center of his aching chest. "I'm an idiot."

"You are." She didn't offer a teasing smile. There was no warmth in her tone, only bitterness.

He'd wanted to see her upset and angry, to be there for her when she finally let out the feelings hidden behind her smiles. He'd just never imagined her anger would be aimed at him. But it was. She'd faced a criminal on her own, had somehow wound up covered in ketchup, which she hated, instead of getting shot. He was proud of her strength, but she shouldn't have been alone. Not like this. Not for this.

He dried her cheeks with the cloth. "I hope you'll hear me out. Later. For now, just keep breathing."

She nodded, more tears slipping out. He also felt one glide down his face.

29

After telling the EMT Beatrice had gotten carried away rehearsing a theater scene, she was whisked to the hospital. Huxley rode with her while his brothers dealt with Big Eddie. When Axel and Fox met him at the hospital, they huddled together in the waiting room.

"We talked to the neighbors who were milling around," Fox said. "Reinforced the rehearsal story with a malfunctioning prop gun."

Huxley nodded absentmindedly. "And Big Eddie?"

"He knows if he shows his face here again, we'll rearrange it. We also reminded him his boss wouldn't take kindly to being conned with fake death photos. We told him we'd keep quiet if he promised not to hurt Bea's father."

They couldn't protect Franklyn Baker from Big Eddie's boss, but they'd done what they could. Anything to curb Beatrice's worry, not that it helped with Huxley's.

Axel and Fox stayed with him while doctors attached Beatrice to a cardiac monitor and tested for EpiPen after-effects. They waited while she was pumped with an anti-allergy cocktail, followed by six hours of observation, ensuring her symptoms didn't return.

Huxley and his brothers agreed to cancel that evening's show, a first for the Marvelous Marlow Boys. All the while, his brothers didn't leave his side. Not when Huxley's adrenaline crashed and he punched the waiting-room wall. Not when he ignored their offers of coffee and cafeteria Jell-O, or when he yelled at the nurse for limiting visitation because Beatrice needed rest. He ranted while Axel and Fox placated the staff.

He wasn't sure when his brothers had started taking care of him.

Determined to distract him while they waited, they dragged him to the pediatric ward, and Axel thrust a deck of cards at Huxley. Next thing he knew, he was performing tricks for children. Kids with tubes in their arms and noses. Kids with broken limbs.

Some seemed interested in his burned eyebrow and scar, asking what had happened, if it had hurt, like they wanted proof you could live with disfigurement. All of them clapped and laughed as he performed. Their jaws dropped when he guessed which cards they'd picked. An adorable girl, who had lost all her hair, smiled so wide she reminded him of Beatrice.

"Again," she cried.

He entertained her for an hour, his anger and frustration ebbing with the games. Nearby, Axel taught a boy with a casted leg how to false shuffle. Fox entertained a crew with disappearing coins. His brothers wore dopey grins, stopping occasionally to dab the corners of their eyes or press their hands to their mouths. He wasn't sure if he looked as moved as them, but he sure as hell felt it.

This was one of the things he'd missed since Axel's stripping had changed their audience. Performing on stage was in his blood. He loved the rush of wowing a crowd, working the room. But kids were innocent, their awe genuine, and seeing a sick kid smile was inspiring. Even after the day he'd had, it flooded him with pleasure.

"We'll meet you at your apartment," Fox said afterward. "Get a head start on cleaning that mess."

The fake crime scene from hell. He shook his head. "You guys have done enough."

"Our services aren't free," Axel said. "You'll owe us dinner."

"I'll take a bathroom detailing," Fox added. "You can scrub the hard-to-reach places."

"You guys are a pain in my ass." Huxley dragged them in for a hug.

Beatrice was released shortly after. He wheeled her to his car and helped her into the passenger side. She rested her head on the window as they drove, likely drowsy from the medication and overwhelmed by the day. She didn't talk, and he didn't push. He did, however, insist on carrying her into *their* apartment.

He wasn't willing to call it his. Not yet. Not until she flat out told him they were done. Until then, she was his. The apartment was theirs. His heart was hers.

Until he heard her say those words, he had a reason to hope.

Unfortunately, she glared at him when he lifted her into his arms. She could glower all she wanted. He needed to touch her, hold her. Feel her heartbeat against his own. She gave up and cuddled against his chest, or maybe she was just tired.

Once inside, she spoke her first words in hours. "I'm not a damsel in distress. You can put me down." Her arms were still locked around his neck.

He held her firm. "Maybe I'm the one in distress."

She bit her lip.

Axel and Fox were still in the apartment, on their knees, scrubbing the last of the ketchup stains. First flying penises, now fake blood. No one could call their lives dull.

Axel dragged his forearm down his face. "Tell me again how you convinced a gun-wielding criminal to stage your murder."

"I asked him nicely."

Fox lifted his upper body and squatted on his heels. "That makes you a bona fide Marlow."

"You're surly, sneaky, and cocky," she said. "Not nice."

"We're illusionists, and you performed a perfect illusion."

Of course she did. This woman who saw the best in everyone had seen Big Eddie for the heartsick man he was, unable to harm his ex's daughter. Before the EMTs had arrived, the thug kept apologizing about the broken window screen and bee sting. Beatrice had seen through Big Eddie easily then, and she saw through Huxley now.

"I won't stop breathing if you put me down," she said.

She could probably smell his fear. "You might."

"I won't. But I might choke *you* if you keep holding me. I need a shower."

He contemplated dying at her hands rather than letting her go. It could be the last time she let him touch her. Grudgingly, he eased her onto her feet. She swayed a moment, and he steadied her. "Let me help you in the shower."

She glanced at his hand on her arm and leaned into him. Then she sighed. "Thank you, but I'll be fine."

He sure as hell wasn't fine.

She walked down the hall to the bathroom and closed the door. He hung his head and rubbed his eyes.

"Give her time." Axel jammed the last of the ketchup mess into a garbage bag. "She just staged her death and nearly died."

"Easier said than done," Huxley mumbled. Ketchup or not, he couldn't stop picturing her lying in a pool of blood, struggling to breathe. He couldn't stop berating himself for his moronic texts. If he hadn't broken her trust, she would have told him about her flight change. He would have met her at the airport. She wouldn't have dealt with Big Eddie alone.

Weak from the day's events, he trudged to the couch and fell onto the cushions, not a care to the warped frame.

Fox removed the broken window screen. "I'll get you another." He tossed it toward the door, then planted his hands on the kitchen counter and surveyed the apartment. "Day from hell."

Axel joined Huxley on the couch. "You can say that again. But the hospital was fun—the kid part."

Fox and Axel traded stories about the kid Axel couldn't fool and the girl who'd heckled Fox. As rewarding as their time had been, Huxley didn't join in. He kept glancing at the bathroom, listening for a thump or a sign Beatrice's medication had caused her to pass out. He should have forced his help on her, ignored her glare, and carried her into the bathroom. All he heard now was streaming water.

"Um...guys."

Fox's wary tone brought his focus back to the living area. "Why do you look panicked?" The color had drained from Fox's face.

Axel sat straighter. "You never panic."

Fox studied something to the side of the couch. "In all the chaos, we didn't check what the bullet hit."

Huxley didn't have any pets to worry about. No hidden roommates. "I don't care what it hit, as long as it didn't hurt Beatrice."

Fox crossed his arms and shifted from foot to foot.

Huxley and Axel traded worried looks. They stood and walked around to face whatever it was that had Fox acting like not Fox. They both stared, dumbfounded.

"Shit." Axel's eloquence.

"Fuck." Huxley's.

Their father's puzzle box lay in shambles, pieces scattered over the hardwood floor.

Nine years, they'd tried to open it. Nine years, they'd failed. If there had been a parchment inside, the vinegar vial had probably broken and eaten whatever wisdom Max Marlow had wanted to impart. The bullet could have destroyed any other contents.

He squinted at the mess. "Guess we should search the wreckage."

"Yeah," Fox agreed, but nobody moved.

The will had said the world would be his oyster once Huxley opened that box, but his girlfriend had almost gotten shot, she nearly died from a bee sting, and his theater was the laughing stock of New Orleans. He wasn't even sure if Beatrice was still his girlfriend.

The world didn't feel particularly oyster-like.

As they stalled, the bathroom door opened and Beatrice walked out, a towel knotted over her chest. His body tensed. "You okay?"

She nodded. "But I'm tired. I think I'll sleep awhile."

She might be okay, but he still wasn't. Not remotely. He wanted to pull her into his arms and whisper apologies until his throat was sore. Instead he followed her to her room. They loitered at the entrance. "I'll just be out here. If you need anything, let me know."

Tipping back on her heels, she tilted up her chin and met his desperate gaze. He tried to grovel silently, sending mute pleas through the miles separating them. Her gray eyes pooled with emotion. "We'll talk later."

Unable to resist, he tucked a wet strand of hair behind her ear. "Later."

She closed her door, and he let his forehead fall against it. Just over a week ago he'd stood like this, after his last poker game, the night he'd heard her sigh from the other side. He'd ached for her then, had nearly busted through the door, and crushed his mouth to hers. He'd ended up writing her a love note instead.

She felt farther away now, beyond his reach. A fact he wouldn't accept. This wasn't over. It couldn't be. Today's scare had drilled his idiocy home.

He would not lose Beatrice Baker.

"You might wanna see this." Axel was crouched next to Fox, amid the puzzle box debris. From the corner of his eye he noticed the two men studying something in Axel's hand.

With a last wistful glance at the closed door, he joined his brothers. "It's a key," Huxley said, stating the obvious. Axel held it out to him, and Huxley ran his thumb along the rounded top and jagged end. "It's for a safe-deposit box. He left one like this to Mom."

Whatever had been inside that particular box, Huxley had never seen a sliver of it.

Axel jumped to his feet. "Seriously?"

Huxley kicked stray pieces of the shattered wood. "Find anything else?"

"The bullet's lodged in the baseboard. We'll have to pry it out and patch it up later. And there's this." Fox held up a frayed bit of scrolled paper. "There was a message inside. The shot broke the vinegar tube in the box. No way to know what it said."

So that was it. Nine years of waiting on a message from his father that would never come. He wasn't sure what he'd hoped it would say. An explanation as to why he'd trusted Huxley with everything, to know his father was proud of him after all—anything to make him feel better about his lack of action the night Max Marlow had died.

In the end, it didn't matter. Huxley hadn't dented that fated barrel. He hadn't forced his father to risk his life. He should have reacted sooner, but he hadn't caused his father's death, just like he hadn't caused Beatrice's bee allergy or her gambling aversion.

But he did break his promise to her, along with her heart.

He fisted the key. "We'll visit the bank in a couple days, after I deal with the hearing. The bank manager can help us figure out if this was an additional key to the box Mom emptied or another one. And I might miss the next couple shows." His attention drifted back to the only place he wanted to be. "In case Beatrice needs me."

"She needs you," Axel said. "You'll see. And did you know there's a butt-ugly unicorn painting in here? Tell Bea to stick to the portrait stuff."

Huxley cuffed the back of his brother's head. "I painted that, moron."

Axel rubbed his skull. "Then you should stick to illusions."

Fox hefted the ketchup-filled garbage bag over his shoulder. "Everything will work out as it should."

Which was precisely what worried him. He wasn't sure he deserved Beatrice Baker.

The boys left. Oppressive quiet hung in the air. He showered, ridding himself of ketchup and graffiti remover, and the stench of bad decisions. Hair wet, he folded himself back onto his shitty couch and spun his father's key. *The world will be your oyster.* The only oyster he wanted had shut him out of her room. He looked at the pink pony Beatrice had given him and frowned instead of smiled. He couldn't stomach watching TV. His brain was too slippery to read. He chose painting instead. The astringent smell made him feel closer to Beatrice.

He hadn't finished the background yet. He decided on a star-filled sky, midnight blue like his cape, with twinkling gold stars. A two-year-old could do a better job, but the back and forth of his brush soothed his rattled nerves. Color mixing calmed his mind. One hour passed, then two. Blue and gold paint smeared his hands and jeans. His neck hurt from swiveling to check Beatrice's still-closed door. She hadn't made a sound.

Why hadn't she made a sound? How long was a bee sting survivor supposed to sleep?

He dropped his paintbrush. Five strides later, he was at her door, ear pressed against the wood. He couldn't hear a damn thing, and his shoulders stiffened. She didn't want him in there. She'd made that clear. But if he complied, he'd yank out his hair by morning.

He eased the door open.

He walked to her bedside and crouched by her head. Her lips were slightly parted, the covers pulled up to her chin. Soft breaths filled and left her lungs, lulling him. It took all his willpower not to crawl into bed next to her and gather her in his arms, but she didn't want to be gathered. He hadn't groveled yet. They hadn't talked.

He traced the slope of her cheek. "I love you," he whispered.

The words he should have said before her flight. What he would say when she woke up.

He stayed crouched, staring at her so long a cramp seized his thighs. He stood, but he couldn't leave. He sat on the floor, propped against the wall as night encroached. The hardwood was murder on his ass. He didn't care. Arms resting on his bent knees, he watched Beatrice Baker sleep, because Beatrice Baker was a woman who made sleep fascinating.

30

Bea woke with cottonmouth. Her throat ached. It felt like an anvil pressed on her chest. Fake dying was the pits. Stretching her arms and legs, she yawned and peeled an eye open. Blue-tinged darkness slipped through her curtains. Her clock read five a.m. Body heavy, she pushed to sitting and scrubbed the grit from her eyes.

Her heart hiccupped at the sight before her.

Huxley was on her floor, tipped on his side, one arm under his head, his long legs askew. His *Hogwarts Alumni* T-shirt had ridden up, exposing a section of burned flesh. Her fingers itched to touch him.

He was the first thing she'd thought of when that gunshot had sounded. Not a montage of art sculptures and waitressing jobs, or New Year's celebrations with her dad and dancing with her mother. She did think about her mother now, though, a woman whose zest for life had saved Bea's.

Your mother lit up a room. Big Eddie hadn't been wrong about Molly Baker. Her excitement and joy over the mundane had been infectious growing up. It was a reminder that smiling through adversity wasn't all bad: Molly's natural effervescence had inadvertently saved Bea's life. She should thank her mother for that. She should also tell her life wasn't all smiles and some hardships had to be faced, just like Bea had to face Huxley.

His worry since the shooting had been like a pheromone tractor beam, drawing her to him—the way he'd *had* to carry her, the pain in his eyes. She'd wanted him in the shower with her more than she'd wanted to wash off the ketchup smell, but she'd held her ground. Trauma couldn't be the thing to toss them back together.

She sat cross-legged, facing him, and picked up his large hand. Dark paint stained his knuckles. Lighter gold was caked into his cuticles, like he'd been painting. She feathered her fingers over the marks.

His eyes fluttered open. "Bea?"

"You always use my full name."

A sleepy smile pulled at his lips. "Beatrice."

A statement this time, her name always so perfect in his deep baritone. She wanted to hear him say it over and over and pretend he hadn't taken her money. That he hadn't played *just one more game.* Forgiveness was the path of righteousness. Her father had told her that once, after thanking her for lending him cash. Hollow words at the time, but she clung to them now.

For Huxley, she wanted to be righteous.

He blinked a bunch and dragged his body upright. "Jesus. The floor's hard." He rolled his left shoulder. "You okay?"

"You keep asking me that."

"You gave me a scare."

"Ketchup is terrifying."

He didn't laugh. A look of devastation washed over his face. "I thought I lost you."

She wasn't sure if he meant physically or emotionally. Probably both. "I'm still here."

"You are."

They stared at each other.

"Can I make you some tea?" he asked, his voice sleep-roughened and raspy along the edges. "There might be chicken soup in the freezer."

She shook her head. All she wanted was him—his arms, his strong body, his scars cocooned around her. That raspy voice in her ear. Being with him was like eating dessert before dinner. Sometimes, sadly, dinner had to come first. "Can we talk now?"

His handsome features tightened. "Yeah. Sure. Of course."

They relocated to the couch. She only wore her oversized *Smile* T-shirt and underwear. Feeling cold and exposed, she tucked her bare legs under her. Or maybe it was the impending talk that had vulnerability chilling her limbs.

A hall light cast the darkened room in a soft glow. No remnants of the staged crime scene remained. "You cleaned up." Looking around was easier than facing Huxley.

He sat beside her, a short distance away. "Fox and Axel did."

Silence settled. Not uncomfortable, exactly, but not the ignoring-TV-because-they-couldn't-stop-touching kind. He tugged at his disheveled hair. She picked at her nails. Her frazzled attention snagged on the unicorn painting. It had a background now, deep blue with gold stars—the same colors staining his hands. It resembled his galaxy cape.

Her mind tripped back to the first night she'd seen his cape. The night she'd vandalized Huxley's car. A cowardly act performed instead of telling Nick his actions had hurt. Instead of telling her father his betrayal had cut her to the bone.

She sought her inner strength this time and faced Huxley. "Asking to use my money to gamble, no matter why, was wrong."

He inched closer. "It was."

He didn't try to talk over her or offer apologies and empty explanations. He waited.

"I trusted you. That's why I gave you the money. I may have told you I wanted to help if the theater had problems, but you had to know using my savings to stake a poker game wasn't what I meant."

"Rationally, yes."

Her voice rose a notch. "Then why do it? If you knew it would upset me and ruin what we have, why use my money for a stupid game?"

His chest jerked, like he'd been punched. His posture sunk on an exhale. "I've lived the last nine years trying to make my father proud and ease my guilt over his death. I thought fixing up the theater would end all that. But when I saw flying penises spray painted on it—"

"Flying penises?" Not even their intense talk could cover up that detail.

Huxley's lip curled into a snarl. "Being the prick he is, Oliphant had some spray painted on the theater. He has a thing for phallic pranks."

Don't laugh, she told herself. *Now is not the time to smile.* She flattened her lips.

His eyes darted to her and away. He scrubbed a hand over his mouth, chuckling. "Only you could make me laugh about that." But their discussion wasn't funny. He cleared his throat. "Seeing the graffiti was rough, but Oliphant also threatened to expose the building's other issues, and I just... snapped. Not sure how else to describe it. It was like that threat and the stupid spray paint colored over every effort I'd made the past nine years, leaving only me standing there, watching my father's locked barrel, wondering why he hadn't pushed through the top yet. It felt like I'd done nothing but disappoint him over and over. So I convinced myself you'd understand, when deep down, I knew you wouldn't."

His shoulders rose and fell heavily. "It wasn't rational, and I'm ashamed of myself. Sorry doesn't begin to cover the apology you deserve. I'm also willing to do whatever it takes to make this right."

Before she could reply, he stood and walked to the kitchen. His bare feet scuffed the floor, his sweatpants riding low on his hips. She shouldn't be thinking about his hips. Or riding. But his earnest apology was tearing down her walls, the regret in his voice palpable. They didn't need dinner before dessert. In fact, they needed to order every dessert off the menu to make up for the last two days.

Ready to accept his apology and focus on dessert and the riding of his hips, she opened her mouth to tell him so, but he returned with an envelope.

He sat and held it out to her. "This belongs to you. It was never mine to use."

The sweetness on her tongue turned acerbic. Thoughts of dessert fled, and she barely refrained from tossing the envelope across the room. She didn't want gambling money. *Dirty* money. It would only remind her of everything she'd lost. School. Her father. Her childhood. Huxley's choice. She wanted to forgive him and forget this incident had ever happened, but here he was, shoving it in her face.

"I guess you won." Her words sounded barbed.

Huxley flinched. "Won?"

She tipped her chin toward the envelope, refusing to touch it. "The poker game. I guess this means you won."

He swallowed slowly. "Did you read my texts?"

"The first handful, but it felt like reading my father's messages, with him pleading and explaining. I deleted the rest." Bea didn't want to listen to his explanations now. She thought she had. She'd wanted to be righteous enough to love him regardless of his faults. *She* certainly wasn't perfect. But her mind felt tangled. A thorny rosebush of love and hate.

He dropped the envelope between them, and the tired lines of his face snapped taut. "I *never* played, Beatrice. I texted you in the heat of the moment and planned to, but I never touched your money. I never agreed to the game. I'd like to say I figured it out on my own, but Edna barking at me and a talk with my brothers helped me realize throwing my life away for the theater isn't what my dad would have wanted. It's not what *I* want. *You* are what I want. So, no." He pushed the envelope toward her. "This isn't gambling money. It belongs to you. As does this."

He tapped his breastbone, over his heart. "I'm in love with you, Beatrice Baker. The rest is a backdrop. Window dressing. You're the main event I can't live without."

His face shimmered through her teary gaze. Her heart must be allergic to happiness; it swelled three sizes. "You didn't gamble?"

"No." He leaned close and cupped her cheeks. "I'd walk away from the theater if it meant keeping you. I'd paint a thousand flying penises over it, if you'd forgive me. I'd eat your crunchy eggs every morning. There are no partly sunny days without you, Honeybee. You make me a better man."

Her chin trembled and her tears spilled free. If she'd taken off like she'd planned, packed her bags and disappeared from his life, she'd have lived believing he'd betrayed her. Her past, like his, could have stolen this moment from them. They'd both reacted emotionally before sense had kicked in. For her, it had taken a unicorn painting and gunshot to wake her up and keep her there to face her pain. But she was awake now, and Huxley's lips were inches from hers, his strong hands cradling her cheeks.

"I love you, too," she said.

Her words were magic. The greatest illusion of Huxley's time. "You love me?"

"I do. And your unicorn painting."

"The painting is awful."

"Perfectly awful."

He had never known relief as sweet as this. "How can you love this idiot?"

"Are you trying to talk me out of it?"

He kissed her instead of replying, slow and deep, savoring every taste.

She nipped his bottom lip and pulled back, a shy grin on her face. "I actually painted you something, too. It was going to be a surprise." She wiggled away from him and pulled a small canvas from under the couch. "I mean, I guess it's still a surprise, but if you don't like it, it's okay. I wasn't quite finished."

He was ready to tell her he'd love anything her hands touched, but the second he saw the painting, he couldn't speak. This portrait wasn't like her others. There were no tiny squares or funky details. Beatrice had painted a candid image of his father, his head tipped back, a glint in his eyes and sly smirk rounding his cheeks, as though he were about to share a secret. "I've never seen this picture before," he said, his voice rough. "Was it from a photograph?"

She picked at a rip on the couch. "Edna had some old albums. She let me go through them, and the second I saw this picture, I fell in love with it. I hope I didn't overstep."

He laid the painting gently down and pulled her onto his lap. "It's perfect. You're perfect." He buried his face in the curve of her neck. The non-bee-sting side. "And we should probably burn my painting. It was an embarrassment before. It's atrocious now."

She slipped her legs around his waist and nestled against him. "Never. I love it. And I'm sorry I didn't read your other texts."

"Doesn't matter," he mumbled against her skin.

He cradled the back of her head, his other arm latched around her waist. He couldn't hug her tight enough or hold her close enough. His ribs felt like they were cracking, his chest shifting below his skin. It was a familiar sensation, this invisible tearing of his tissue. It reminded him of his near-death beating.

Much of the incident itself was hazy, but the hospital afterward was hard to forget. The stabbing pain. The operations. The itching that had made him want to rip off his skin.

Healing often hurt more than injury.

Like now.

He hugged Beatrice closer and replayed the sound of the gunshot, her ketchupy body prone on his floor. How she couldn't breathe. That he'd almost lost her to his idiocy.

His bones shifted invisibly again.

Yes. This was the pain of healing. *Yes.* This was the start of something better.

He didn't ease his grip. "I want to kiss you, but you need rest."

"I've rested plenty."

He pulled his head back. "You sure?"

She answered him with a soft kiss. It had only been two days since he'd last tasted her lips, yet he was parched. Dehydrated from missing her. Her sparse clothes were the perfect cure. He caressed her thighs and round ass. He flipped them over and lay her gently down. "Can you handle more than kissing?"

"I'll hurt you if you stop. Just not too rough."

"Oh, Honeybee. I plan to make love to you slow and deep. Does that work for you?"

"It definitely does," she whispered. "But maybe not on this crappy couch."

He laughed and carried her into his room. The second he had her down, her knees parted for him, inviting him in. He was hard, wanting to grind against her and mark her skin with his teeth. But this wasn't a moment for abandon. This was the time to show Beatrice the extent of his love. Prove he'd bow at her altar for as long as she'd have him. He stripped her leisurely, covering her in kisses. He stroked and caressed her and worshipped her body with limitless devotion.

He hated parting from her for a second, but he left to grab a condom, returning swiftly. He groaned at the sight of his gorgeous woman lying on his bed. The left side of her neck was swollen, her eyes puffy from crying. She was the most beautiful sight he'd ever seen.

His clothes joined hers on the floor, then she sat up and rolled on the condom, fisting him and guiding him to her. Guidance he didn't need. She was his North Star, a steady light in an ever-changing sky. He pressed in slow as a summer sunrise, letting her heat wrap him, her color blind him. The promise of a new day ahead.

He nosed the tender flesh of her neck. "Don't ever fake die again."

A tear slipped out as she canted her hips, taking him deeper. "Don't ever buy ketchup again."

"Never," he murmured.

They moaned as they met. They held their breath as they parted—a reminder to always find their way back. They made love slowly, tenderly, their briny kisses bitter and sweet.

31

Bea stood at the kitchen counter, tapping on her phone. "Is it okay if Della comes?"

"Sorry, did you say something?" Huxley had her caged from behind, his insatiable mouth busy on her collarbone. Only the counter kept her from toppling forward.

She wiggled against him. "If you don't stop, we'll be late meeting your brothers."

He pulled her neckline down and exposed her shoulder. "Don't care."

She tipped her neck, giving him more access. "But you've waited nine years to learn what your father left you."

"*Mmmm.*" He'd devolved to incoherent sounds, and everything hard behind her got harder.

She'd happily spend the next year like this, trapped between the counter and Huxley's hard place. That's what happened when you staged your death, almost stopped breathing, and nearly broke up with the man you love. But today was important.

She swiveled around and pushed at his chest. "Huxley Marlow, don't make me punish you."

He quit pawing at her. "Will there be whipped cream involved in this punishment? I'm still dying to know what you do with it."

She had some delicious ideas up her sleeve. "Yes. There will be whipped cream. Right now, however, there will be beignets, then there will be a trip to the bank. Fox told Della about the safe-deposit box and wants to know if she can come. He said you're ignoring your phone."

"Of course she can come. She's family."

Bea knew Della didn't want to be Fox's family. Not of the sisterly sort. But Della probably wanted to be there for Fox today.

Huxley had done some preliminary work and discovered a different deposit box his mother hadn't touched. It may have been left to Huxley, but he wanted his brothers with him, to stand together while they uncovered this last piece of their father. Della obviously wanted to support Fox for this emotional moment, the way he'd always supported her. Bea was thankful Huxley understood.

She went to place a thank-you kiss on his cheek, but he moved to capture her lips. When they came up for air, she placed two beignets on a plate and headed for the door.

"Where are you going with my breakfast?"

She turned to catch Huxley adjusting himself in his briefs. Her mouth watered. She contemplated abandoning the bank plan and having something else for breakfast, but today was more important than her lusty fantasies. "We're eating outside."

"We have a perfectly good counter. A table, too."

"Beignets taste better outside."

"That's ridiculous."

"It's a fact."

"A ridiculous fact. And we're not dressed for it."

Her tank top and flannels were just fine. His briefs were maybe a tad skimpy. "Throw on one of your nerdy T-shirts."

"No."

"Then come as you are. Mrs. Yarrow won't mind. She'll take extra-long watering her peonies." One look at him in his briefs, and their neighbor would turn the hose on herself. Bea planned to keep a close eye on the spray-tanned woman, who cornered Huxley at will, trying to coax him to see her *azaleas*. She still wasn't convinced the married woman hadn't sent in the rogue bee.

"Inside is fine," Huxley said, unmoving. Obstinate.

She took a page from his book and growled. "Then I'm tossing in one of my poker chips."

"You'll have to be more specific."

Rule One of forgiving her man and moving on was talking about their issues. Not letting them slumber in her dormant volcano of unaired grievances. Rule Two was taking advantage of the fallout. "You don't get to almost bet my savings and get off scot-free. I've earned favors."

"Yeah, okay. But..." He rubbed his nape and glanced at the floor. At the spot where she'd staged her death. "There are bees outside."

Oh. Bees.

Her frustration deflated. Huxley Marlow was a tall man. He was a proud man. He'd withstood a near-fatal beating and had kept most of his family together. That didn't make him invincible. "There will always be bees."

"But the outfit I ordered for you hasn't arrived yet."

"Outfit?"

"A netted one. It has a face mask and everything."

"You're insane."

"I'm determined."

To keep her safe. He didn't need to say it. His crumpled brow spoke of his vulnerability, and warmth engulfed her chest. She wasn't sure she'd get used to being worried after and cared for. She wasn't sure she wanted to get used to it.

Plate of beignets in hand, she joined him in the kitchen and traced the long scar down his abdomen. "Life is unpredictable. You could get hurt. I could get hurt. But we can't walk through the world bubble wrapped. Or in a net suit."

He ran his thumb over her bottom lip. "Then how do I protect you?"

She leaned into his touch. "By eating beignets outside with me and dancing in jazzy clubs and painting and performing together. Loving me is protection enough."

He inhaled deeply, his breath rushing out on a sigh. "I can do that."

Pac-Man T-shirt on, he joined her outside. They sat on the curb, side-by-side, enjoying their beignets, *after* they'd both searched the scene for bees.

"Yoo-hoo." Mrs. Yarrow waved from her garden. She bent forward, her cleavage ready to make a getaway.

Huxley waved distractedly. "Roses look great."

But he hadn't taken his attention off the pastry in his hands. He finished it in four large bites. Bea nibbled hers. It was too good to inhale, crispy and chewy, sweet and rich, bits of cloud-light powder sticking to her lips. She couldn't keep from moaning. Before she popped the last morsel in her mouth, Huxley stole it, barely chewing his prize.

She went to swat him, but he grabbed her wrist and licked the powdered sugar from *her* fingers. "You're right," he said, crowding her space and jostling her too-full heart. "They taste better outside."

Everything tasted better with Beatrice Baker. *On* Beatrice Baker, specifically. Huxley also couldn't imagine facing his father's safe-deposit box without her at his side. The sterile room felt small with five of them inside. Fox and Della were at one end of the steel table, Beatrice and him opposite.

Axel drummed his hands on the left side. "Remember that diamond heist when we were kids? I always wondered if Dad had something to do with it."

Huxley fit the key into the box but didn't turn it. "There aren't diamonds in here. It's probably another riddle."

Axel bounced on his feet. "It could be his stash of ruby rings. We never found those."

Stolen by their mother, likely. "Don't get your hopes up."

For Huxley's ninth birthday, his father had sent him on a scavenger hunt through the theater. It had taken him a month to figure out the clues. He was sure the Wolverine comic he'd coveted lay at the end. Instead he'd found a picture of a dove. Irate hadn't begun to describe his nine-year-old self, who'd expected his long-awaited comic. Max had told Huxley the real dove would be his if he mastered a flying card illusion. Huxley grumbled, but eventually gave in and learned the magic trick. Two weeks later, he became the proud owner of a dove. And had become addicted to magic.

Huxley didn't expect ruby rings from Max Marlow, or an oyster world, or answers to impossible questions. He expected games. Eccentric keepsakes.

Still, Huxley didn't twist the key.

Beatrice smoothed her hand along his lower back. "You don't have to open it today. It's been nine years, another few days or weeks won't matter."

"No freaking way," Axel said, impatient as always. "I wanna know what he left."

Fox rolled his eyes. "It's your call. I'm good either way."

So was Huxley. For the first time in too long, he looked ahead and saw a life with possibility. Not a daily grind of bills and obligations.

The court hearing yesterday had gone as expected. They had a fine to pay and had thirty days to repaint and fix the façade. Together, they'd make it work, and gradually repair the interior. His brothers would share the theater burden from here on out. He also had a watermelon girl who filled his days with sweetness. What he didn't want was for this mysterious box to throw their newly ordered world off-kilter. He liked his current kilter just fine.

He released the key and crossed his arms. "The theater's doing better, but we're still short cash." Beatrice's hand tensed on his back. Before she could pull away, he tucked her into his side. "Gambling is out, as is picking pockets." He aimed a glare at Fox, who stared back blank-faced. "But I have another suggestion."

"I suggest we open the box," Axel said again. Considering he always opened his Christmas presents early, his impatience wasn't surprising.

"I'll get to the box. But whatever's in there, it changes nothing. We need more cash flow, and I think we all enjoyed our time at the hospital."

Beatrice scrunched her adorable nose. "Because watching medicine get pumped into my veins is fun?"

"Cool, actually," Axel said. "But we killed time in the pediatric wing. Entertained the little farts with magic."

As if the girls had an automatic maternal switch, they both *awwwed*. Beatrice had a moony look about her he'd like to bottle. He wondered if she wanted kids, little Baker-Marlows with her zest for life and his sleight-of-hand skills. He certainly liked that notion. So much so, he'd happily dump his condom supply.

The powerful devotion he felt toward her didn't surprise him. What was surprising was the matching dreamy expression on Della's face...an expression aimed at Fox. The sneaky brother. The serious brother. The brother who slipped his arm around Della and tugged her to his side. He whispered something in her ear. Della nuzzled his neck.

"Oh my God." Beatrice's shocked voice must have matched Huxley's expression. "You told him!"

"Actually, no," Della said, her starry-eyed gaze locked on Fox. "He told me."

Axel's attention swiveled between the apparent couple. "Told you what?"

Fox stared at Della like he'd discovered gold. "That I couldn't live another day without her."

Beatrice clutched Huxley's arm and sighed. He chuckled, unsure how he'd missed the signs. Della must have been the source of Fox's rant the other day.

Axel waggled his eyebrows. "This mean I can't ask her out?"

Fox snarled at him.

"Ignore the idiot," Huxley said. As fun as taunting Fox could be, they needed to get back on track, and he had a business venture to propose. "I'd like to volunteer at the hospital every month or so. It won't help pay our bills, and I'm happy to do it on my own, but if you guys are keen, I'd also like to set up a magic school. As a side gig to our nightly shows."

Beatrice gasped. "Can I be in Hufflepuff?"

Della raised her hand. "Ravenclaw all the way."

Ignoring the girls, Fox eyed Axel's *Top Gun* T-shirt. "He'd have to wear clothes."

Axel resumed drumming the table. "Not if I teach adult classes."

"What do you think?" Huxley directed the question to Fox. The levelheaded brother.

"I like it. We could host a theater show for the kids. A performance at the end of the sessions. Get their parents involved."

Beatrice snuggled closer to Huxley's side. "I think it's a stupendous idea. And I'm sorry I missed the hospital show." She pressed to her tiptoes and tried to kiss his cheek, but he stole a proper kiss, deeper than appropriate for their audience. He didn't care. He'd never waste another opportunity to taste her lips or confess his love.

"It must be the Elder wand," Axel said, obnoxious as always.

Beatrice pulled away, a mischievous glint in her rainstorm eyes. "It *is* the most powerful wand. Fifteen inches, they say."

Della snickered. "Huxley must be a skilled wizard. He should teach wand mastery at his school."

Beatrice lowered her voice, as though sharing the secret to their Flying Playing Card routine. "He has a PhD in wand mastery."

"Does he specialize in direct hits or stamina spells?"

Axel mock-puked. "We passed TMI Street two blocks ago."

Fox tightened his hold on Della. "You don't need to know about Huxley's wand aptitude."

Huxley beamed at his girl. "You're getting a raise. I'd also like you to be my assistant for our next hospital visit."

She shimmied her shoulders. "I'd be delighted."

To his brothers, he said, "Marlow Magic School. No wand classes or stripping. You two in?"

They made eye contact and nodded. As good as a blood oath in the Marlow Family.

That left the box. His father's last gift to his boys. Huxley hadn't tried to locate Xander or Paxton yet. They'd disappeared without a trace five years ago, and he'd never searched for them. They knew where their family was. He figured they'd make contact in their own time, but the box's contents could change things. Unless it was a box of magic beans.

Swallowing hard, he grabbed the key. "Here goes nothing."

Beatrice pressed her fist to her mouth.

Axel rubbed his hands together.

Fox flattened his lips, while Della kissed his jaw.

Huxley opened the lid, and everyone gasped. "The Marvelous Max Marlow," was all he could say.

Five gold bars glinted from the box. A proverbial oyster for each of the great man's sons, probably meant to ease the burden of his death. Or maybe not. The puzzle box had been near impossible to open for a reason. Max Marlow hadn't wanted to hand over an easy inheritance.

As Huxley watched Axel whoop and Fox stare at the bars with tears in his eyes, as Beatrice slipped her arm around his waist, her affection sweeter than any sum of money, he finally understood why. If forced to choose between them and his father's gift, he'd throw this box and its contents in the river. Nothing was more important than keeping the people he loved close.

THE END

Do you want more Beatrice and Huxley?
Visit Kelly's website for a free epilogue!
www.kellysiskind.com

READING GROUP GUIDE

1. When you first meet Beatrice, she prides herself on being a glass-half-full person, always looking for the positive in situations. Do you consider this a flaw or a strength? Are you someone who looks for the silver lining in situations, or do you focus on the negative?

2. Huxley's life was defined by his father's death. If he had reacted sooner and had saved his father, do you think he would be as close with his brothers today? What do you think would have happened to the theater and their relationship if the building had been left to Axel or Fox?

3. At one point in the novel, Beatrice says she likes her mother but doesn't love her, and that she loves her father but doesn't like him. Do you have relationships like this in your life? Do they add value, or are they people you should consider letting go?

4. Huxley has spent the majority of adulthood putting his brothers' needs before his own. How did meeting Beatrice help him learn that putting himself first was just as important? Are you defined by caretaking roles in

your life? Do you think carving out "me" time is valuable? What things do you do to take a breath and focus on yourself?

5. Maintaining tradition isn't as important in today's society, but Huxley clings to his father's theater and his dated magic routines. Why do you think he couldn't let it go? Should he have sold the theater after his father's death? Would he have been better off starting fresh in a different job or working at a different place?

6. How has Beatrice's relationship with her father pushed her to be a better person? In which ways has it held her back?

7. Beatrice kept getting sucked into her father's drama, even though it impacted her life negatively. Should she have cut him out of her life sooner? Why do you think it took her so long to walk away? What would you have done?

8. Do you believe meeting Huxley was the reason Beatrice finally learned to let out her emotions? Do you think she would have continued running from her problems and hiding behind her smiles on her own?

9. Huxley never got to read his father's final letter in the shattered puzzle box. What do you think it might have said? Where do you see Huxley and Beatrice in five years?

10. New Orleans is a character unto itself in the book. The city is filled with so much music and color and amazing food. Have you traveled to New Orleans? If so, did you enjoy it? If not, is it a place you want to visit? Which other vibrant cities could have been the backdrop to this story?

ACKNOWLEDGMENTS

This authoring gig only works because of you, my awesome readers, and this book was a blast to write. I drafted it before traveling to New Orleans, but I spent a week there while revising. There's something special about visiting settings and using that exploration to add life to the page, and New Orleans has enough vibrancy to fill ten libraries.

I'm ridiculously fortunate to work with my agent, Flavia Viotti. Your enthusiasm and hard work are astounding. This partnership has inspired me both as a writer and a person. I can't thank you enough for believing in me and this book. My editor, Shannon Criss, knew exactly what this story needed and pushed me to make it shine. The whole EverAfter team, in particular the tireless Laura Kemp, have been a great support throughout this book's journey. You all saw something in this story you loved, and I couldn't be more grateful.

So many other people helped breathe small and large breaths of life into this book, some with tough love, others by proofing or reading early drafts and telling me it didn't suck: Jamie Howard, J. R. Yates, Kristin B. Wright, Heather Van Fleet, Shannon Moore, Tammy Cole, Meghan Scott Molin, Mary Ann Marlowe, Jen DeLuca, Shelly Hastings Suhr. Thank you all, times a million. If it weren't for Michael Mammay, Huxley's poker scene wouldn't have been nearly as accurate.

Aside from the above, and others I have probably forgotten to mention, there are so many writers who are there for me when I need them: Brighton Walsh, Beth Miller, Rachel Lacey, Tara Wyatt, Brenda St. James, Michelle Hazen, the everlasting CD, the Badass Bitches, my Pitch Wars family, my Fab FB Babes, my Golden Heart crew, and oh my God… where would I be without you all?

A special shout-out to Mary Ann Smith, who designed me a stunning cover. It is beyond perfect. Seeing my vision so gorgeously executed was a thing of beauty. Emily Smith-Kidman, you are a PR guru. I could never have navigated this release without you.

As always, mad love to my patient husband who doesn't (often) complain when I lock myself in a room for hours on end. You are my favorite happily ever after.

To all the ladies who hang out with me in my Facebook group, Kelly's Gang, you keep me laughing and make social media a fun place to visit. Love you all! And finally, to my readers and the many bloggers who live and breathe romance: thank you from the bottom of my Chardonnay-filled heart. Knowing people are out there reading my words is the best high there is. Your support means the world.

Don't forget to visit my website to read a special
free epilogue from Huxley and Beatrice!

xoxox Kelly

ABOUT THE AUTHOR

A small-town girl at heart, Kelly Siskind moved from the city to open a cheese shop with her husband in northern Ontario. When she's not neck-deep in cheese or out hiking, you can find her, notepad in hand, scribbling down one of the many plot bunnies bouncing around in her head. She laughs at her own jokes and has been known to eat her feelings. She's also an incurable romantic, devouring romance novels into the wee hours of the morning.

For giveaways and early peeks at new work, join **Kelly's Newsletter.** (https://www.kellysiskind.com)

If you like to laugh and chat about books, join Kelly in her Facebook group, **Kelly's Gang.**

Connect with Kelly on social media:
Twitter: https://twitter.com/KellySiskind
Facebook: https://www.facebook.com/authorKellySiskind/
Instagram: https://www.instagram.com/kellysiskind/